MAX,
WELCOME TO
MY IMAGINATION.

FOLLY

MAX,
WELCOME TO
MY IMAGINATION.

FOLLY

A NOVEL

BILL NOEL

iUniverse Star

New York Bloomington Shanghai

Folly

iUniverse Star
an iUniverse, Inc. imprint

iUniverse books may be ordered through booksellers or by contacting:

iUniverse
1663 Liberty Drive
Bloomington, IN 47403
www.iuniverse.com
1-800-Authors (1-800-288-4677)

Because of the dynamic nature of the Internet, any Web addresses or links contained in this book may have changed since publication and may no longer be valid.

This is a work of fiction. All of the characters, names, incidents, organizations, and dialogue in this novel are either the products of the author's imagination or are used fictitiously.

ISBN: 978-1-60528-015-8 (pbk)
ISBN: 978-0-595-61306-9 (ebk)

Printed in the United States of America

CHAPTER 1

I met Jim Lionetti on a chilly, early April morning and learned to hate him. It wasn't his fault—he was dead. I was standing on a desolate, rough stretch of sand on the east end of Folly Beach, South Carolina, looking down at him.

I'd arrived at daylight to photograph the morning sun as it lit the deserted Morris Island Lighthouse. About a quarter mile from the nearest road, gunshots startled out of my peaceful sunrise experience. I barely heard the sounds over the roar of the ocean slapping against the rocks and brisk wind whistling through the scrubby trees, but instantly, I tried to wish myself invisible. Failing at that, I inched my way through the sea oats and shrubs toward the source, and then I saw it—fewer than a hundred feet from where I'd left my tripod standing—a hunk of clothes and flesh lying on the beach.

As I hurried closer for a better look, three thoughts hit me. First, I'm no doctor—though I had a suspicion that the soul of whoever was in the clothes had already met his maker, or someone much worse. Second, while the gentleman was obese, the pool of red liquid growing in the sand beneath his head and the empty socket where a left eye should have been, told me the cause of death wasn't a heart attack. The third and most frightening thought was that the murderer could easily be standing very close, getting ready to send me on a trip I wasn't ready to take.

That got my attention. It scared me enough that I took one quick look around and briskly walked toward the water. Though I didn't see anyone lurking in the shrubs, I needed to distance myself from the unwanted find. Down the beach a way, at the water's edge, I forgot about my Monday morning venture to capture the images of the lighthouse and lost the cheese crackers I'd had for breakfast. Then I hid.

I crouched for what seemed hours in the rocky area north of where the corpse was resting before I finally got the nerve to dial 911. Actually, it was only fifteen minutes.

Being six hundred fifty miles from home, I was surprised to hear the phone answered with a pleasant, "Folly Beach Police Department. How may I help you?" The voice's mood changed drastically when I said I wanted to report a murder. I gathered that wasn't the common response to the "How may I help you?" question.

When I told him the murder had occurred within the last half hour and that the killer might still be nearby, his "helpful guide to responding to citizens' calls" came up lacking, and he barked out some police code that I interpreted as, "We got a murder here. Get the chief!" The formerly calm voice finally asked where I was and where the body was. I told him that I was on the old coast guard station property at the end of the island, and knew only that I'd driven to the end of East Ashley Avenue, parked by a rusting barricade and walked about a quarter of a mile on a sand path to where I had the best view of the lighthouse. He said he knew where I was and was sending officers. He asked my name. I told him and spelled it three times at his request. He cautioned, "Mr. Landrum, you best not leave the area." A caution not needed—I was too busy shaking to go anywhere. To reach my hiding place, I'd even used my tripod as a crutch; not its intended use, but handy at the moment.

CHAPTER 2

I pressed the *end call* button, and slowly regained my ability to walk. Believing—or just wishfully thinking—that the killer was miles away, I walked back along the sand trail to where I'd parked, and stopped at what had once been a coast guard station, now only a concrete, graffiti-covered foundation with eight steps in front that went nowhere. The rest of the building had been demolished.

I was now within site of the turn-around where, I hoped, the police would shortly be. With nothing to do but sit and be eaten by sand fleas, I tried to reconstruct what I'd seen.

It wasn't long before a white Ford Crown Victoria, overhead blue lights flashing, headed toward me. Its siren wasn't on, which was a relief to me—I didn't want to be a spectacle in the center of a curious crowd.

Two officers were quickly out of the car and headed toward me, each with a hand not subtly covering the handgun on his belt. With half the distance covered, the first called out to me.

"I'm Officer Robins and this is Officer Spencer," he said. "Are you the one who reported a murder?"

I resisted making a sarcastic remark, "No, I'm the killer waiting for a ride to town," and said, "Yes."

Officer Robins, who looked like he had been around awhile, especially around food, was clearly the superior officer—at least in seniority. He asked to see some identification, so I fished out my driver's license, which he handed to Officer Spencer and told him to record the "salient" (policespeak?) information. Spencer, unseasonably tanned and looking like a junior in high school, took the license and made notes.

"Please take us to the body," commanded Robins.

We walked back down the path, me feeling safer knowing I was flanked by two armed officers. But their own nervousness as they scanned the overgrown areas on each side of the trail didn't contribute much to that feeling.

"The body is just ahead where the trail ends at the beach. Turn right at the corner and you'll see him," I said, feeling like a tour guide.

"Stand here and don't touch anything," cautioned Robins once we were within twenty feet of the corpse. It was easy to follow those directions. There was absolutely nothing around to touch except sand, and I didn't know how to avoid that. I volunteered that I had only got within three feet of the victim the first time, so there shouldn't be any contaminates from me. From watching television (not public broadcasting), I thought these comments would be helpful. Officer Robins wasn't the least bit impressed. Water, encouraged by the wind-blown tide, was now lapping around the body, wiping out any chance of finding footprints.

I gazed at the pitiful spectacle of what had once been a man—now unaware of the salty water rolling in around him, soaking his clothes, making his pale, cold hands glisten in the early light, and washing out the empty, bloody socket where his eye had so recently been.

Robins saw the body wouldn't be going anywhere on its own and told his young partner to go to the car and get the crime tape. Once Spencer was gone, we moved over to a cluster of large, bench-sized, black boulders at the water's edge. We sat, and the questions began.

Noticing my Nikon camera and tripod, he started with, "You didn't happen to take a picture of the killer, did you?"

He was serious. Ridiculous as the question was, I thought I'd better answer appropriately, "No, sorry." But I was thinking, *Well, you don't know if you don't ask.*

"Why were you on this deserted beach this early in the morning?"

"I'd heard this was a great place to photograph the lighthouse, and that just after sunrise would be the best time. I got here before seven and was walking around trying to find the best spot to get my shots."

"How'd you stumble upon the body?"

"Stumble," didn't strike me as policespeak. I shared that I hadn't. "I must have been a hundred feet or so over that way when I heard two shots and immediately walked toward where I thought they'd come from until I saw the body lying there."

"Did you see anyone else?"

"No one."

"How about cars or trucks where you parked?"

"None. I noticed a couple of drives off the end of the road. It was still pretty dark. If anything was parked there, I didn't see it."

"Did you see anything out of the ordinary after you got here?"

That was tougher. "I've never been here, so I don't know what's 'ordinary.' Nothing seemed unusual; I didn't hear anything other than surf, wind, and shots. That's it."

Officer Robins didn't appear satisfied, but I was saved when his obedient partner reappeared, rushing back from the car carrying a roll of the ubiquitous yellow crime scene tape. The gusty ocean winds, the tide lapping in, and the soft vegetation presented the officers with their greatest challenge of the morning—how to string tape around the crime scene.

The sand and the body were already wet from the thin sheets of rushing water that always precede the tide. But now the waves themselves were pushing closer. It would have been difficult to attach the tape to anything in the water. Even I could figure that out, and I've never strung crime tape in my life. The beach section was nearly as difficult, but at least the sturdy sea oats provided a minimal tying structure. My contribution was carrying some of the nearby larger rocks to hold down the tape in the sand. I was afraid they were going to commandeer my tripod, so I laid it out of sight. But all the while, I was wondering what the purpose of stretching tape was, when, if they didn't hurry, the tide would shortly pick up the corpse and carry it out to sea.

With that accomplished, Robins suggested the three of us retreat to the deserted concrete structure. I suspected they wouldn't want me to photograph their finished handiwork to be used in a police journal as an example of creative tape stringing. He'd already called the station and requested assistance from the County of Charleston's sheriff department. He said Folly Beach doesn't investigate murders; it was the sheriff's department that had the detectives and resources for that. He seemed relieved. He told Spencer he thought he recognized the body as "… that big time developer from Charleston—Linenett, or something like that."

The name meant nothing to me—unfortunately, that would soon change.

CHAPTER 3

After just under an eternity, another Crown Victoria, unmarked and dark blue, pulled up to the barrier separating the old coast guard station property from the real world. Two detectives—I presumed—exited. They didn't seem to be in nearly the hurry their predecessors had been. They slowly walked through the sand to where we were encamped, looking carefully at everything as they came. I was thinking they'd better get a move on if they were going to reach the body before the tide did. Robins and Spencer walked over to the new arrivals and whispered a few words before they came my way.

The lead detective was an attractive, well-dressed female in her mid-thirties. After a strong handshake, she introduced herself as Detective Lawson. She also introduced her partner, a male in his early sixties, but I didn't catch the name.

They asked me to continue waiting on my perch of concrete while they went to the scene. It was interesting watching the newcomers in their nicer clothes and in shoes definitely not designed for sand walking. The local officers, now old hats on the scene, led the way and trudged down the middle of the trail, kicking up little clouds of sand that settled on the detective's shoes. A little resentment?

This was the first time I hadn't had an armed escort since the police arrived. Fear crept back into my consciousness. To put it aside, I tried to remember if I knew anything I hadn't shared.

Going over the events one by one, I remembered that I had parked my Lexus at the chained-off entrance just before sunrise; hadn't seen anything or anyone *out of the ordinary,* as Robins had put it. I had taken my camera and tripod out of the trunk, put on a light jacket and my trusty, canvas fedora-shaped Tilley hat, and walked down the only path. I had assumed it led to the view of the light-house. Where the path met the beach and the Atlantic Ocean, I had wisely decided not to walk any farther that direction, so turned left and followed the beach around a gentle bend until I found a better view. The lighthouse was about three hundred yards offshore and backlit by the rising sun. I set the tripod so the camera angle would have water in the foreground, the lighthouse, and then the sun. I hoped to silhouette the structure, using a telephoto lens. All set up, I began to shoot. I doubted I was getting what I wanted, but continued bracketing shots in hope of catching the light just right. Still, I hadn't heard or seen anything other than a few birds windsurfing between the lighthouse and me, and the sound of the waves.

On a warmer day, I would have spent more time experimenting with camera settings and shots, but by that time, there was enough light to handhold the cam-era and use a fairly quick shutter speed to get a sharp image, so I'd begun to move around freely. Besides, I hate tripods.

North of the spot where the path meets the beach, I'd taken more shots of the vegetation, small trees shaped by the strong winds, unique rock formations, birds, and a small pond that struck me as out of place. The smell of decaying fish had grown increasingly noticeable.

I had previewed many of the photos, deleted some, and kept most to review later on my laptop—the whole time in my own peaceful world light years from civilization. If not for a few man-made odds and ends, I could have been on the moon.

That was when it had come to an abrupt end.

*   *   *   *

Detectives Lawson and No Name—I need to get better at remembering names—were now cautiously walking back the path toward me. At the same time, a second Folly Beach cruiser slid to a halt in the gravel at the increasingly crowded parking area beyond the stanchions.

"Morning, Chief," Detective Lawson said to the tall, thin, partially graying gentleman joining the three of us at the base of operations. This had to be the most activity the concrete foundation had seen since the thriving days of coast guard protection.

"And a pleasant good morning to you as well, Detective. I hear we've a situa-tion here. Where're my men?"

"We left them at the beach guarding 'the situation.'"

Way too syrupy considering the circumstances, if you ask me.

"If you're going down there, Chief, have one of your officers return to initiate some crowd control at the entrance. Word of 'the situation' is reaching some of your locals."

A small group, mainly construction workers who had walked from a nearby beach house being built, gathered outside the property line.

"And, Chief, by the way, the victim is James Lionetti, the developer from Charleston. Once word gets out, your island will be the center of much attention. Get ready for it."

The chief headed down the path toward the beach without giving me a glance, but the two detectives turned their attention to me. "Now Mr. Landrum," Lawson said in a firm but feminine voice, "I know you've told the other officers what you saw and found. Please repeat it for us."

After having had time to reflect on what I'd actually done and seen, I did a better job reliving the experience. When Detective Lawson finished hearing my story and asked me to repeat it again, I was a little disappointed. But considering my choices, I started over.

The second telling sounded the same to me. But then again, I'm not a detective, and didn't know what could be detected from my retelling. But while I was telling it, someone breeched the invisible crime barrier and interrupted my monologue.

Detective Lawson, looking up from her notes, firmly said, "Tammy, please stay behind the stanchions. I'll get with you in a little while."

The newest visitor was an attractive woman in her mid-forties, who looked a little like Diane Sawyer. She was shorter—although I really don't know how tall Diane Sawyer is—but this woman appeared to be five one or two.

"She's a reporter for the Charleston newspaper," Lawson said. "One of the best, but still the media—not always our friends."

After I'd repeated the story a second time for the detectives and answered more questions, they said they had enough—for now. At least neither of them asked if I'd taken a picture of the killer.

"Mr. Landrum, we'll be here the rest of the morning," said Lawson. I don't want to keep you longer than necessary. This has been a traumatic few hours, but I do have one more request. I'd like for one of our detectives to go with you to where you're staying and get your fingerprints and the clothes you're wearing. Have any problem with that?"

She said *request*, but it sounded more like an order. I didn't have anything to hide, and these weren't my best clothes anyway. "No problem," I said.

"Okay. Wait by your car and we'll be with you shortly."

It was a strange feeling knowing I was the center of attention for the twenty or so gawkers watching me walk to my car with my tripod slung over my shoulder, and camera and gear in my hands and pockets. And it was a frightening feeling, knowing the killer could be among them. I had stowed the equipment in the trunk and was coming around to get in, when the reporter—Tammy according to the detective—blocked my way. Not rudely, but with a pleasant smile on her face and a cell phone to her ear. But I still would have had to push her out of the way to get in. A move that I didn't think very wise, considering all these onlookers.

She clicked off her cell phone, put it away, and broadened her smile. "Sir, I'm told you found the body. I know you can't talk now, but could you call when you're free? I'm with the newspaper in Charleston and would like to get your comments and perspective."

Before I could say, "yes," "no," or "go jump in the ocean," she thrust a card in my hand and I looked at it. Tammy Rogers, the *Post and Courier*, it simply stated, and listed several numbers and an e-mail address. I remembered Detective Lawson saying Tammy was "one of the best," and I figured that was a ringing endorsement. I understand police generally detest watchdogs from the media. Now I used the line I'd practiced on Detective Lawson. "No problem."

Detective No Name appeared and asked if I was having a problem with the reporter. I said no, and he said he would follow me home. I started to tell him how to get there. He interrupted and said he wouldn't lose me, that his car was much more powerful than mine, and he had years of experience chasing bad guys. I never doubted his claim, and resorted to a highly articulate, "Okay."

I led the detective on a low speed chase, reminiscent of OJ and the Los Angeles police of several years ago. It really wasn't a chase, but I felt that way with a police car on my tail following me through every turn. We continued down Ashley, running parallel to the beach, took a couple of other turns and arrived at my newly rented humble abode on West Cooper Avenue. When we got there, I did a fine piece of detecting myself.

"What's your name again?"

He couldn't stand the pressure and caved, "Brad Braden."

And I thought this detecting stuff was difficult. He went abruptly from being Detective No Name to Brad Braden—how could I have forgotten such a poetic moniker?

It took two tries to get the door lock open—I was more nervous than I thought—and ushered him in. We went in, and I immediately went to the bedroom to change.

"Do you need my underwear?" I thought he said something like *no way*, but maybe he just said "no." I came out in fresh gear and handed him my clothes, neatly folded and piled and with the shoes sitting on top. He promised to return my six-year-old, raveled-around-the-cuffs khaki Dockers, faded Tommy Hilfiger red polo shirt, and nearly new black socks. I was more distraught about giving up my aging Nunn Bush deck shoes. I wore them every day and would have to go shoe shopping soon.

The fingerprinting process was intimidating. He spread out his stuff on my dining table. He was just doing his job, but I felt like a criminal as I rolled each finger in a stamp-pad looking ink tray. This was the first time I'd been demeaned in this particular manner—I had been demeaned in other ways—so I doubted he'd find much to hang on me from my far less than checkered past.

Before Detective Braden left, I did one other bit of fine detecting. I asked what the Folly Beach Chief of Police's name was. He said he thought it was Chief Newman. I doubted his mother gave him the first name *Chief*, so I assumed it was his title. His first name will remain a mystery a while longer.

"If you think of anything else," Braden said, "regardless of how insignificant, please let the Folly Beach police know, or give us a call at the number on this card. He handed me a card with Detective Lawson's name on it. "If you're thinking about leaving the state in the next couple of weeks, please let us know."

Despite the use of the word *please* twice, the last part of what he said didn't leave me with a warm, fuzzy feeling. Even with the island to move around on, I felt suddenly claustrophobic. Still, when Detective Braden closed the front door, I realized how lucky I was to be among the living. And how I was wishing I could just walk to breakfast this morning and read about others' trials and tribulations. I also realized I was hungry. After all, my breakfast crackers were somewhere back on the beach. But worse, thoughts of a killer out there wondering what I'd seen put a dark cloud over my mind.

And then came another thought, one that made me catch my breath; I remembered the card the Charleston reporter had given me, and the warm smile she'd shared during my time of trauma. So, I thought, I can kill two birds with one stone—the phrase seemed to fit. I'd share a few minutes with a friendly face and get the word out that I hadn't seen anything at the crime scene. If Mr. or Ms. Murderer knew this, he or she would have no need to pay attention to me.

I called the cell phone number and was disappointed to hear a digital version of her real voice saying she wasn't available, and instructing me to please leave a message. With a sinking feeling, I hung up.

But not five minutes later, my phone rang, and Ms. Rogers greeted me.

"I see you called, Mr. Landrum. Is it possible for us to meet? I'd like to get your answers to some questions about this morning?"

I'd already decided it was acceptable; that was why I'd called.

"Sure, could you meet me in the restaurant at the Holiday Inn? I'm only about three blocks away; we could get some breakfast. I don't know about you, but an early-morning murder gives me an appetite."

"That sounds good; I'll meet you there in a half hour."

CHAPTER 4

I could have walked the three blocks to the Holiday Inn, but I was feeling light-headed and decided to trust my foot on the gas pedal rather than using my legs for transportation. Actually, I wasn't all that unfamiliar with the Inn; I'd been here before, as you'll soon see. The hostess at One Center Street Bar and Grill, the hotel's restaurant, welcomed me to the almost empty dining room. A Monday morning in early April is not a busy time at the only chain hotel on Folly Beach. She offered me the choice of any table. I chose one overlooking the Atlantic and the impressive Folly Pier. She saw me looking at it and offered that the pier was 1,045 feet long with 170 benches. Two facts I doubt many have verified. I told her one other person would be joining me, so she brought water for two, and coffee, and left me to wait.

A few minutes later, Ms. Rogers, in all of her trim five feet and one inch glory, confidently strolled into the dining room and immediately walked toward my table. Thanks to the sheriff's department, I was wearing different clothes than when she had seen me earlier. I'd like to think she recognized me because of my charming smile and wonderful personality. It was really because I was the only male in the room.

I stood. She greeted me with her outstretched hand, no cell phone this time, and thanked me for meeting her. I asked if she were hungry and hoped she'd say yes before we did any talking. I was approaching famished but didn't want to order unless she wanted something. She said yes, and I quickly signaled the waitress.

Without even glancing at the menu, Ms. Rogers ordered grits, wheat toast, and black coffee. I was from farther north, so I skipped the grits and went directly for a power breakfast of two eggs over easy, bacon, very well done if not burnt, rye toast and hash browns.

Not ordering grits was a mistake.

"No *grits?* You are either very sick and traumatized after this morning's find, or you're a damn Yankee," she exclaimed with a rather strong—and I suspected slightly feigned—southern belle accent. The pleasant smile that went with the words *damn Yankee* didn't hurt her Diane Sawyer looks a bit. "You better just be sick," she continued, and without taking a breath, she asked, "Are you aware that this very weekend, just sixty miles from here, the entire world will be celebrating grits at the World Grits Festival?"

"No, Ms. Rogers, I'm not ... or I *wasn't.*"

"First, it's Tammy, and second, you had better start eating them—grits, I mean—here or you'll not be treated kindly. And, third—I forgot third earlier—Mr. Landrum, those thousands of grits lovers who will be converging on little St. George this weekend will be attending concerts and celebrating everything there is to celebrate about grits. You could go and compete in the 'Rolling in the Grits' competition. I'm sure you don't need to ask how you win *that* world famous competition."

I paused and gazed at her from under my brows, trying to figure out just how serious she was about all this. The fetching, wry curve of her lips and the way she returned my gaze told me *not very.*

Gaining more of a voice I replied, "It's Chris, and I don't see how it could take long to celebrate everything there is to celebrate about grits. And please don't even *attempt* to tell me about the Rolling in the Grits competition."

A little smile was beginning to appear, and I concluded that our breakfast conversation would continue without her throwing a plate of grits in my face.

"We better get down to business," she said. "Since I saw you this morning, I've spoken with Detective Lawson, Chief Newman, two of our reporters in Charleston, and some of the construction workers gathered at the coast guard property. If you don't mind, would you walk through everything you saw and did out there? Starting at the beginning?"

I didn't go clear back to getting out of bed and heading straight to the bathroom. I began my story with getting out of the car at the coast guard station, and after having rehearsed the story three times for the police, I got through it with a minimum of wasted words. Ms. Rogers—Tammy—took notes and interrupted me only once. That was by the time our breakfast arrived—my northern version, her southern.

When I finished my well-rehearsed story, she asked question, after question, after question. I don't believe I told her much more than I'd shared with the police, but her skilled questioning was impressive. In spite of the fact that she was a petite bundle of energy, she not only listened, but appeared to understand what I had been experiencing and feeling.

She was even interested in the time I was spending traipsing around the area and photographing about everything I saw, and in the fact that I'd purchased a new wide-angle lens before leaving home and was intent on using it as much as possible. I was pleased someone appeared interested—the police sure hadn't been.

We finished my story, and she asked if I knew who James Lionetti was.

"I only heard his name this morning. I have no idea who he is—or was."

"Well, you came across a very influential body." She took a couple of bites of her grits—which produced such an expression of absolute bliss as to leave me totally puzzled—and continued. "He was one of Charleston's, and most likely, South Carolina's largest developers. I won't bore you with all the details. Buy tomorrow's paper, and 'read all about it.' From the few folks I've talked to this morning, the consensus is that he was a sleazy, fat, egotistical, backstabbing, son of a bitch. Those were the nice comments."

"One of his 'colleagues' said that the only reason he wasn't a bigger backstabber was that those who knew him wouldn't let him get close enough to stab them. The person who told me that didn't want to be quoted—surprise!"

"He's—excuse me—he *was* married to old money. His wife—there I go again—*widow* is from a several generation Charleston family that made its fortune in cotton and whatever else was popular at the time. They lived in a mansion near The Battery, her family home by the way. She is deeply involved in the Charleston arts' scene—a strong supporter of the annual Spoleto Festival, and she almost single-handedly supports two of the area's acting companies. As you can imagine, she is loved by the patrons of the arts. In fact, she is loved by the arts people almost as much as he was hated by the development community."

After a few more bites of what looked to me like soggy, bland grits, she said, "The biggest challenge for the police will be to decide if they want to list the potential suspects alphabetically or in chronological order. Either way, it'll be long." She stopped eating and looked straight at me, obviously serious. "Are you sure you didn't take a photo of the killer? That sure would make my story easier and please the photo editor to no end."

I took more bites from a real breakfast, and sadly told her there were no pho-tos of the killer. At least none that I'd taken. I could tell that she was about fin-ished with her breakfast of the South and was somewhat distracted. I assumed she was mentally working on her story. I was sitting quietly, wondering if she were through with me and what I was going to be doing next, when the ringing of her phone interrupted the silence.

After a brief, "Yes, I'll be back in about a half hour; tell him I'll talk to him when I get there," she hung up, said she had to go, and motioned for the check. She threw a twenty on the table and asked for a receipt, then abruptly stood and asked that I call if I thought of anything else. She did thank me for meeting with her and strongly suggested that I acquire a taste for grits. I couldn't tell whether she was a crime reporter or a food critic.

After watching her walk quickly to the door, her heels clicking on the tiles, I asked for a refill of coffee and sat staring at the ocean and the sparkles of sunlight the mid-day sun was skipping off the breaking waves.

The question kept going over in my mind, "What have I got myself into?"

CHAPTER 5

Before crossing the Folly River last Saturday morning—that was two days before this murder fiasco—I had seen something on the side of the road that reminded me why I was here; something I had seen five years ago on my first visit that had gnawed on my unconscious ever since. It was a boat—or to those who live on Folly, more accurately, *The Boat*. It hadn't served any nautical function in seventeen or more years. In 1989, Hugo, the most powerful hurricane to strike South Carolina in more than a hundred years, picked up the thirty-foot boat from who knows where and deposited it at the side of the road to welcome friends and strangers to Folly Beach, "The Edge of America."

No one ever claimed the displaced vessel. The residents, showing their sense of humor and perspective, decided to leave it there and make it an ever-changing community billboard. It now regularly sports new paint with messages ranging from "Happy Birthday, Laura," "Happy Anniversary, Fred and Marilyn," "Will You Marry Me, Jane?" and a collection of less socially acceptable messages. All it takes to change the message is a coat of white paint and multi-colored letters painted by someone who usually remains anonymous—correct spelling and grammar optional!

The Boat wasn't what brought me back to Folly. But it was a symbol of the reasons I returned—a depiction of the character of the island, of the character of the residents, and of the laid-back atmosphere that prevails here.

My few days here five years ago had been a lot less memorable than this visit was turning out to be. I had attended a three-day Human Resources Conference in Charleston. I'm a human resource specialist for a multi-national health care company headquartered in Louisville, Kentucky, and had been asked to partici-pate in a panel discussion on the implications of recent changes in federal legisla-tion on sexual harassment in the workplace—a topic that sounds much more exciting than it really is. My part of the conference ended Thursday afternoon, and I wanted to head to the nearest beach for three days in the sun. A look at a map of South Carolina showed that a place called Folly Beach met my criteria—that is, it was the nearest. The only thing I knew was the name and that it was only seventeen miles from the hotel where I was staying. A quick Internet search revealed a Holiday Inn on the beach. It was late summer, most of the kids were back in school, and the hotel had a room available for the weekend. Perfect!

I arrived late in the day, caught a brief glimpse of *The Boat* on my drive in, thought it strange, but didn't give it another thought, and drove directly to the Holiday Inn. Folly Road dead-ends in the parking lot of the hotel, so finding it did not present a challenge. I had a wonderful room on the sixth floor with a great view of the beach, Folly Pier, and the Atlantic Ocean. It had all the accou-trements you'd find in a normal chain hotel room. It was clean, convenient, attractive, and had a nice restaurant and swimming pool only an elevator ride away.

By Saturday afternoon, I'd experienced everything one could experience at the wonderful, nice, convenient, chain hotel. The property was everything a Holiday Inn should be—a consistent, predictable stay, which is to say that I could have been staying at any nice chain hotel anywhere in the world.

But I wanted something different, and so I began to explore the surrounding area on foot. A five-minute walk from the door of the hotel took me up Center Street (the name of Folly Road when you get on the island) to the center of town. Center Street is roughly the east-west center of the island as well as the street through the center of the "business district." A good choice for a street name, it seemed.

The island is only about seven blocks deep, so it doesn't take long to explore Center Street. On the other hand, it's more than six miles wide, so walking the entire beach was outside my range. The size and shape of the island was quite appealing; the west end is anchored by a county park and the east by an aban-doned coast guard station overlooking the Morris Island Lighthouse.

In strong contrast to the feel and atmosphere of the Holiday Inn, the island is anything but sterile. Even the street names are indicators that something is differ-ent about Folly. Here in South Carolina, you find streets named Huron, Hud-son, Erie, and the ever-popular southern street named Arctic Avenue.

"What's the deal with the strange street names," I'd asked the bubbly and usually informative desk clerk on that long ago day.

"What's strange about them?" she asked.

Surely I wasn't the first person to ask her this question.

"Doesn't it seem a bit odd that some have the same name as some of the Great Lakes up north," I asked, attempting to clarify. "Also, what's Arctic have to do with your lovely southern coast?"

"Don't have a clue," she responded after another moment of deep contemplation.

That succinctly summarized the collective wisdom of others I'd asked during that stay. Some questions just shouldn't be asked.

The mix of housing appeared to be some old, some older, and some oldest—mostly small, fishing village-like structures. Of course there were a few, very few, new McMansions but they stuck out like, well … McMansions.

The nine-floor hotel was the tallest building on the beach; one four-story condo complex the nearest competitor, and everything else came in a distant third. Folly Beach was clearly different. I began to suspect there were more true "characters" in its two thousand residents than in all the rest of the state. That judgment was based solely on the appearance of the houses and stores.

That brief stay had ended way too soon. I'd had to leave early Sunday for my eleven-hour drive home. On the way out of town, my eyes caught sight of *The Boat*—a picture that returned several times in memory over the next few years. That old, dilapidated vessel came to symbolize the Folly Beach that would play a significant role in my life.

*   *   *   *

So now, here I was. I'd looked forward to this day for months—in fact, for years. I'd accumulated four weeks of vacation and had expected to spend it all on Folly and in the surrounding area. Other than a nice, long vacation, I had another, deeper motive—to find and purchase a vacation home.

CHAPTER 6

The first thing I had to do last Saturday was to find somewhere to stay for the month. Some would call it poor planning that I hadn't found a place before coming. I like to think it was only that I wanted to get in the laid-back, unhurried spirit of Folly Beach. Besides, April wasn't a busy month, and there should be plenty of places available.

The first realty company I spotted was Island Realty, so I pulled into the parking lot, my tires crunching on the crushed shell and gravel. It was still morning and also early in the season, so that not many of the rental vacationers had arrived. The lot only had one car, a twenty-plus-year-old Oldsmobile. It was covered with rust, so I doubted it would be classed a collectable of that now defunct division of General Motors. Island Realty was a small frame house that had gone commercial. On the door was a hand-printed sign saying, COME IN. Interesting—why else stand on the porch and look at the door unless you wanted to come in? I vowed not to ask, and as directed, I went in.

The lobby looked more like the office of a mom-and-pop motel in Kansas. Pictures and pleasant furniture and florescent lighting gave it a cheery feel. There was a brochure rack on the wall, and a sign-in clipboard lying on a cheaply wood-paneled counter. In the corner beyond the counter, on an old battleship gray metal secretary's desk, an IBM Selectric typewriter was humming away—I knew it was a Selectric because I had had one in my office a thousand years ago. That was before the typewriter went the way of the mimeograph machine. But on a small table in another corner sat a computer—not turned on. I suspected that was the case most days. Looking at me from behind the typewriter was the smiling face of a seventy-plus-year-old lady in a loud green and yellow floral-patterned dress.

"Hi! Want to check out?" she asked brightly.

"I sure hope not! Especially at my young age." I said, hoping to equal her smile. "I just got here and want to find somewhere to stay for a few weeks."

"Oh." From the look on her face, you'd have thought I'd asked where I could park my spaceship. "Usually folks who come in in the morning are going to check out. Our realtors don't get here until after two on Saturday. I'm sorry— and I'm being rude. I'm Louise. Is your family in the car?"

Just the kind of thing someone named Louise, in a flowery dress, eligible for AARP membership for the last quarter century, would ask.

I explained I was the entire family.

Unable to get the assistance of a professional realtor this "early" on Saturday, I asked Louise if she could help me. I told her I was looking to rent a small house or cottage for the month. The size wasn't that important; and I didn't expect it to be on the beach, or even facing the marsh—although that would be nice. I was here alone, and price *was* important. Her interest picked up significantly when I told her I was here to buy a house for a part-time retirement home "at the beach."

"Well," she said, "folks usually rent their houses from us several weeks and months before they get here. Gosh, many do it *years* in advance so they can get what they want. They stay the same place every year. I don't think we have much available. But let me check."

After that mini-lecture on the correct way to rent a house, she was now look-ing through what appeared to be an old journal. I was afraid she was going to have to fire-up the computer; I doubted her ability to maneuver through it and find what I was looking for.

"Let's see," she said, "it looks like there are three houses vacant. No, I'm sorry, only two. The Lamkins are coming in on the fifteenth for a week, so their house wouldn't be available all month. We have a nice house out on Ashley Avenue. It's about twelve blocks from the center of town east of here. Just turn on Ashley and look for our sign in the yard; you can't miss it.

"I've been in it a couple of times and it's nice," she said. "Three bedrooms and three baths, it shows here, but I couldn't swear to that. I don't remember three baths." She was rambling now. "This shows it would rent for seventeen hundred. High for April, if you ask me, but that's what it says."

I now knew why she wasn't one of the realtors; most likely she was the elderly maiden aunt of the owner.

"What about the other house?" I asked.

"I'm not sure about that one. I don't recall ever being in it. It was rented for the winter through Memorial Day weekend, but the folks renting it—such a *nice* family, have two little kids; they were from Pennsylvania—had a family emergency and left last week. This says it's a little smaller than the Ashley house, but it looks the same to me from the outside. It rents for fifteen-fifty. Three bedrooms and two baths—doubt you'll need both baths though, since you can use only one at a time. It's on West Cooper. Just head toward the ocean and turn right on Cooper. It's on the right. We should have a sign up there too."

She closed the book, laid it sharply down on the desk, and as she pulled out a drawer, I heard the jingle of keys. "Tell you what," she said. "Why don't I just give you the key to both houses. You can take your time, walk through them, and let me know if either works. How does that sound?"

That sounded like something a real rental agent would say, so I jumped at the offer.

"Now don't steal the keys," she cautioned as she handed them to me.

I doubted I could get much for two keys—even on E-Bay.

"Worry not," I said. "I'll bring them back within the hour."

She handed me a map of Folly Beach and, with a black Sharpie fine point, marked the locations of the two houses with little x's. The map had been photocopied from another map—most likely from another realty company—and had an Island Realty sticker pasted on the front. She didn't ask me not to steal the map.

I thanked her and set out on what I thought would be one of my biggest adventures and challenges of the month. I was wrong; very wrong.

*   *   *   *

Both houses, from first glance, appeared to predate Hurricane Hugo—which itself was years ago—and to have survived. Actually, judging from their style and age, they might have survived the Civil War. Rustic, quaint, full of character—all words I would learn to use when describing many of the houses on Folly. But my first reaction to each was, "What a dump!"

The Ashley house hadn't been painted since the 1960s. It had been sea green at one time—one time very long ago. From the street, I saw that it had a nice screened-in front porch, and once in the living room, discovered a fairly new carpet. The owners obviously took more pride in the interior than in the outside. Everything was neat and clean. It had several windows—always a nice feature. What it didn't have was proximity to town. I could walk, but it would have been more than an easy stroll.

The house on West Cooper was about the same age. I could imagine the owners of this house fighting for the Confederacy, and the Ashley owners proudly taking up guns for the North. Of course neither house was really that old. The exterior of the West Cooper Street house sat perched above a concrete block carport, and from the front, the arrangement looked like a giant letter "T." The purpose for the elevation, I suspected, was to keep the living space above the tide rushes from visiting hurricanes. And the place was still standing, so the architectural tactic had obviously worked. The house had a walk-around open porch spanning the front. On the porch were two white plastic chairs—the kind you see stacked at all self-respecting grocery stores during the summer.

The front room was a sunroom with eight windows around the front and sides. Unfortunately, the view was quite *un*spectacular since it was only of West Cooper Avenue and a shack across the street. If it hadn't been for the shack across the street, some trees, two houses on West Ashley Avenue, some more trees, one large house on West Arctic Avenue, and the dunes, I would have had a view of the ocean. That sure beats what a citizen of the state of Missouri has to look through, or over, to see the Atlantic. I was lucky.

There was a toilet and sink in the living space, but the shower was in the second bath adjacent to the "laundry room" beside the carport—in other words, downstairs and almost outside. Louise was wrong; I *would* need both bathrooms. The house had a washer and dryer, cable television, minimal furnishings, and was located less than two blocks from town. That clinched it.

Good to my promise, I crossed the threshold of Island Realty forty-five minutes after I'd left. "Aunt" Louise—I'm sure she won't mind adopting a new nephew—greeted me and seemed disappointed when I told her I had chosen the house on West Cooper. Maybe it was because she had never been in it. She took my credit card, handed me a second key, and a five-page handout of rules that gave me some interesting reading material. As I was about to leave the office, I noticed there was no sign saying GO OUT. I had my hand on the doorknob when Louise told me that when I was ready to seriously look for a house to buy, I should call Bob Howard, "the best realtor on Folly Beach." Coincidentally, Mr. Howard worked for Island Realty.

*   *   *   *

While it was yet morning on this Saturday, the first day of April, I headed to my rented house. From having absolutely no plan to moving-in seemed to me a major achievement.

Even before I unlocked the door, I met my neighbor. I was standing on the porch with a suitcase in one hand and key in the other when I became aware of him.

"Hi, you a realtor?" boomed the low, strong voice of a tall, thin black man. He walked across the yard from the well-manicured house on the right.

When I replied that I wasn't a realtor but was moving in, he said, "I saw you looking at the house a little while ago and assumed you were a realtor deciding whether you wanted to show it. The family that was living here left just last week."

"Hi, again," he said, coming to the foot of the steps and looking up at me. "I'm William Hansel. You can call me Bill or William—I answer to either; don't really have a preference. I've been able to avoid that dilemma over at the College of Charleston where I work. Most just call me Dr. Hansel." A not-so-subtle hint to his academic credentials and status.

I hadn't even got to my name, much less where I work and what most people call me, when he proceeded to tell me he was a professor, tenured, in the hospitality and tourism program. Still at the door with a key in one hand and a suitcase in the other, I didn't ask him more about his career. Truth be known, I hadn't yet asked him anything. I hoped I could just tell him who I was and start moving in. So I said, "Bill, I'm Chris. I'll be vacationing here all month. It's good to meet you." Then gesturing with the suitcase, "I'd better get in and get the air conditioner started."

Either Bill took the hint or just didn't know what to tell me next. He said he would talk to me later. I didn't doubt that for a second.

Bringing in my two suitcases was simple, and the hang-up bag of clothes was a quick carry. The more difficult, and more tedious, move was bringing in my photo-printer and camera equipment.

✻   ✻   ✻   ✻

Work was simply work. My true passion for more years than I want to remember has been photography. During my youth, I had owned most of the popular inexpensive kinds of cameras of the day. After college, I'd graduated to a cheap thirty-five-millimeter, then to a twin-lens, medium-format camera, then even to a Hasselblad for a while. But wanting a handier camera, I had gone back to the thirty-five millimeters, starting with an old Nikon, then to the most recent auto focus models. Five years ago, kicking and screaming, I had entered the digital age, and had started over again in learning what to do after I tripped the shutter. I had learned on a fairly simple point-and-shoot model, and was now using a ten megapixel Nikon, single-lens reflex camera. If you're familiar with cameras and photography, this makes sense—if not, sorry.

One of the fantastic features of digital is that it allows you to take your darkroom wherever you go—if you want to lug a printer, that is.

"Can I give you a hand," my new neighbor asked as he reappeared beside my car.

"Sure," I said, hoping I didn't show too much surprise at his kindly offer. "This printer moves much easier carried by four hands."

Adding his two, we gingerly lugged the Epson photo-printer up the stairs to its new residence in bedroom number two—a bedroom that looked out toward the ocean. (That sounded so much better to me than saying "overlooking the shack across the street.") Normally, I would have left the printer at home, but I'd never been away from it for a month, and I was afraid it would think I'd deserted it. Besides, I hoped to use it often while down here.

"So what line of work are you in, if you don't mind my asking?" said Bill.

"I don't mind at all," I said. "Next May, I will have been a mostly happy employee with a large health care company for thirty years. Somehow, because of the way the stars are aligned, a little luck, and a decent company buy-out plan, I'll soon be able to retire. Not that I'm counting—but that's thirteen months, fifteen days from now."

"I'm glad you're not counting," said Bill with a small smile. "What's your specialty?"

"Good question," I said. "Six years ago, I took a lateral move from marketing to the human resource department. The official reason was reorganization in the marketing department. My take was that they were moving some of the old codgers out of the fast-paced marketing operation. That was fine with me; same salary, less stress and travel."

I supposed I'd said enough about my job, since Bill appeared to have lost interest, which was fine with me.

On top of the carport, we found a card table that would serve as a printer stand with room left for my laptop computer. I'd be able to download the images from the camera, edit and subject them to the wizardry of Photoshop, and then send them to the printer.

With Bill watching, I got my third most important room in the house in somewhat acceptable shape (the bedroom being first, bathroom second, living room—with the television—fourth. Then any room besides the kitchen next). Only when that was done did I start to explore my home away from home—with

Bill at my heels. The couch had, or more accurately, at one time *had* had, a light colored tropical pattern that was now more of a squashed pea green. The only chair was sturdy but far from attractive or comfortable. I supposed it was still there because it had refused to fall apart.

On a better note, the television was a modern, twenty-five inch model with a remote that actually worked. The flooring in the kitchen showed a great deal of use—I wouldn't be contributing to its wear much further. The counters had held many a meal, but the fixtures worked well. The refrigerator functioned as intended. My main interest was the freezer. Would it keep ice cream hard? That was my acid test for the kitchen appliances anywhere I went.

There were several lamps, but none of them had a bulb. The former residents must have thought there was a light bulb shortage in their native Pennsylvania, and taken all they could find home with them.

"I've got some bulbs at the house you can use until you get some," Bill offered.

"Thanks, but I need to go to the store in a little while anyway," I said. I didn't want to be indebted to someone my first hour on the island. But the offer did give me a warm feeling about my neighbor.

Bill said he had pestered me enough for the day and left almost as quickly as he had arrived. The light bulb shortage reminded me I really needed to start a list of things to get at the grocery. I'd noticed a Piggly Wiggly on Folly Road before crossing over the river to the island.

The temperature was in the upper seventies under a cloudless sky, so I decided to walk along the water. After the quick five minutes to the public beach, I was able to stroll along the primary feature that had brought me here—the Atlantic Ocean with its strong waves, soothing sounds, and sand stretching in two directions as far as I could see. This was almost heaven. I spent an hour walking past the pier to a point where small houses dominated, then returned to the beach section that was located just before the Folly Beach Park. There I sat in the sand and enjoyed peace and quiet—if you overlook the sound of waves. I didn't overlook the sound so much as I soaked it in. Then I headed back to reality and my new, most favorite house on West Cooper Avenue.

I completed my must have list, and headed back to the Piggly Wiggly in that strip center just off the island where I nearly froze in the overly air conditioned store as I shopped for the necessities—ice cream, chocolate syrup, candy, three bottles of wine (two Chardonnay and one Cabernet), chips and dip, bread, mayonnaise, Velveeta cheese, peanut butter, and coffee. I also stocked up on such luxury items as toilet paper, paper towels, coffee filters, and diet Dr Peppers. I also picked up one of those multi-colored folding chase lounges to take to the beach. And I reminded myself not to forget the light bulbs.

By the time I returned from the store, I was feeling the effects of that morning on the road, finding a place to stay, the walk on the beach, and the trip to the grocery. That's an activity that exhausts me every time. No partying tonight; I was ready for bed. Sleep came quickly.

CHAPTER 7

My first full day on Folly was a Sunday—I used it as a day of rest. I took a leisurely shower beside the carport. Excuse me, in the lower level bathroom, and walked the two blocks to town and The Lost Dog Café. I had seen the restaurant on my first visit but hadn't gone inside. It was to become my breakfast—and often lunch—restaurant of choice. The welcoming sign read "Lost Dog Café, Coffee and a Bite." Clever, I thought. Who gets the bite, you or the dog? In any case, it wasn't your ordinary Bob Evans. The décor was "early amateur-construction-worker-built" booths along one wall, mismatched wood chairs at several tables in the middle and along the front window, and a stand-up bar counter along the other side. Everywhere you looked, you were facing photographs of dogs, dogs, and dogs. Dogs looking at you, dogs on the beach, dogs looking at the Folly Pier, dogs frowning, dogs smiling; simply a doggone lot of photos of canines.

The Lost Dog Café was *the* place for breakfast. I was lucky to get a booth; all the tables were filled with locals. I say *locals* because of the dogs—real, not photos—tied up outside the door, and judged that the patrons weren't tourists because they didn't have sunburned foreheads and shoulders. As soon as I was seated, a waitress approached me, quite pleasant to the eye with short, cropped hair, a big smile, and a "Lost Dog Café" polo style shirt that featured the restaurant and the pleasing shape of the wearer.

"Good morning," she said, "I'm Amber, and will be doing everything I can to make your breakfast experience as positive as possible." That well-rehearsed introduction would bring a smile to the face of the dourest patron. It did for me.

For one thing, I liked her voice. It had a nice, warm timbre that went well with her eyes and the way she met my gaze. There was a little more than a touch of the South in her words.

"Well, Amber," my words stumbled a bit as I tried to bring my attention back to the menu she'd handed me, "what would you recommend so my breakfast experience is as positive as possible?"

Suddenly her rehearsed veneer was gone. She gave a little laugh. "Thanks for listening to what I said; most folks just say something like, 'coffee with cream.' Did you see the chalkboard outside listing today's specials?"

I said no and asked what I'd missed.

"To me, the best thing we serve—other than my charm—is the Belgian waffle. We generally have it on weekends. That's why it's on the board outside and not on the menu. Go figure!"

I wasn't in any mood to try to figure anything; after all, I was on vacation. So I said I'd take the waffle. Amber seemed pleased with her sales pitch, and happily went off to place the order.

I watched her walk away, but when she disappeared into the kitchen, my gaze strayed up to the surrounding walls. Getting a little unsettled with all those dog photos staring at me, I was glad I had picked up a copy of the Charleston newspaper on my way in, even if it had cost a dollar fifty—six quarters in the language newspaper machines understand.

Before I finished the first three news sections, Amber reappeared with the best item not on the menu—my Belgian waffle.

"I've worked here for going on nine years," she said, "and I don't recall seeing you before. Are you a tourist or some jewel thief hiding from the law?" She sat the plate in front of me and then straightened as if really waiting for an answer.

I asked how many jewel thieves she'd waited on in the nine years.

"Don't rightly know; they seldom reveal their occupation when I ask."

Not seeing much future in that line of questioning, I told her I was somewhere between a typical tourist and a permanent resident, and that I planned to be here all month. I avoided the jewel thief question.

"Well," she said with little tilt of her head, "welcome to Folly—it's full of charm, personality, and mystery." (At the time, I had no idea how accurate that really was.) "You're always welcome at The Lost Dog. If you ever come in when I'm working and you don't sit in one of my sections, I'll make sure the cook poisons your food."

I said I'd keep that in mind. And by the way, she was right about the waffle—fantastic!

The rest of my day was hardly worth mentioning. I spent an hour walking up and down the beach; walked to the end of the Folly Pier; then took my newly acquired beach lounge chair down to water's edge and rested the day away.

After a hardy peanut butter sandwich supper chased with a bowl of ice cream, I spent the rest of the evening setting-up my laptop to the Internet and my printer.

*   *   *   *

You already know about Monday—not exactly how I planned to spend the day, but, as the old card players would say, "You got to play the hand you're dealt." Of course a lot of those old card players also died from the cards they were dealt.

CHAPTER 8

The first thought I had Tuesday was *Thank God, I'm alive*. That was quickly followed by *How did I make it through yesterday?* After all, how often do I hear of someone being murdered, and how often am I that close to a murderer—especially one that had my life in the crosshairs of his gun?

As I view life, the best way to get past fear is to avoid its causes—a helpful technique I'd learned years ago in college.

Keep busy, I told myself when I got up before sunrise. I quickly showered in the "guest bathroom." (How many names can I come up with to describe that carport shower?)

The sun was just throwing its first gold over the island as I walked down Second Street past the Rolling Thunder Roadhouse Café—an upscale dive catering to the locals—toward the Charleston Oceanfront Villas. After many years working in marketing, I appreciated the charm of using the term *villas* to describe a large condominium complex. To be honest, The Villas, the only large condo on Folly, looked like a tall, thin stucco-sided building that had fallen on its side and now covered two blocks of prime oceanfront property. The four-floor complex—excuse me, *villas*—stood on pilings and had parking underneath. That allowed those who lived in the more Folly-like houses across the street to peer through the open space underneath and get a glimpse of the beach. That is, if they could see around the American and imported SUVs and new European luxury cars clogging the villa's lot.

I turned on East Arctic—hardly an iceberg in site—and walked the short distance to the Holiday Inn. I said hello to the friendly and "way-too-cheerful-for-that-time-of-day-receptionist and made straight for the complementary coffee bar. I interpreted *complementary* to mean for all visitors and residents of Folly. As the courts would say, "a broad interpretation." And it's possible that the management had a more limited view of those who should partake.

Then I walked outside to the newspaper racks and bought the Tuesday issue of the *Post and Courier,* Charleston's daily newspaper.

In spite of Ms. Rogers's—Tammy's—having told me, I didn't realize how important James Lionetti was until I saw the front page above the fold article about his murder. This was, I hoped, the only time my name would ever appear on the front page of a major newspaper. In any case, I was eager to see what was what. So there beside the hotel entrance—not wanting to press my welcome by going back in and drinking their free coffee—I leaned casually against the stucco wall, and nodding occasionally to those who came and went, read Tammy's banner headline article on yesterday's murder.

FOLLY BEACH—The body of James F. Lionetti, a prominent Charleston real estate developer, was found Monday morning on a deserted stretch of land on Folly Beach.

According to Larry Keeling, a spokesperson for the Charleston County Sheriff's Department, the death is being treated as a homicide. Sources close to the investigation indicate Lionetti was shot multiple times just before 8:00 AM. A vacationer to the island, Chris Landrum from Kentucky, heard two shots, found the body, and called the police. There are no known suspects.

The body of the sixty-seven-year-old developer was found on the east end of a beach on property that formerly housed a coast guard station.

Lionetti's wife, Sally Roosevelt Lionetti, a well-known supporter of the Charleston art scene, told the police that her husband left their Church Street house at six thirty to visit his development properties. One of the properties is a duplex on the beach at Folly, about a half-mile from where the body was found. The construction crew told investigators they had not seen Lionetti that morning.

Lionetti, owner of Lion Development Company, was well-known in the area as a hard-nosed, aggressive businessman. Richard Finnell, president of the Charleston Metro Chamber of Commerce, said, "I'm shocked by such tragic news. Jim has made an indelible mark on the face of Charleston; his efforts provided growth opportunities for businesses in the city and numerous high-quality housing units. He will be missed."

A Folly Beach resident and fellow developer, Frank Long, expressed shock. "Jim was not only a strong competitor, but a friend and someone who would stand by you once he made a commitment."

Over the past thirty years, Lionetti developed some of the area's largest shopping complexes, apartment buildings, and luxury condominiums.

The article continued with more information about Lionetti's family and requested that anyone knowing anything about the shooting should contact the Charleston County Sheriff's Department.

Reading the story clearly brought home the terrible impact of yesterday's murder on the community. I had somehow hoped the entire day had been a dream. It wasn't.

I was struck by how neutral the article seemed—especially after hearing Tammy describe what she knew about Mr. Lionetti's dark side. The rumors and "sizzle" were absent from the story. This was a watered-down version, totally devoid of what she had described to me as the "cruel, unethical practices" of the late developer.

The main thing the article didn't contain was news that someone had been arrested for the crime. No one had; I wanted too much, too soon.

*   *   *   *

I spent the rest of the morning and part of the afternoon walking the neighborhood. This gave me a chance to pick-up fact sheets on several houses for sale, and if there wasn't information available, to take photos. To put it mildly, a walking tour of the area was fascinating. At first glance, many of the houses appeared dilapidated and in terrible repair. But on closer inspection, they were solid, appeared weatherproof; most were clearly lived in and not just beach houses for weekend rental. I was surprised how many had children's toys and swing sets in the yard. And a couple even had trampolines—although in Folly style, they were in the front yard and not in back where the world I know keeps them tucked away.

And along the way, I was snapping shots of things that provoked my interest.

"Hey mister," the young voice came from somewhere to my right, "why are you taking pictures of 'Old Blue'?"

I was so intent on capturing the light reflecting off old beer bottles attached to a tree trunk, I hadn't seen the young boy leaning on the fence in the next yard. I grinned at him.

"Hi," I said, a little embarrassed at being caught.

The tree had been cut off at about four or so feet, the remaining trunk impregnated with gutter nails placed at an upward angle, and the beer bottles placed over the long nails. The tree or stump—or whatever it was—looked like a blue Christmas tree with an attitude. I assumed this work of "Folly art" was what he meant by "Old Blue."

"What's your name," I asked.

"I'm Sam. That's short for Samuel, but I hate that name. Mom says it'll sound better to me when I get older."

"So Sam, what's the story with 'Old Blue'?"

"Mr. Black, the guy who lives there, says that with 'Old Blue,' it's always Christmas here. His tree don't rot or fall apart like all the other Christmas trees."

"That makes sense," I said.

"Yeah, but I keep telling him the bottles should be red. Whoever heard of a blue Christmas tree?"

"I have to agree with you there, Sam," I said, although from what I've seen, a blue Christmas tree on Folly didn't seem out of place at all.

"I better keep going. I'm taking photos of some of the interesting things I see."

"There'll be a lot of them," said Sam, showing a keen sense of perspective far beyond his ten or so years of age.

Sam, of course, was right. I saw at least three old pick-up trucks and mini-vans with many miles on them and almost as many hand-painted messages as were on *The Boat*. I must've been out of it, not realizing that true pet lovers painted portraits of their dogs and cats on vehicles.

Most every abode presented me with a "photo op." I took advantage and shot about a hundred images before my walk ended. I noticed a Folly Beach patrol car a couple of times during the day and almost expected the officer to stop and ask why I was photographing houses, cars, and—"unique," to put it mildly—yard art.

By late afternoon, I had been fairly successful at keeping myself busy enough to not think much about the terrible events of yesterday. I'd accumulated eight fact sheets and photographed several others. I'd had fun photographing what I really liked taking pictures of—unique items in an unusual environment and from a little different perspective on what most others photographed.

Who wouldn't take a photo of a bumper sticker on an old Ford Edsel that said "I Brake for Unicorns!" Someone once told me I make the mundane look good. Although, some of the images turned out to be so mundane that I deleted them on the spot. Anyway, I think the comment was a compliment.

I returned home and began the tedious process of downloading the day's photos from the camera to my laptop and cataloging them.

After they were downloaded, I made a duplicate set by burning the images on a compact disk. Like most digital photographers, I've had the hard drive in my computer crash and take my photos with it. It only takes once before you learn to make copies. When I'm away from home like I was in Folly, I just burn a CD each day of what I've taken and leave it in the car. I'm even so anal I'd brought along a copy of Photoshop in case something happened to my laptop. I was never a Boy Scout—but I did read their handbook, especially the "be prepared" part.

*   *   *   *

With the photos downloaded and the duplicate disk burned, I put the memory card in the car and took out one of the other five I'd brought for the camera.

My feet were telling me I'd had a busy day. Unfortunately, with my "keep busy" exercises completed, my mind wandered back to yesterday morning. The fears that I'd been numb to earlier in the day kept bouncing around in my head and occasionally vibrated through my entire body. I kept thinking there must be something I'd forgotten that might be helpful to the police. Had I actually seen the killer sometime before I headed to the beach? Had I noticed his or her car along the road or down one of the drives near the entrance to the coast guard property?

No matter how many times I asked, the answer was the same. I didn't remember seeing anything, hearing anything—other than shots—or smelling anything. Since I've never had any indication that I was a psychic, I eliminated that possibility.

So I watched *NCIS* and a rerun of *MASH* before drifting off to sleep.

*   *   *   *

It was raining so hard the next day that I didn't walk to the Holiday Inn for a cup of their complimentary coffee. Instead, I took time to look at some of the magazines whoever had lived here last left on the coffee table and on the yard sale end table by the couch. The age of most of the magazines made the selections at my doctor's office seem hot off the press. The most recent issue was two years old.

Issues of *Fitness* (which I quickly skipped), *Vegetarian Times*, *American Cowboy*, *Maxim* (which I had to review twice because I'd skipped *Fitness*), *Surfing*, *Teen World*, and even the magazine I would nominate for being the "most out of place on Folly," *Architectural Digest*, were all available for my reading pleasure. Few had mailing labels. They'd obviously been bought from convenience stores here and there and brought to the island by their new owners, only to be left for future residents' use and enjoyment. Someone must have bought *Fitness* and actually read it—amazing!

I got tired of the magazines and scanned a couple of *informative* brochures left for those who followed. There was one published by an organization called Birds Are Us—honest! Under the heading, Folly Beach, I learned there were one hundred sixty-eight kinds of birds that you might see. My knowledge of birds is limited to basic colors—blue jay, redbird, blackbird, and robin (I know that's not a color, but I know one when I see it). I wouldn't recognize a Whimbrel, Bells Vireo, or Soro if it sat on my shoulder, said hello, and then pooped!

My mind wandered, as it will when looking through such exciting magazines as *Vegetarian Times* and *Teen World.*

I think my conscious mind was trying to identify what my unconscious mind was nagging me about—maybe something that had occurred before the shooting. At last, while sauntering through an article on mountain camping in *Outdoor Life*, it came to me. I had seen, or thought I had seen, a navy blue "something" in the brush near the dunes on the side of the trail. I couldn't remember any more than its color and that it had looked soft, possibly a jacket, sleeping bag, or blanket. At the time, I had been more focused on setting the aperture in the camera to get a quick enough shutter speed to capture the sea oats with enough light so they didn't appear to be black weedy looking things—what some would call *art.*

I had viewed the result as a vastly underexposed image. Getting used to a new lens in a new environment with wind and the early morning chill was challenging me. But I did remember seeing something. Did it have importance to the murder? Could it have simply been something discarded by a previous day's visitor? I had no idea, but I thought I should tell the police. So I fished my cell phone out and dialed.

I didn't want to disturb the detectives from Charleston, so I called the local police, and received the familiar, "Folly Beach Police Department, how may I help you?" I couldn't tell if it was the same person who'd answered the other day, but the sentiments were the same. I explained who I was, and thought about saying that I hadn't found another body, but simply said I wanted to talk to someone about the investigation. This time the man didn't yell for someone to get the chief—a good sign. I gave him my location, and he said he would have an officer "visit."

*   *   *   *

It must have been a slow day for crime on the sleepy barrier island, because a cruiser pulled in front of my house and two officers were standing on the doorstep in front of me within fifteen minutes. I recognized young Officer Spencer from my memorable first encounter with the police. His partner introduced himself in an efficient, professional tone as Officer McConnell. McConnell was older than Spencer, which wasn't saying much. The couch I invited them to sit down on was older than Officer Spencer.

McConnell was also a head shorter than Spencer. A wiry little guy, full, I thought, of the bravado short men sometimes use to make up for what they lack in height.

Once I started telling my story, I felt foolish trying to describe how I really wasn't sure what I had seen, but that it was *some*thing. Officer Spencer, who must be the official note taker on the force, diligently wrote down everything I said. At least I think that's what he was doing. He could have been writing a note to his mother for all I know. The other officer appeared distracted as I told what I had seen. Actually, what I *hadn't* seen. He seemed more interested in my camera equipment sitting there on the kitchen table.

I finished my story. Officer Spencer said thanks for bringing this to their attention. Officer McConnell asked if I had photographed the object. I said I didn't believe so. He spent a couple of minutes telling me how he had visited this house a few years ago when some friends of his sister owned it.

The officers said they would share the new information with the chief and the detectives from Charleston. And then, with a polite "Thank you, sir," they left.

It was still raining as they pulled away. I turned and went into the bedroom that had the view clear out to the ocean, fired-up the laptop, and began reviewing the photos from Monday's aborted photo shoot. Or would that be more appropriately called "photo session aborted by a shot?"

Leaning close to the screen, I analyzed what I was seeing. The images of the lighthouse were average at best. With the structure some three hundred yards away, I hadn't gotten the angle I'd wanted. But then I was used to taking "average at best" shots, so I wasn't too discouraged. I told myself I'd have to get back and try again. The photographs of the dunes, wind and water-worn boulders, and the sea oats were better than I'd anticipated. The new wide-angle lens was proving to be a wise investment; it captured many features I hadn't noticed when shooting. Because of its ability to see more than I noticed, it also highlighted trash bags littering the sand, shadows where I wanted none, and in two frames, my left foot!

CHAPTER 9

It was late afternoon now, and the rain had stopped and patches of blue peeked through the early spring clouds. I grabbed my camera and walked two blocks to the Folly Beach Crab Shack where I was escorted to a hand-painted wood table on the patio. After studying an extensive menu that listed several "Shackwiches" (Their word, not mine!) of fish, fish, and more fish, I ordered the Flounder Crunch Sandwich with coleslaw. I was tempted to order a bowl of the famous she-crab soup but deferred to another visit.

The days were warming up, and soon thousands of tourists would be coming to the island for vacations. It was relaxing and even a bit rejuvenating sitting on a "beach rustic" wooden chair looking out on Center Street. If it hadn't been for the Holiday Inn, I could have seen the Atlantic Ocean. I finished the sandwich and listened to the ever-present Jimmy Buffett parroting the advantages of beach living. There were only a couple of other *diners* on the patio, so I didn't feel the need to vacate the seat and atmosphere. Besides, the sounds of Mr. Buffett were a vast improvement over the low humming of the fan in my laptop that I had been listening to all day.

"I hear you found yourself a big ole dead body," boomed a voice from immediately behind me. I had just left the Crab Shack and was walking away from the beach. Startled as I was, I didn't believe God would be speaking to me here on Center Street in downtown Folly Beach. Besides, the sound was very human. I turned, and there, about three feet behind me, was verification.

A gray-haired gentleman was following me step for step. He looked to be a little younger than I, about five-eight, trim, hair thinning on top, wearing a gold

University of Idaho long-sleeve sweatshirt. Though he was carrying a hand-carved cane, he didn't have a noticeable limp.

I stopped. He stopped.

"Howdy, and welcome to Folly Beach," he began, putting out his hand. "I'm Charles—not Charlie—Fowler. I saw you around here yesterday and the day before, always looking like you were headed someplace."

Not knowing the proper etiquette for Folly introductions, I kept it simple and told him my name and that he could very easily have seen me. That said, I didn't have to use my power of speech again for several minutes.

"You must be a *professional* photographer," he said.

When I looked at him as if to ask why he had come to that conclusion, he began his discourse. "Facts my friend. 'Facts are stubborn things; and whatever may be our wishes, or inclinations, or the dictates of our passions; they cannot alter the state of facts and evidence.'" Appearing not to want to get caught by the plagiarism police, he added, "John Adams, old, dead United States president."

Continuing, in his own words, I assume, and as he spoke, pointing to each item. "You always have that heavy looking camera over your shoulder. That fancy, expensive looking hat on your head says you are not the normal visitor. And you wear that silly looking vest with those ninety pockets to hold more stuff than any normal human would ever need. I see those only on obsessed fisherman and an occasional photographer. Now that I think about it, that vest should be worn by magicians. They could hide all the critters and balls and handkerchiefs that keep appearing from nowhere."

The need to take a breath slowed him a little, but not for long. "So, that all makes me believe you're a professional photographer."

If I'd been carrying a fishing pole, he would have thought I was one of those obsessed fishermen.

I fixed him with my best inquisitorial gaze—narrowed brows, steady eyes, the whole thing. "Where did you hear I'd found a body?"

"You don't have to be the genius of Folly to know that," he said. "The sleazy developer guy's murder is the biggest thing to hit this island since Hugo. I don't know who you are, just know you found him. Everyone here knows that. Mind if I walk with you a spell?"

What choice did I have? So I resumed my walk with Charles—not Charlie—Fowler in step beside me. I decided not to stray off the main drag, even for a "spell." Maybe Fowler was the murderer. He was carrying that cane; it looked like something a whaler caught in the doldrums might've carved. It looked old. Even more suspicious, he wasn't using it to walk with, just touching the ground with it once in a while, a couple of times smacking the palm of his hand with it. Murderer ... or was he just a quirky native? Deciding not to ask, I simply took the cautious route.

In less than a block, the silence got to him. "By the way, who are you, and why're you here? The newspaper just gave a name and said you were a tourist? Very few of us believe that's the truth. And, did you see the killer and you're just not telling anyone?"

A rough count identified at least three questions more than I had planned to answer today, but I thought, *Why not?* I briefly got a few facts out of the way and told him I'd been born in Louisville in 1949 making me an early baby boom generation kid. I gave him the abbreviated version of why I was here and made a point of denying I had seen the killer. If I was walking next to him, I didn't want him to have any doubts about my ignorance.

"So what about your work background? I suppose you have one," he said.

I clearly saw that no question was off limits to my new friend, Charles. Why disappoint his efforts? So I told him.

"A bunch of years ago," I said, "I earned a degree in psychology and took a job as a counselor at a neighborhood youth center. I wasn't making enough money to live off of, but I was using my training. Then I was given an opportunity to take a job in the marketing department at a mid-sized health care company, where, though I wouldn't be using my academic training, I'd be making an excellent salary. The mid-sized company grew to international proportions. I grew with it. End of story."

"Sounds boring to me," he said. "But hey, I guess it allows you to walk around taking pictures. Could be worse."

I didn't disagree.

"I like photography; haven't had any training," he said, apparently tired of my resume. "My camera is about as old as my car, a 1988 Saab soft top. It's a Minolta; the kind that takes film. I take a lot of pictures but seldom get any of them printed. It costs too much. I really wanted to learn to paint, but decided I'm just too lazy. Besides, the camera does a much better job of getting what the scene looks like than I would."

Time for another breath and to wave at someone across the street. Charles—not Charlie—Fowler was comfortable and at home on the streets.

It was my turn. "How long have you lived here?" I asked.

"I came here from Detroit in eighty-five. I was thirty-four and figured I was about half way through life. I wanted better weather and less work. Up north, I was a landscaper—at least the season for landscaping was fairly short up there.

But in the winter, we did a lot of the snow removal; parking lots, apartments, malls. That kept me way too busy. Before that, just out of high school, I'd worked in the big Ford factory for eight years. You don't know nothing about work until you've spent time in one of those factories."

He paused. I would rather him talk than me, so I led him on a little. "And what do you do for a living now?" I asked.

"Well, mostly nothing," he said. "I live in a little apartment behind the River Café near the marsh. I do some work—cash only—for local contractors. They need day laborers sometime. And when I get real industrious, I help a couple of the local restaurants maintain their properties and clean-up some evenings and between the lunch and supper crowds. Any odd jobs that are out there, people let me know. It doesn't take much money to live in a cheap apartment, let the restaurants feed me as pay, and use my Schwinn bicycle to serve as my second favorite means of transportation. As you might already see, my number one way to get around is what we're doing right now."

"So what's the deal with the University of Idaho shirt?" I asked. "Did you go there?"

"Hell, no. I've never been west of Michigan. Besides I don't think anyone lives in Idaho. I'm not sure where it is—Idaho that is, not the university. I don't think there *is* a university in Idaho. How could there be if no one lives there? Did you ever meet anyone from Idaho? Ever been there? I don't think Idaho exists."

Confessing that the answer to both questions was no, I shared that I saw Idaho on a map once. There are Idaho potatoes and I assumed someone must be there to harvest them. "Any idea what the name Vandals on the shirt comes from?"

Showing his sense of perspective, or just gab, he replied, "I assume it's what they call someone who goes to a university that doesn't exist in a state that ain't there."

"You don't have ties with the University of Idaho or the great state of Idaho— or you don't act like you do—so where'd you get the sweatshirt?"

"Found it a while back on the beach," he said. "It was wet and covered with sand and a little seaweed. Just assumed it floated over from Idaho and was deposited there by divine intervention—just for me, of course."

Who could challenge that logic? I simply agreed. I gently broached the subject about Charles's relationship with Mr. Lionetti. "Did you know the gentleman I found?"

"Nope, never met him. But from what I hear, you won't hear many folks referring to him as a *gentleman*. People who knew him tend to use the words *pond scum*, *chiseler*, or *thief*, before *gentleman*."

We reached the community park on the edge of the island. The crowd was thinning out, and I decided not to walk farther with my new *friend*. From his tone, I could easily imagine that he *was* the one who'd shot Mr. Pond Scum.

"Charles, I need to get back to the house and make a couple of calls. Maybe I'll see you later," I said.

"Oh, I suspect so—if you stay around here." As he walked away, he had a smile on his face.

CHAPTER 10

Around eight, I was surprised by a call from Tammy Rogers. Her editor wanted a human interest story about the tourist who found a body. "Not an everyday occurrence, you know."

She had told him she was more comfortable reporting hard news, but that she'd follow-up and see if I would agree. "So," she asked, "can you meet me for lunch tomorrow?" I could, and safely—I hoped—avoid grits at *lunch*, so I agreed.

"I won't have much time," she said. "Why don't we meet at the Anchor Line Restaurant on Folly Road? It's on your left just after leaving the island."

I was skeptical. I'd noticed the "restaurant" a couple of times in passing and thought she was using the term loosely. To me, it looked like a dive, or whatever you called a run-down, weather worn building in this part of the country. So, of course, I said, "What time?"

I got there early so as to get a feel for the place. The gravel-covered parking lot was nearly empty; the three cars probably belonged to employees. On one side of the parking area was a large refrigerated locker the size of a mobile home. It was covered with paintings of smiling fish and boasted a sign that said, "Get hooked on FISH." The painted fish couldn't read or they wouldn't have been smiling.

The restaurant itself was a two story wooden building with a teal and white addition between it and the road. Entering the screen door, I was faced with a rough-hewn wooden counter beneath a large menu board. An article from the *Post and Courier* nailed to one of the columns soothed my fears. The Anchor Restaurant had been named the "Best Fried Seafood Restaurant" in the Charleston Area for 2005. Maybe there was hope. Hope for all but the fish.

A young woman in a white cap and apron came out from the kitchen and told me to sit wherever I wanted, and to come back to the counter to order. The temperature outside was pleasant, so I sat on the patio overlooking the marsh.

It wasn't long before Tammy arrived with her captivating smile and with her cell phone to her ear. After a few pleasantries, we walked inside to order. She, being more accustomed to the food of the area, ventured out and ordered the fried oysters. I stuck with the traditional fish sandwich and coleslaw. The young woman set Styrofoam cups before us and told to get our drinks from the large stainless containers at the end of the counter. Someone would bring the food out to us.

"So, what's life been like since Monday morning?" she asked, switching to reporter.

I gave a brief summary of the last three days and shared my uneasiness about knowing there was a killer loose, possibly somewhere nearby. I confided how lucky I felt not to have been caught at the scene by the killer, and my anxiety at the narrow escape. She was kind enough to ask about my search for a house. I told her that I hadn't seriously begun the process and that I hoped to get with a realtor next week.

A boy who looked like he was just out of high school brought two heaping plates to our picnic table. Obviously, the Anchor Line Restaurant was keenly concerned that its food be presented in the best light. It arrived on Styrofoam plates that matched the cups. The white paper towels complimented both cups and plates.

I asked Tammy if the police had made an arrest.

"You sure stumbled on the body of a real sleaze," she mumbled, a bite of fried oyster competing with her words. "The police aren't saying much; they have several suspects, but no one is the clear frontrunner." She swallowed, took a sip of her drink, and continued.

"They say there are several other potential suspects, but the police gravitate toward family and money when starting any investigation. The wife, Sally, clearly didn't pull the trigger, but she had several reasons to want her beloved husband dead. Some of her friends say she was tired of his bullying—bullying her, her friends, and his business associates. They stop short of saying he physically abused her, but I wouldn't be surprised to find out that he did. One of our reporters says there're rumors of her having an affair with an actor in one of the community theatres she's such a big financial supporter of."

"That sounds promising," I said. "I need some news like that."

"Yes, and there's another reason for thinking she might be involved. Her beloved late husband never hesitated to reach into her family money to back his projects. He was successful—at least according to his PR flacks—but his development empire was literally and figuratively built on sand. A collapse was not only possible, but probable. Last year, one of his larger apartment complexes bit the dust—or sand—when his financing fell through. I hear he lost several million in that deal. So that's what I've learned so far."

I was beginning to understand why she was a successful reporter.

"Another suspect is Frank Long, the developer I interviewed for my article on the murder. He lives on Folly and has for years. His wife's a realtor in one of the big regional James Island firms. Mr. Long was a competitor of Lionetti's. The two had fought over properties many times. Long considers Folly his turf and, because of the limited development opportunities, fights whoever attempts to interlope. The only problem is that Long was one hundred twenty-five miles away in Columbia at a meeting Monday morning. The range of bullets is getting better, but that's quite a stretch."

We finished lunch, but Tammy was determined to continue with the list of suspects. "Another one of your—now that you're almost a Folly resident—locals under investigation is Wynn Stamper. Stamper grew up on Folly and is the island's strongest 'anti-development' proponent. He owns nine or so houses on the island in addition to his own and uses them as rental property. Every time Lionetti drove to Folly, Stamper seemed to know and started a protest. He also opposes about everything Frank Long wants. Simply stated, Wynn Stamper hates developers. His idols are the little old ladies who sit in front of the bulldozers so they can't demolish their old family homes or the oak tree they swung on as a child, or some outhouse that has sentimental value. Unfortunately for Stamper, he has absolutely no alibi. If this were a horserace, he'd be my early favorite."

I excused myself and went back in for two more cups of tea. Activity in the restaurant was picking-up; the smell of fried fish permeated the place.

When I returned, Tammy said she had been talking enough and that it was my turn. "After all, I am supposed to be interviewing you," she said. "Have you heard any gossip about who might have wanted Lionetti dead?"

I told her about my new acquaintance Charles, but quickly added that he didn't seem to have a list of possible candidates. "No one else has directly mentioned the murder to me, but I've had some interesting stares."

"Have you ever spent time in Charleston?" she asked, between bites.

"Not really. I was there was a few years ago at a conference, but I didn't see much of the city."

I was surprised when she said, "I'm off next Wednesday and Thursday. If you want, I'd give you a tour. We could have lunch. No conflict with business, because my editor won't want me to do any more follow-up stories on you—unless someone kills you between now and then."

Surely she was kidding about my possible demise, but her words sent a chill down my spine.

I didn't have to consult my Palm Pilot to know I had nothing on my calendar for either day. We agreed that Wednesday would work.

"Let's meet on The Battery," she said. "It's easy to get to from here, and there's plenty of free parking if you arrive early. Free parking is at a premium in Charleston—you need to grab it when you can. I'll meet you by the cannon at the north end of Battery Park at nine."

After a long, rather warm handshake, she left the restaurant. This was turning out to be a very nice day. I was feeling better—*much* better about being here.

*   *   *   *

The next day was warmer than Thursday had been. With my trusty Nikon over my shoulder and Tilley on my head, I took a brisk walk—as brisk as a walk can be in only two blocks—to The Dog. It was still before seven thirty, so I had a fairly wide option on seats. I chose a small table by the window because I liked watching the quiet town awakening. I hoped it was in Amber's section—I didn't think I could take a poisoning.

Amber was quick to the table with my coffee. This was only my second visit, but I guess I'd been accepted as a regular; I hadn't mentioned coffee to anyone.

It amazed me how fresh and cheerful she was this early in the day. I attributed it to my charm and her happiness to see me—right! Kidding aside, Amber's charm and personality would make any breakfast taste better. The Belgian waffle was not on the menu, so I ordered the more traditional Dog breakfast—the breakfast burrito.

"I hear you've made a quick impact on our town," she said after writing down my order. "There've not been more than a handful of murders on the island in my nine years here, and you just go out on a hike and find us one."

I chose not to correct her hiking comment. She didn't need to know my aversion to healthy activities. I weigh one seventy, not horrible for someone five-nine. Besides, I hear one seventy is the new one fifty. Or, maybe I dreamed that.

But I shrugged and said, "It sure wasn't my intent to find a dead body when I set out Monday morning."

"My son Jason thinks you are some sort of famous adventurer," she said. "Of course, he's only nine and everyone is some sort of adventurer to him. He believes we live in the jungles of Brazil and not on lazy Folly Beach." She glanced at the arrivals gathering around tables like early birds around a feeder. "Better go—customers are waiting."

On the way in, I'd bought Charleston's *Post and Courier*, and now opened it to see if Tammy had any bylines. The death of Mr. Wonderful, Jim Lionetti, was already off the front page. There was a follow-up by her in the metro pages about his funeral; it would be attended by "everyone who is anyone" in the development and real estate community. To celebrate sticking him in the ground, I suspected.

Another piece hidden in the back pages said the police were "exploring some promising leads in the murder." I hoped that was accurate. I didn't feel in any immediate danger, but the thought was always there. If the killer believed, even for a second, that I'd seen him or that I knew something that might lead to him, I doubt he'd hesitate to come after me.

The breakfast burrito arrived, and with it, Amber with more of her local insights.

"I hear our mysterious police chief and that female detective from Charleston were on very friendly terms Monday over at your murder site."

Amazed as usual about what people know, or think they know, I asked her where she'd heard that, and why she called the chief "mysterious."

"Hon, I hear everything; couldn't even begin to remember *where* I heard it. It doesn't really matter; everybody knows about him and her anyway." She paused. "But in fact, the man's a blank to most of us. He was already on the job when I came. He's been chief for about a dozen years. Retired from the army where he was an MP, they say. Rumor has it he was once in Special Services, or one of those secret groups. He was stationed in Charleston and saw the Folly Beach chief's job as a way to supplement his military retirement. We only have about a dozen cops and they're also the firemen—pretty simple job. Mostly traffic control during the busy summer days. They have fun trying to arrest the surfers who are stupid enough to surf near the pier. They seem to think it's a felony if the kids surf within two hundred feet of it. I've never seen the police out there with a tape measure, but I guess they know somehow how far two hundred feet is." She looked around to see who might need a refill on coffee. Apparently no one did, and she turned back to me.

"So, Chris—that is your name, isn't it?—back to the chief. Actually, I think his official title is Director of Public Safety, although I don't know how someone can direct safety. He lives here all week than disappears on his days off." She leaned close enough that I whiffed her perfume. Then she added *confidentially*, of course, "Now the rumor is, Chief Newman's been seen in several restaurants in Charleston with the big city Detective Lawson. And, not just having police-type discussions—sitting much closer together than that requires; sharing desserts if you know what I mean. Monday's happy talk about them at the murder site sure fanned that rumor flame."

Not much caring what Chief Newman and Detective Lawson were up to, I was thinking of something else. "Amber," I said, "since you appear to know about everything around here, who *was* it that ruined my Monday?"

She shrugged her pretty shoulders. "Good question," she replied. "For one, Jim Lionetti. Local money is on the wife—because none of us want it to be any-one from here, and it's a lot easier to blame it on a woman. Besides, she has enough reasons for wanting him dead.

"Raymond, at the convenience store, thinks it was Wynn Stamper, an islander who's against development. One of my regulars thinks it's our new mayor. Mayor Amato is *pro*-development, and the theory is he was getting kickbacks from Lion-etti and something went wrong. I've even heard one or two think it was our local character, Charles Fowler—you may have seen him. He's usually tooling around on his old bicycle. I think he's a nice guy, but you never know. My son thinks it was a hit man hired by the King of Ethiopia, because Lionetti was getting ready to start building skyscrapers in Africa. I wouldn't put much stock in that theory."

Since I'd spent some time with Charles Fowler, I was more than a little curi-ous to get Amber's take on him.

"So what do you know about Fowler?"

"Occasionally works in here … if we're really busy. He'll bus tables and clean up around the restaurant. Don't think he's got a regular job. He seems okay, and he's never come on to me." She wiped a mock tear and grinned. "That's a little unusual."

"You think he's gay?"

"Don't know. I'm sort of a flirt," she laid her hand on my shoulder, something I wasn't used to a woman's doing, "—you might have noticed. Most guys either try to get to know me better than I'd like or make suggestive comments. Charles hasn't done either—hurt my feeling a little I guess. Maybe I'm losing my touch."

I smiled and tried to reassure her. "Well, Ms. Amber, I don't think you've lost anything."

She grinned back, obviously pleased. "Thanks," she said. "If you want to see some of the *lesser-known* charms of Folly, just say the word. I'd be glad to show you around, especially between one thirty, when I get off, and four when Jason gets home from school."

So what was I supposed to do with that? I just smiled up at her, and she winked down at me.

As she walked away, I wiped a bead of sweat off my brow. I hadn't noticed her being *that* much of a flirt before. So I decided to get my camera and walk around before it got too hot in The Dog.

*   *   *   *

I headed toward the marsh on Second Street, an area I'd only seen once, although it's only a couple of blocks from where I live. Hardly anyone around, and the foliage was getting thicker. Maybe not the best place for a fellow in my situation, but still ... Before I'd taken a dozen photos, I heard the hiss of bicycle tires on the pavement behind me, and the now familiar voice of Charles Fowler.

"Doing your photo thing again, I see," he called.

I looked back over my shoulder. "Good morning, Charles," I said. "How are you this beautiful day?"

"Well, I'm doing well. Thanks for asking."

This was my first look at the Schwinn both he and Amber had mentioned. It was old—vintage old—no fancy gearshifting stuff or hand brakes. The navy blue paint had been around a while, but it looked waxed and fresh and caught the light just right—testimony to his having kept it out of the weather except when riding it. The fat tires looked brand new and their white sidewalls hadn't a spot of dirt or grease.

The brake groaned a little as he brought it to a stop beside me, and astraddle the seat, leaned his elbows on the wide handlebars. Also, crosswise on the handle-bars was the cane I'd seen the first time we met.

"You look mighty chipper and alert there on your bike," I said.

"'A little flattery will support a man through great fatigue,'" he said. "James Monroe—dead United States president."

I chuckled. "Okay, you win. What's with the quotes from presidents?"

"Christopher, it's not just presidents. They're all dead and the quotes are fairly obscure. Anybody can quote Roosevelt, Kennedy, Lincoln, Washington, those famous ones. Has anyone ever quoted Monroe, James Garfield, or Chester Arthur to you?"

"To be honest, I don't recall anyone ever quoting Roosevelt, Kennedy, Washington, or even Lincoln to me," I said. "But you're right; Monroe, Garfield, and Arthur's words have not been spoken in my direction—at least to my knowledge."

Mr. Fowler hadn't answered my question about the quotes; I realized he might never get around to it, and I changed the subject.

"I was just talking with someone about you at breakfast," I said.

That got his attention. "Who?"

"The lovely and talented wait staff person, Amber, at The Lost Dog Café."

He frowned, and in an undertone, said, "Did she tell you she thinks I'm gay?"

That wasn't exactly what I thought he'd be asking.

"Not directly," I said, hoping he'd leave it at that. He did; I must be living right.

He simmered in silence a moment, and then piped up with, "This is a pretty day for taking pictures, isn't it? Where're you headed?"

"Oh … I was just walking. I haven't spent much time on this side of Center Street and wanted to shoot some of the houses for sale and anything else that catches my eye."

"Sounds good," he said. "Mind if I tag along?"

"Not at all." In spite of myself, I was beginning to trust him. But why?

"Good," he said. "I'll leave my bike here and walk with you." He got off and guided the bike off the sidewalk and leaned it against a tree. Of course he didn't leave the cane.

"Will it be safe?" I asked, thinking more about whether *I'd* be safe.

"Sure, everyone knows it's mine. Say," he changed the subject abruptly, "in case I ever decide to class-up my image, where do you get one of those Tilley hats?"

"Around here, I don't know. I got this one in Canada years ago."

"Oh well," he muttered, "I'm not ready to change my image anyway, so that's no problem."

We continued north on Second Street and turned on West Indian Avenue away from town. Charles pointed with the cane to a road called Sandbar Lane, said that's where he lived and invited me to visit. I said I'd consider it. He said if I came to his apartment, he'd show me a restaurant with some of the finest food around and a fantastic view of the sunset over the marsh and the Folly River.

Thoughts of food always get my attention, and the idea of a sunset over the marsh appealed to the photographer in me, so I promised I'd take him up on that sometime soon. We passed several houses, some fairly new, large and elevated, clearly hurricane-proof. And there were the older homes that had withstood hurricanes for many years.

Charles was interested in the photos I was taking. My typical subjects were anything but typical, and he seemed to identify with that. He patiently waited while I lined up shots of flowers growing through thorny weeds and rotting tree limbs, of houses that could best be described as shanties surrounded by rusting cars and mildew-covered hulls of small fishing boats, and of mailboxes wrapped in ropes tied to look like they were holding seagoing vessels to the docks.

"I never thought you could actually take photos of such ordinary things and consider it art," he said.

I tried to explain that art was more than pretty paintings or photos. It involved the capturing of the artist's impressions, feelings, and image of the way he wanted things to be. I myself didn't fully understand what I was saying, so I didn't expect him to, but he said he did. Politeness is not one of his strengths, so maybe he did.

When we got to the end of West Indian, he pointed to a nice, although fairly old, house and said it was owned by Wynn Stamper, the anti-growth landlord. I recognized Stamper as one of the leading candidates in the murder of Mr. Lionetti.

Charles was musing half to himself. "I've heard Wynn say on several occasions, 'To grow, Folly must stay the same.'"

I was afraid to say that quote sounded more like something Yogi Berra would say.

He—Charles, not Yogi—continued, "Stamper owns a bunch of houses here; rents them to the tourists and the snowbirds several months a year. He doesn't want any development. Why should he? It would just cut into his stock of places to rent—bucks out of his britches." Charles had a far away look in his eyes.

"I don't own quite as many homes as Wynn," he said, "—zero for me, a bunch for him—but I've talked with him some. He's a nice fellow. And, we have something in common—sort of. He rides around town on a little Honda scooter, and of course you know about my two wheel means of transportation. He named his *Kiwi*. That's the name of the green color on it; it's green and white. A cute little thing, by the way. Maybe I need to name my Schwinn. *Blueberry*, or *Bluebell*, or … something. I don't know." We walked on.

At the end of the street, Charles told me that all the land in front of me used to be the Seabrook property. The Seabrook family owned much of Folly Beach in the 1920s, deserted stretches and mysterious with a dense forest. We soon turned away from the Seabrook land, so it still remained a mystery, at least to me.

Charles finally got enough nerve to ask if he could look through my camera's viewfinder. I told him sure, took the strap from around my neck and handed it over to him. He put it to his eye, fiddled with the adjustments a moment, and then let out a low whistle. He'd never held a camera with a zoom lens before.

"My gosh," he exclaimed, "that brings it in close!"

When I told him he could take photos of anything he wanted, he was shocked. I reminded him that with the digital camera, it didn't cost anything to take the photos.

I could see the light dawn in his face. "So can I snap a couple?" he reluctantly asked.

"Absolutely! Go ahead."

While Charles—not Charlie—was busying himself with my camera, I finally garnered the courage to ask, as carefully as possible, the question that had been on my mind. "Charles ... where were you the other morning when Lionetti was killed?"

He didn't even take the camera down from his eye. "Asleep, of course—it was early in the morning."

His answer wasn't very comforting, but it made sense. And that's all he offered.

We were soon back to his yet-to-be-named navy blue vintage bike. It was, of course, still there. As quickly as he appeared, he said he had to go and tooled off toward the thriving metropolis of Folly Beach.

The temperature was hovering in the mid-eighties now, with the harsh, at least for photographic purposes, sun directly overhead. I thought it was time to fix myself a gourmet lunch of peanut butter and jelly sandwich and chips—eat your heart out, Emeril Lagasse.

CHAPTER 11

After a week of exploring the housing market by walking and picking-up fact sheets, it was time to secure the services of—according to *Aunt* Louise—"the best realtor on Folly Beach." A phone call to Island Realty told me Mr. Howard was out with a client but would return my call. I was a little disappointed that Mr. Howard wasn't waiting by the phone to hear from me. I released my frustration by downloading and burning a CD of the morning's photos and reviewing the images. I was curious, too, about what Charles had taken.

What he had taken was a lesson watching me shoot commonplace subjects. I didn't see anything artistic or interesting in two of his photos—one of a broken Diet Rite bottle, the other a wadded-up Snickers wrapper. Maybe I didn't know as much about art as I thought. I was also curious as to how he managed to get two out-of-focus images of a birdhouse—especially with the auto focus Nikon. We obviously needed to work on his technique.

The phone interrupted my critique. "This is Bob Howard with Island Realty. Louise tells me you're lookin' for a house. She's also a bit worried about your taste since you rented the West Cooper house instead of the one she was pushing. But hey, that's her damn problem not yours. What can I do for you?"

At least he didn't mention my fame as a finder of dead bodies. I asked him if he could show me some houses. After a few words about size and a rough price range, we settled on meeting Monday.

Evening came, and I found that another busy day of doing almost nothing had worn me out. I drifted to sleep thinking about the highly popular and exciting "World Grits Festival" taking place up the road in St. George. Not quite "visions of sugarplums," but considering the source of information, a pleasant memory.

*   *   *   *

Saturday began cloudy and windy, but, no rain was forecast, so I ventured over to the Holiday Inn for coffee and to buy the *Post and Courier*. I had mixed feelings. Did I really want to read an article about me? Yes? Sort of? No. Who needed that kind of publicity? But it didn't matter. The article was there or it wasn't. This time I took the paper inside and sat on one of the comfortable chairs in the wide corridor overlooking the pool and the Atlantic.

I was almost convinced the article wasn't there, when I caught the headline "Not Your Everyday Find."

FOLLY BEACH—Monday didn't turn out exactly as planned for Chris Landrum, a Kentuckian vacationing on Folly Beach. The semi-professional photographer and human relations executive for a multi-national company from Louisville, was exploring the deserted coast guard station on the north end of the barrier island. "My plan for the morning was to get a couple of nice photos of the Morris Island Lighthouse, maybe even one or two of the waves lapping at the beach at sunrise. Hearing gunshots and finding the body were nowhere on my radar," said Landrum.

Much has already been reported about the murder of developer and one of Charleston's best known citizens, James Lionetti. His family is suffering a terrible loss. His friends are both saddened and angered by the sudden taking of his life. And, the County of Charleston's sheriff's department is vigorously investigating leads in this tragic event.

By simply being at the wrong place at the wrong time, Landrum's life changed as well. "Leading a life filled mostly with peace and calm, I didn't know, and still don't know, how to react," said Landrum. "I don't think I've even felt the full impact of being within feet of someone intentionally taking the life of another. And, more frightening, I could just have easily been the next victim," Landrum continued.

"It was pure luck that I didn't stumble upon the killer. If I had, I wouldn't be telling this story. I guess it's even more amazing that I never saw anyone, considering we were only a few feet apart." He continued, "Ironically, I was concentrating so much on taking photos that I was not aware of what was almost directly in front of me."

Mr. Landrum, 56, is on Folly Beach to enjoy a month-long vacation and search for a real estate investment. "I fell in love with Folly Beach a few years ago and want to spend much of my retirement time on this strange, yet captivating, island."

    Will the events of Monday morning change Landrum's plans? "I would be less than honest if I said no. I don't believe I can answer that now. Perhaps in a few days I can think more clearly and make the decision," said Landrum. "I still have the feeling I'm being watched, and with so many new faces I'm seeing, I'm always wondering if I might be facing a killer.

    "Sure, this has been terrible for me, but my deepest sympathies go to the family of Mr. Lionetti."

I laid the paper down in my lap and gazed out at the ocean. It could have been much worse. I hadn't come across as a blithering idiot, and Tammy was kind in what she used and what she omitted. The article was filler so the paper could sell more ads, but I frankly enjoyed my moment of fame. I was sorry it had to come at someone's ultimate expense. And it struck me that I might be the only person sorry for the untimely passing of Mr. James F. Lionetti.

I bought an extra copy and headed home to get my camera. I was crossing the parking lot to the sidewalk and saw Charles riding his bike my way. This was the first time I'd seen him first. I was beginning to take control of our encounters, or so I thought.

"Morning, Charles. Where are you headed in such a hurry?"

He veered to my side of the street. In addition to the ubiquitous cane across the handlebars, there were two butcher paper-wrapped boxes in the big wire basket that was a fixture over the rear wheel.

"I have to deliver a couple of packages for Jim at the surf shop. He uses me occasionally as a cheap substitute for UPS—besides the delivery is only six blocks from the store. The men in brown usually get irritated when they pick-up something at the store, take it back to Charleston for processing, then the next day, deliver it six blocks from where they picked it up. So, United Parcel Charles comes to the rescue. What're you doing?"

"Just heading home to get my camera, then to The Dog for an early lunch. Want to join me?"

"My big delivery should take about thirty minutes," he said. "I'll come over."

When I got to the house, I remembered that I'd actually brought three cameras on this trip, two single lens-reflex models, and an older one, my first point and shoot digital. It was sort of an accident that I'd brought them all; even the most prepared Boy Scout in me saw no reason for three cameras. But I could lend the older one to Charles so he could get used to digitals. He could download the photos at the library on one of their computers. Though I doubted they had the Photoshop software, they should have something a little less sophisticated, and that would be good enough. I grabbed my Nikon, the extra camera, my Tilley, and headed to The Dog.

*　　*　　*　　*

Charles was there waiting. He waved me to a table that I hoped was in Amber's section. I didn't want my food poisoned, and I did enjoy talking with her. As I approached the table, he was eyeing my gear.

"Chris, I can't help notice—your camera inventory has doubled. What could possibly be twice as good to photograph here?"

I unslung the older digital from around my neck and held it out to him. "I thought you might want to borrow one for the next three weeks," I said.

For the first time since I've known him, he was speechless—not even a quote from an obscure, dead president. I guess they didn't do much photography around the White House in those bygone times.

"I couldn't do that," he finally said with obvious feeling. "That's a great camera, and you barely know me. If I dropped it, I could never pay to have it fixed."

"Look," I said quietly, "I've had this one several years. I've dropped it more times than I would admit. Besides, I'd rather you drop this one than the other one I let you use."

He tilted his head and looked at the camera, a sort of gesture of relinquishment. "Well, that makes sense. Okay, I'll let you lend it to me." He took it in his hands and turned it this way and that, looking at it. Then after another pause, he said, "That's the nicest thing anyone has done for me in a long, long time. Thank you."

"But, you can't have my Tilley," I said, hoping to break this rather embarrassing, bonding moment.

Then I pulled a chair up beside him and spent a few minutes giving him the abridged version of how to use the camera. Knowing much of what I said wouldn't stick, I gave him the manual.

When Amber took our order and brought our food, I noticed she wasn't as cheerful as usual. She almost acted jealous of Charles for taking away from our talk-time. In fact, she came and went with hardly a word.

With his plate of food sitting in front of him and his fork poised, he pointed with a nod. "See that guy in the light blue shirt talking to the lady over there?"

In view of the fact that I wasn't traveling with a Seeing Eye dog, it would have been hard to say no in a restaurant the size of The Lost Dog Café.

Not waiting for my reply, he said, "He's on the city council. Their meetings are the best show on the beach. Especially since we don't have any movie theatres, strip joints, and only a handful of churches. Not many performances a week, but the one thing you can count on happening in our city council meetings is the good citizens of Folly discussing—and cussing—growth versus things staying the same. It's gone on ever since I've been here, and I doubt it started because I arrived. When the council wants variety, they debate how badly they want or don't want surfers in the city."

"Do you go?" I asked.

"Nah, but everyone hears about them. The mayor, Eric Amato, is pro-growth and development. He only got elected because the heavy favorite, an equally strong anti-growth advocate, suffered a heart attack and had to withdraw from the race a week before the election. Amato's name came up again yesterday as a suspect in this murder thing. Seems someone saw him with Lionetti the week before—over at Lionetti's duplex project."

"Do the police know about that?" I asked.

"Suspect so. If the rumor's out there, they hear it too."

Back to his original subject, "If you want to be entertained, go to the meetings. Today's the eighth, right? The next meeting will be Tuesday at seven thirty. The council chambers are in City Hall."

Between most every sentence, Charles was saying hello to someone coming in or leaving. He was also giving me a capsule version of the who, what, and why on each of those someones. Unfortunately, he didn't have a manual to give me, so I was going to forget most of what he said.

Before we left, Amber finally warmed-up enough that I didn't worry anymore about stomach pains. I promised I'd return soon, and she seemed happy about that—and with the way she smiled at me as I walked out, so was I.

✳   ✳   ✳   ✳

I woke early Sunday thinking I should make amends with Amber, so I headed to The Dog. That would give me more "quality time" with my most favorite wait staff person. As soon as I opened the door, she was right there asking me where I wanted to sit.

"Anywhere you want me to," I told her. That got a smile.

"For now, why don't you take the first booth? Later, we can discuss where else I'd like you to sit."

Ahhh. Well ... she must have meant in case her stations change.

"We have your waffles on special again today. Want one?"

I said sure, and she took the order to the kitchen. When she returned, I asked what she did before coming to Folly. The restaurant was nearly empty, and she had time to talk.

"I left a highly successful career as a McDonald's manager trainee," she said. "I never got past the trainee part, so I'll never know if I would have been a highly successful McDonald's manager. They wanted me to be a manager so they could work me seventy hours a week and not have to pay overtime."

I told her I didn't know anything about that, but I knew she was now a highly successful wait staff person at The Lost Dog Café. She was pleased at hearing that, and she didn't express a desire to be anything else.

She brought the waffle, and, this time, she sat. "I've been thinking. How did the killer get away from the coast guard station? You said you didn't see any cars there. Right?"

I was busy with my knife, distributing the butter over the waffle, but being keenly interested in this subject, I nodded.

"Then what happened to Lionetti's Mercedes?" she asked, leaning closer.

My gaze was playing between her blue eyes and the syrup I was pouring on my waffle. "I don't know," I said.

"But you would've noticed if there'd been a big Mercedes sitting there when you arrived. What I'm really thinking is that the murderer must have taken the car after he killed Lionetti. The keys would have been on the body and easily taken—easily after he was dead."

I hadn't thought about any of this for the last few days. The mind is full of great defense mechanisms; and one of those lets you forget unpleasant stuff. That was my favorite.

"If that's true," I replied, "then Lionetti would've arrived *after* me, and the killer came with him or was waiting. If he was already there, how did he get there? If he came with Lionetti, why would they be at the deserted coast guard station at sunrise?"

I thought, but didn't say, that either way, it must have been someone local. At least someone with knowledge of the area.

"I said I'd been thinking about it," she continued. "I didn't say I had it figured out. How it all went down just has me confused. By the way, that was a nice article in yesterday's paper. Was that the same woman reporter who wrote the story about the murder?"

I said yes, and wasn't sure what Amber's look meant. Using my untrained in "what do women's looks mean" eyes, I couldn't tell. But it didn't look good.

Before I left, she reminded me of her generous offer to show me the high-points of Folly.

I remembered.

✳   ✳   ✳   ✳

I headed toward the Folly River, then onto East Indian Avenue. I had driven down the roads closest to the marsh before now, but hadn't spent time exploring them.

The morning sun cast strong shadows from the live oaks. The marsh had a totally different personality than the ocean side a short distance away. It was as calm as the Atlantic was rough. The houses facing the river were more remote, removed from the mild activity of downtown. I was photographing the peaceful sites along the marsh side streets, but my mind was wandering back to the events a week ago and to Amber's questions.

Since the coast guard property was off-limits to private development, why would a prominent developer be there, especially so early in the morning? The newspaper said he often left home at six-thirty to visit his construction sites. I assume that that morning, he'd driven his Mercedes. But the development on Folly wasn't that close to the coast guard station, so why did he go *there*? The most confusing part to me involved the question of what had happened to his car. I would swear it wasn't there when I arrived. It definitely wasn't there when I called the police. Either the murderer came with him, or there were two killers. One to drive *their* car away and one to drive Lionetti's. I hadn't heard any specu-lation about *two* suspects.

Besides, I was only a lowly tourist trying to enjoy a vacation and buy the home of my dreams at the beach. I'd leave the detecting to the professionals. "Now," I said to myself, "focus on focus."

But then thoughts of Amber's offer bubbled up in my mind, and … Well, I was thinking about that more than concentrating on where I was, and suddenly I realized I'd already reached the end of Huron, five or so long blocks from Center Street, taking pictures all the way. So I walked away from the marsh and headed back toward my rental.

When I got there, Dr. Hansel was working in the yard. I stopped to see what words of wisdom he was going to share today. He didn't look professorial in his wrinkled, dirty shorts and sweat-stained "Hard Rock Café, San Francisco" T-shirt.

"Well, well," he said, "I didn't realize how big a celebrity I had living next to me. Not only did you get a mention last week when you found one of our most outstanding citizens in a state of demise, but now you get a story just about you."

I was embarrassed about how he put it. After all, it was a terrible tragedy, and all I did was stumble on a body.

"Yeah, the newspaper contacted me and asked for a few comments. I didn't realize what they'd do with it."

"Care to share a glass of iced tea and conversation?" he asked.

I couldn't come up with a reason to refuse, and cold tea sounded good. He went back into the house, came out with two tall glasses, and we sat on a bench under one of his live oaks.

I sipped my tea and found it just right. "What brought you to Folly?" I asked. "I know you're at the university, but why the beach?"

"Good question. I suspect you've noticed that I'm black, or *African American* as we now say."

"I admit it; I did notice," I said with a smile. He sipped his tea and smiled in response—a good sign.

"What you might not know is that out of the entire full-time population of more than two thousand folks here, a whopping sixteen are black. That's progress, I guess. Ten years ago there were five. Most of the sixteen are in three families who live by the marsh. So you can see that my decision to move here wasn't based on a desire to be close to my fellow descendents of slavery."

"So why?" I asked.

He thought a moment, gazing at the toe of his shoe. "I've always liked the beach and the ocean. My doctorate is from the School of Hospitality Management at Penn State, but I have had very little real world experience in travel and hospitality. I worked a couple of years for a large travel agency planning corporate outings. I did that only because I had to as a requirement for the graduate school. During those two years, I traveled to San Francisco three times and thoroughly enjoyed driving along the Pacific Coast Highway looking at the sites and the beauty of the West Coast. I also traveled to Ireland and spent several days exploring the coastal region of that very green country. In other words, my roots may be in the dusty, barren, central region of Africa, but my heart and interests are with the ocean. After all, before I was an African, I descended from the sea—correct?"

I didn't know about that, but said noncommittally, "That's interesting."

"I've always marched to the beat of a different drummer," he added. "My degrees are in hospitality management, but all I've ever wanted to do is teach. My family is in the north. My wife died of cancer in ninety-nine. And now here I am in South Carolina. And though there's a large black population in Charleston, I'm here on a very colorless Folly Beach. Colorless unless you count the varying degrees of sunburn."

"Bill," I interrupted, "I'm glad you're here. The tea is great, and the conversation enjoyable. But you've answered my question, and I've got a feeling you've heard something about who killed the developer?"

He stared into the glass for a moment, sloshed the ice around a bit, and then, taking his time, drank the last of his tea. "This may be off base," he said, "but I'm heavily involved with two groups that are organized to save the Morris Island Lighthouse. I won't go into all the details, but talking with a few of the members in Preserve the Past, they believe the murder had to do with the project. Especially since the murder took place within site of that historic landmark."

"Any names?" I said. "What would be gained by killing Lionetti? He couldn't develop the coast guard property or the lighthouse, could he? It's standing in water."

"Sure. That's true, but considering everything bad that's been said about him, my friends think he would have profited somehow."

None of this made sense to me, but I knew next to nothing about the lighthouse *or* the development possibilities. Besides, I'm not a tenured professor, nor am I a doctor of anything.

I could see by the way he was glancing at his rake that Bill was getting anxious to get back to his yard work. I wasn't ready to volunteer to help, so I thanked him for the tea and I said we'd talk later.

CHAPTER 12

Bob Howard knocked on my door promptly at nine Monday morning. When I opened the door, I was surprised to see a man in his sixties, about six feet tall, burly, with a short white beard and white hair around the edges of his mostly bald head. Santa out of season, I thought.

He greeted me with, "Hi, I'm Bob Howard, the best realtor in the second largest of the three very small island realty firms."

I was never good with word problems and was having trouble figuring where he ranked on the list of realtors, but I said hello and that I was Chris Landrum.

He gave me a sly, knowing look. "Ya think I'll be safe ferrying you around?"

So much for him not knowing about me. "I suspect so," I said. "I doubt anyone will take a shot at me as long as I'm accompanied by such an important escort."

"Not a good start," he said, "you shoveling bullshit on me right here on your front porch." He said it with a smile … or maybe that was a smirk.

I could feel the makings of a good relationship, and asked if he had something to show me today.

"First, tell me why you think you want something over here," he said.

"Twenty or so years ago," I began with us still standing there on my porch, Howard leaning on a pillar, arms folded over his ample chest, "I went deeply in debt and bought two brick duplexes in a middle class residential section of Louisville. For years, I regretted that move."

"Been there, done that," he interrupted. "Go ahead."

"During the first two years, the roofs needed replacing, so did the furnaces and air conditioners. I added new water heaters, and a couple of other big-ticket items had to be repaired. My property management checkbook didn't see black for years. But later, because of the growing real estate market, I was able to sell the two properties for a substantial profit. My early regrets turned into a nice return."

"Been there, but haven't done that yet—the substantial profit that is," he said. "That's why I'm out working today while you're enjoying your damn vacation. But enough. I'll give you an overview of what's available. I won't ask you exactly what you want, because 'buyers are liars.' You think they know, but they seldom buy what they say they think they want." He was already down the steps and expected me to be right behind him.

A *really* good start. After our first few minutes together, he had already called me a liar. What was that comment I made about our relationship? But on that pleasant beginning, I ran back inside, grabbed my camera, and followed him to his car. His choice of wheels gave me an even better idea of who this man working for me was—or more correctly, what I was up against. His "Realtormobile," as he put it, was a purple, two-door Chrysler PT Cruiser convertible.

He was opening the driver side door when he saw me staring. "Don't even think about calling it purple—it's Dark Plum. It's perfect for island real estate shopping. It has nice wide doors for easy client access, nice leather seats for a smooth slide for wide asses, a convertible so clients can easily see the skyscrapers. What more could you want?"

Skyscrapers? The tallest building on the island was the nine-story Holiday Inn, with a couple of four story condo complexes coming in a distant second. Leather seats, great, nice and hot on those wide posteriors, and weren't realtors supposed to drive four door cars for easy client access? But I wasn't the "best realtor in the second largest of the three very small realty firms on the island," so what did I know?

"And it was made in the good ole US of A," he continued. "Not in Japan like so many cars out there. So how could I go wrong with this—the perfect realtor car?"

I doubt that's a line he uses on his Asian clients, and I believe I've heard that the PT Cruiser was made in Mexico. Regardless, this was a good time to keep my mouth shut.

"I've chosen a few properties that'll give you an idea what's available. They range from a fine, fairly new condo on the beach to some of the more traditional Folly homes in the South Carolina architectural vernacular—clapboard with tin roofs and overpriced. Are you aware that the average single family house on Folly Beach costs more than six hundred thousand dollars?"

I guessed it was my turn to speak, so I said no, I wasn't, but I had known it was high. He kept talking.

"Today there are almost ninety properties here for sale. In the last two years, they've appreciated twenty-five percent. I think this tiny island has finally been found."

He drove down Center Street and turned at the Holiday Inn. I hadn't noticed it before, but Center Street dead ends into Arctic Avenue. If you turned left, it was a one-way street, and if you turned right, it was also a one-way street, but going the other way. In other words, you couldn't go wrong. We turned right.

"Let's start with a condo in the Charleston Oceanfront Villas," he said.

I was familiar with the four-story stucco building that dominates the beach for the next two blocks.

"This is the largest complex on Folly—ninety-six condos. The one that's presently available is on the third floor. Owned by a doctor in Atlanta—some sort of specialization I can't pronounce."

From the parking area under the building, we took the elevator to the third floor where he showed me a nice, three-bedroom, three-bath unit, fifteen hundred square feet listed for nine hundred thousand. The view, directly overlooking the Atlantic and The Folly Pier, was extraordinary. Both the living room and the master bedroom had a balcony with sliding glass doors. The master bath had an oversized Jacuzzi. The furnishings were upscale with all the amenities—three wide-screen televisions, new kitchen appliances, and fairly nice art on the walls. There were even three attractive black and white photos framed above the king sized bed in the master bedroom. That touch I appreciated.

"The building opened in 1998 and meets all the hurricane standards with concrete and steel materials. It even has two pools." He finished by saying, "These units don't stay on the market long."

I could see why, although the price was way out of my range.

"Let me show you what you can get for three quarters of a million," he said. "I know I'm sounding like a damn salesman when I say this, but you need to know that properties are hot. For example, what we call "days on the market" for properties three years ago, was greater than two hundred. Now they're on the market for less than a hundred days. That average is made longer by trash that'll never sell. Take that for what it's worth."

Before I could figure out what it was worth, we were back in the Dark Plum— I'm a quick study—PT Cruiser turning on West Arctic Avenue, the main road that parallels the beach, then away from the surf to my street. We drove two blocks, almost to the end, and stopped in front of a house Bob described as "cute." From his mouth, "cute" sounded like another of his four letter words. The house, clapboard and very old, was surrounded by live oaks with a little moss hanging from the branches. It had a wrap-around porch and looked similar to what, back in Kentucky, we called "country style."

Bob said it was only two hundred-fifty steps from the beach. I asked, but he couldn't say if they were baby steps, adult steps, paved steps, or whatever. He simply said the beach was a couple of blocks away—and that I could step any damn way I wanted. The interior was even smaller than it looked from outside. There was new carpeting in all but one of the rooms, and the kitchen appliances barely looked used. They would stay that way if they became mine. Unlike the Oceanfront Villa, the house was unfurnished, and by the dust on the floor and musty smell, appeared to have been vacant for months. The price was a *fantastic* three quarters of a million dollars. Should I be looking for a retirement home in the mountains?

"Well, how does this compare in relation to the oceanfront condo?" he asked.

"It has character," I said. "And it's more in the spirit of Folly Beach."

"I couldn't agree more," he said. "This is what this island was twenty years ago and what most of it still is today."

After a quick walk around the exterior, we moved on. Back in the Plum PT, driving back toward town, Bob shared that—fortunately for him, but unfortunately for the folks who don't want Folly to change—the island had been "discovered" by the new money investors in Charleston, Columbia, and as far away as Atlanta.

"That's the main reason for the high appreciation of the properties. Many of the investors want only the lot and consider the house a 'tear down.' They want to build McMansions." He said that with a curl of the lip, but then added, "Now as far as my pocketbook is concerned, I don't care what they want to do with the property. But on a personal level, I hate to see the character of the island diluted by the damn yuppies—or whatever they're called now."

We drove on a little farther before he said, "I have two other condos to show you, but couldn't get us in them today. Besides, if you see more than three properties at a time, they begin to run together. You don't know what in the hell you know."

That made sense, I guessed. After all, he was one of the best.

We drove to Sandbar Lane, about six blocks from the center of town and down a gravel road, where we found a small complex—twenty-four condos, I believe Bob said. They were older than the last building and more weathered. He said this was the most "economical" condo opportunity on the island. I think that's realtor speak for "cheap."

As we were walking up the steps to the second story condo, Bob asked, "What in the hell does it feel like to almost get killed—especially when you're on vacation?"

"I guess it doesn't feel any different from getting killed while sitting in my lounge chair in Louisville reading *Popular Photography*. It's a terrifying, horrible experience. Knowing that a killer is still out there right now makes it worse."

"I wouldn't worry about that," he said. "I think it was someone from Charleston who had a run-in with Mr. Pain-in-the-Ass. I don't think anyone from here is involved. Besides, from what I hear, you're a fairly nice fellow—for a northerner. People are keeping an eye out for you so you don't get killed. You're bucks in my pocket, so I sure don't want anything to happen to you."

I understood why Bob wanted me safe, but was surprised to hear that there were others. I asked him, "So who's keeping an eye out for me?"

"Well, maybe someone who works at a local restaurant, maybe someone who always appears out of the blue on his trusty steed—or is that a Schwinn? A local cop or two, and even Louise in our office. She's taken a shine to you, and she's watching."

It was some consolation to know that I was safe in The Lost Dog Café and in the offices of Island Realty. It was endearing to know that these people were thinking about my safety after my being here just over a week. But it was slightly irritating that Bob had learned so much about me, or more correctly, about my protectors. Word traveled fast. Even with all that, this place was growing on me.

The one-bedroom, one-bath unit was small. The ceilings were only eight feet high so it felt its size, which couldn't have been more than four hundred square feet. The bedroom was on the back, facing the parking lot.

From the window, I saw what I guessed to be the building where Charles lived. It was a one story, weatherworn structure. On the end facing the marsh, there was a large sign that said Restaurant, and a much smaller one that identified it as the River Café. There were also several doors opening onto the gravel parking lot, each with a number—apartment numbers, I assumed. Quaint, very quaint.

Only the living room had a view of the marsh and the Folly River. The paint on the small wood deck was peeling with some rotting wood showing through. The furniture was "low-end condo package," as Bob graciously put it. The price was its main selling feature. At two-fifty it was as low as you could go on the island. It was amazing how a quarter of a million dollars for a one bedroom, tiny, tiny condo began to sound like a bargain! The price was "right," but it wasn't for me.

We got in the car, and before Bob started the engine, he asked, "Well, what have we learned today?" I assumed the "we" was only me.

"I've learned that money means something different here than in Kentucky."

He laughed and said he knew what I meant. "That's why I like clients from New York or even California. They think everything here's cheap. A much easier sell, for damn sure. But," he went on, "other than the Folly currency conversion rate, what else?"

"Clearly the condos are easier to maintain and have better views," I said. "But something doesn't feel right."

"Other than cost?"

"Yeah, but I just can't put my finger on it. Maybe after we see a few more, I'll have a better idea."

"Let me pull a few others, and we can get together Friday morning to take a look. Same time," he said.

I was beginning to see the true salesman in the blustery, unique person of Bob Howard. He'd not only already set a day but also a time for our next tour, and I didn't get a chance to say no to either. I told him I looked forward to another ride in the PT Plum, and with all details confirmed, he headed to my house. I wondered—had he planned to leave me stranded in that parking lot if I didn't agree to our next meeting?

We'd pulled up in front of the house, when my realtor pulled another question out of hat. He looked at me and grinned. "Has Amber offered to serve you more than food?"

I looked at him maybe twenty seconds before I answered. It didn't seem like the sort of question a man should ask about a woman. But I relented. "Sort of," I said. "But I think she's just being nice."

"Don't put money on that," he said, the grin gone now. "Her plan is to find a father for her son Jason. She's been dedicated to that task for years. Hooked one or two, I hear, but the damn line broke before she reeled in her catch. Some of the know-it-all experts around here say she's a nice kid, but that the closest she ever came to a brainstorm was a light drizzle. My highly perceptive judgment of others says they're wrong, about the drizzle part, that is."

I tended to agree, but I'd never tell him so. But he wasn't done.

"She likes you—watch out. That is, unless you want a ready-made family. But also, don't forget, that would eliminate all the one bedroom condos we look at."

He said that last part with a saccharine smile. My realtor—thoughtful to the end.

*   *   *   *

I wasn't ready for an instant family, so rather than go to The Dog, I walked to The Rolling Thunder Roadhouse Café for lunch. It didn't open until three, so I was early and walked the additional block to the beach. Much to think about; a new home, relationships, future, the price of eggs in China, etc. Things would soon start coming together—I hoped.

The Rolling Thunder Roadhouse Café was appropriately named. It was near the beach, but this second story bar, grille, with its neon beer signs, dark interior with the main light over the pool tables, and a jukebox in the corner was more like a local hangout than a roadhouse. It was too early for the regulars and karaoke (too bad!). I had a burger, beer, and brevity of conversation. All three tasted good.

With a burst of energy, I walked back to the beach and even waved at one of the police officers who actually stopped his car for me to cross the street. Maybe they really are watching out for me, I thought. I went down the public walkway to the sand for what was becoming a tradition—a daily walk along the shore.

The temperature must have been in the lower eighties, pretty warm, so I cut my walk short.

*   *   *   *

Tuesday started with light showers, reminding me of Bob's comment about Amber and the brainstorm. Having thought about it some more in the night, I decided Amber had much more upstairs than the people Bob was talking about were giving her credit for. And what she might really lack in that department, she certainly made up for in heart.

Anyway, I put on my trusty Tilley—and other clothes—and walked to The Dog. A hot cup of coffee and a smiling Amber greeted me at the door. I followed her to the table of her choice and ordered an egg and cheese bagel sandwich. The restaurant was nearly full of construction workers who were getting a slow start because of the rain, so Amber was busier than usual. But along with the bagel, here she came with the latest gossip.

She set my meal in front of me and leaned close. "I hear our police chief and that detective were at it again in Charleston Saturday evening," she said. Her eyes glistened with pleasure.

According to Amber's source, they'd been spotted at one of the fancier restaurants sharing a steak, "—and more," she grinned. I reminded myself to be careful who I shared steaks with in South Carolina. I nodded for her to sit down in the empty chair to my right.

"Can't," she whispered. "The place is too busy. What do you want?"

"I'm thinking about going to the city council meeting tonight," I said. "If the chief's there, you want me to ask him about his trips?"

She turned instantly serious. "I don't think that's a good idea," she said.

"I was teasing," I said—too subtle, I suppose. By now the rain had let up and the restaurant was emptying quickly; construction must go on. Amber made a quick round of her tables, gathered up her tips, tucked them in a pocket, and then came back. "Really," she said, "don't do that."

I paused with a bit of bagel inches from my mouth, and smiled. "I see Officer McConnell and the other officer whose name I never can remember sitting in the back booth," I said. "I could go ask them."

After threatening me with a pancake over the head, she said in a voice just above a whisper, "You'd better not be saying anything to Rod about his boss. As far as Chief Newsom is concerned, Rod's number two on the force, so Rod's pretty loyal."

"By Rod, do you mean Officer Rodney McConnell?" I teased.

The blush on her face told me she definitely was referring to Officer McConnell, and that he either is, or was, more than her customer. I wondered if he was one of the ones who got away.

With the tables mostly empty now, she paused long enough to explain. "Rod and I dated after he joined the force seven years ago. He was new to town, and I'd only been here a short while. We even talked about getting married, but his personal life and schemes kept getting in the way."

"Schemes?"

As she began, both officers slowly walked toward the door, and her voice trailed away.

"Good morning, Mr. Landrum, Ms. Lewis," McConnell offered with a polite salute. "Mr. Landrum, have you thought of anything else you saw at the coast guard station last week?"

I shrugged. "Sorry, afraid not. If I do, I'll be sure to call."

When the door jingled shut, Amber continued. I could tell she wanted to sit, but with a couple of her tables still occupied, she thought better of it.

"Rod always has a plan to strike it rich. He came over from Charleston and thought this is where he'd leave his mark. Something about being a big fish in a small pond, I think he said. I remember he had this *brilliant* idea to open a 'time-share' restaurant on Center Street. He said it would be a snooty little coffee shop in the morning and an ice cream stand in the afternoon. At night in the summer, it would be a sub-sandwich shop, and in the winter a steakhouse."

"What happened?" I asked.

"Unfortunately, no one would finance it. No one wanted to "share" the time-share. That, and he spent about a month trying to figure out what the sign out front would say. Wondering how he could change the name three times a day. He was even more bewildered when people in the restaurant business told him he would need different equipment, prep space, and a bunch of other things to be three different restaurants on the same day. He said the near-sighted bankers and potential restaurateurs simply didn't know a brilliant idea when it hit them in the head.

"One of the deputies told me Rod even decided he would become a famous developer. Bought two of Donald Trump's books to learn how it's done. He's had a bucketful of other equally ingenious ideas. I wasn't in his life at the time to hear about them. His loss."

She wasn't ready to stop talking yet, making me wonder if she wanted to re-sink her hook into McConnell.

"Him being short—he says he's five-seven, but he's really five-five—he has an inferiority complex anyway. That's why be became a cop. He could be a big man with a uniform, siren, and gun." Pause. "He's a twin, you know."

Of course I didn't know, but didn't want to interrupt her flow.

"His sister has drug problems. She's been in and out of treatment facilities ever since I've known him. Sad, because she's a beautiful woman. Rod always said she got the beauty, and he got the brains. He's half right.

"Actually, he mentioned his sister when he was at my house just last week. Something about his sister's friend living there a few years ago."

Amber had to get back to work, and I'd had about all I wanted to hear about Officer Rod. I told her I'd see her later.

"Don't make it much later," she said, and gave me a smile and a wink.

CHAPTER 13

To make sure I wouldn't have to sit in "reserved" seating, I got there twenty minutes before the scheduled start, entered the city council chambers through bright yellow doors, and found the room nearly empty. I walked back out into the wide corridor and waited with some other early arrivers.

City Hall was a relatively new, salmon colored, two-story building on Center Street. The corridor was light, clean, and attractive, the smell of cleaning disinfectant lightly in the air. There were several familiar faces among those waiting for the meeting.

Police Chief Newman, who was talking to an older lady when I arrived, came over and welcomed me. I told him since I was looking to buy property, I thought it'd be a good idea to see what happened at one of the council meetings. He grinned at me like I'd just escaped from an asylum, said he had to be there and couldn't understand why anyone would voluntarily subject himself to the experience.

At the far end of the corridor, Officer McConnell was in animated conversation with an intense looking man who appeared to be in his early forties. The grade-school-aged Officer Spencer I'd met at the coast guard station was talking and laughing with a couple of middle-aged gentlemen. There were familiar faces from The Dog, but I had no clue who they were.

It was unsettling that after being in town less than two weeks, I knew so many police.

Just before seven-thirty, a stern-looking, white-haired, elderly lady stood in the doorway to the chambers and cleared her throat. It was like an alarm had gone off, and everyone immediately converged on the chambers to grab a seat. She must have been the designated meeting-calling-to-order official.

Most of us sat in folding chairs, and seven of the citizens who had been talking in the corridor moved to the front of the room and took places at a raised, curved table that faced a small desk in the center. The assembled seven, who I quickly deduced were the six members of the council, and Mayor Amato, were all decked out in their finest formal "beach wear." I saw only three ties—two worn by a couple of people in the audience, and one that held back the American flag in the corner.

Mayor Amato gaveled the meeting to order, and the assembled legislators quickly moved through the printed agenda items, Roll Call, Invocation, and Pledge of Allegiance—a pleasant, patriotic, retro activity.

The Mayor's Comments item reminded me that I was in a small town council meeting where concerned citizens gave of their time to legislate and govern a group of people who would disagree on most anything. Small items were as important as the major issues of the day. The mayor was a smallish man, I'd guess in his mid-fifties, bald but for a wisp of reddish comb over. His deep voice and self-confidence belied his size.

"I want to thank the James Island Garden Clubs for donating their time and planting the lovely spring flowers along the causeway. Sally Green, president of the association, is here tonight. Sally, please thank your fellow club members for all of us. Your efforts provide a lovely first impression of our island." A round of applause followed, and Ms. Green (an appropriate name!) was pleased.

"There'll be a revised trash pick-up for the Memorial Day Holiday. Monday's normal pick-up will be moved to Tuesday.

Then he cleared his throat and proceeded with appropriate respect. "I want to make a brief comment on the tragedy that occurred a week ago. It was a sad day for Folly Beach. We share our deepest sympathy and our prayers with the family and friends of Mr. James Lionetti. We pray the perpetrator of this horrific killing is quickly apprehended and brought to justice." The mayor lowered his gaze and bowed his head. "Let's have a moment of silence for Mr. Lionetti."

I slid lower in my chair hoping no one was staring. *Folks, I only found the body. That's all—period!*

A representative from the Folly Beach Art Guild reminded those gathered about the annual Sea and Sand Festival coming Saturday the twenty-second. She asked for a waiver of the "open canister law" from nine in the morning to five in the afternoon. I sat thinking it would be much more fun if the law was waived from nine in the evening until five in the morning, but no one asked. This must have been an annual request, since the council approved it without dissent. The mayor looked at Chief Newman who nodded that he understood.

Next thing up, Mayor Amato recognized Frank Long. Long was trim and handsome—two things that already made me dislike him. He was the person I'd seen speaking to Officer McConnell before the meeting began.

"Mr. Mayor, members of the council, thank you for letting me speak. First, I want to echo Mayor Amato's sentiments about the loss of one of my fellow developers and one of Charleston's better-known citizens. Because of our mutual interests, I'd known Jim for years. We'd even talked about joint-venturing some projects on James Island. As you may know, my wife is a realtor over there. Jim and I met through her. He'll be missed."

Long paused a moment for us to appreciate how close the two had been. I wondered if anyone cared.

"Now for the reason I'm here. I'm a native of Charleston, but have lived on Folly for eighteen years. I know you, your families, our business owners, those who make a living without leaving our wonderful part of paradise. Several of your sons play on the little league baseball team that I sponsor—The Long Hitters."

Cleaver, I thought.

"Like most of you, I don't want chain restaurants here. As we sit here tonight, the closest Starbuck's, McDonald's, and Wendy's are in the Charleston Yellow Pages downstairs by the pay phone—not on our island. I hope you'll recall that I was opposed to the Holiday Inn development. I don't want unlimited growth, and I know that you don't want it either."

A few heads nodded agreement.

"I feel strongly that the lot size restrictions on the perimeter, both on the ocean and along the Folly River, are detrimental to the controlled—and I emphasize *controlled*—growth of Folly Beach. You should allow adjacent private home-owners to consolidate their properties if they choose to build low-density condos or larger homes on the combined properties. You can still maintain the thirty-five foot height restriction and the required number of parking spaces. This easing might encourage folks to build a handful of eighteen unit or smaller condos scattered around the perimeter."

He wasn't speaking from notes, unless they were on his cuff. But it did sound well rehearsed.

"We already have fifty or more homes that don't meet the setback restrictions, most are along the marsh. The next time you have a chance, slowly drive the streets, look at the many dilapidated properties, and ask, 'What's the future of the island—where will our economic growth come from?'"

"Permitting a handful of small condo developments would not increase the beach density appreciably, even during the busiest tourist months. And imagine how such projects would benefit our fine restaurants, stores, and your tax base."

"Now I know this proposal would first need to go through the planning commission, but you, the council members, will be making the ultimate decision. I know that through a technicality, they've already approved a lot consolidation on the beach on the north end. Unfortunately, that was approved for Jim Lionetti. You must understand that I'm a strong proponent of controlled growth on our island, and believe the lot consolidation proposal will achieve controlled growth without harming the character of Folly Beach. Thank you for your time and patience."

There was a whispered murmur around the room, and the sound of rustling cloth and squeaks as people shifted in their chairs. The mayor cleared his throat for attention. "Mr. Stamper, I believe you're next."

"Thank you, Mr. Mayor and members of the council. I'm Wynn Stamper. I know most of you much better than Mr. Long ever will."

There was already an edge in his voice. This was about to get interesting.

"I've lived here for nearly thirty years and own several houses on the island. I've had many more dealings with the businesses here than the previous speaker. As for his comments—bull hockey!"

At first, I had a hard time imagining Mr. Stamper riding the little green scooter Charles had told me about. But after his first comments, I not only could see him riding his scooter, but charging into the council chambers on that trusty steed, brandishing a five-foot-long rapier!

"I, and I dare say most of you, strongly disagree with his self-serving comments. Changing the rules would open a floodgate to developers and others trying to make a buck from us. It would ruin Folly forever."

About an equal number of heads nodded as did for Long. Different ones, of course.

"Folly must stay the same to grow," said Stamper, getting more animated by the word. "No one comes here for skyscraping condos, fast-food restaurants, and crowded beaches. If they want that, they can head up the coast to Myrtle Beach or south to Florida. They come here for peace and quiet. Again, Mr. Long's comments are bull hockey. *Long is Wrong* should be on a bumper sticker and on yard signs in front of each of your houses!"

The mayor cleared his throat again and said in his deep, controlled voice, "Excuse me, Mr. Stamper. Please keep your remarks civil. Personal insults will not be tolerated."

That didn't slow Stamper.

"Remember, Mr. Mayor, most of us are here because of what Folly was and is—at least until now." Then suddenly, "You don't need to stop me. I'm done."

With that, he stormed away from the table and out of the council chambers without looking back. I could almost hear the applause of his faithful, but surprisingly, there was silence. It was a loud silence.

"May I make one more comment, Mr. Mayor?" Frank Long asked as he stood, but made no effort to come to the table.

"Yes. If it's brief."

"Thank you, Mr. Mayor. Mr. Stamper failed to mention that the only reason he's opposed to progress on Folly is to protect his precious rental properties. Everyone knows that."

The mayor leaned forward, and with a stern voice, said, "What part of *civil* didn't you understand, Mr. Long?"

"I apologize to you and the council," Long said. "I thought that point needed to be made."

Without skipping a beat, the mayor asked Lucy Lodgment if she had comments for the gathered city officials.

"Yes, Mr. Mayor, and thank you for allowing me to speak," replied the pleasant looking, very elderly lady as she slowly, very slowly, walked to the table.

"I'm Lucy Lodgment. I live on East Eighth Street. I don't know nothing about what those guys were hot and bothered about. I just want to ask why kids on those little motorized scooter things are allowed to run up and down the streets, sounding like they're racing lawn mowers. Some of 'em aren't old enough to ride a bike, much less get pushed around on a motorized machine. I was told by a friend, whose husband is a lawyer, by the way, that it was illegal for those machines to be rode on our public streets. Now tell me, if it's illegal, why aren't our law enforcement officials doing something about it?"

The mayor was nodding and nervously tapping the table with his pen. "Ms. Lodgment, thank you for bringing this to our attention. I'll have Chief Newman check with our city attorney for clarification." He turned to Newman. "Is that okay with you Chief?"

I guess Chief Newman's nod made it into the official minutes. If not, the mayor moved on anyway.

Thank God, Ms. Lodgment was the last citizen to talk. The council gave first reading to two benign ordinances and then quickly moved to the heading, New Business.

McLaughlin Construction requested permission to work on the next three Saturdays on two houses they were rehabbing. The council granted permission but limited the hours.

On that exciting note, I'd had all the city council I could take. They seemed prepared to go forever, but they would have to do it without me.

Officers McConnell and Spencer were standing outside when I left the building. They were laughing and sharing a joke. "Well, did you learn a lot about our sleepy town during the meeting," asked Spencer as I walked past.

I hesitated and turned toward him. "I guess I learned there's a great divide on the question of development and growth. Nobody seems to be in the middle on the issue."

"It don't take long to figure that out," chipped in McConnell. "We were asked to be here tonight because of possible fireworks between Mr. Long and Mr. Stamper."

I just shook my head. "I think Ms. Lodgment could have taken them both," I said as I walked away.

"You may be right," said Officer McConnell, and he gave me a crisp salute. "Have a good evening."

On my walk home, I thought it was, after all, good to see government at work. Sure, there were silly times and heated moments, but all in all, seeing citizens show concerns about and pride in their community was refreshing. But it was sobering to realize I'd also witnessed an angry debate between two of the suspects in the killing.

And that debate had been moderated by Mayor Amato—another suspect. Strange!

But finally, and more than anything, I was excited about seeing Tammy tomorrow. So what was with that?

CHAPTER 14

I woke early and was anxious to head to Charleston. It was still three hours before Tammy and I were to meet at The Battery. On my way, I stopped for coffee and then headed inland toward the historic city. The sun had been up for more than an hour, but it was just breaking through the clouds. The day was fantastic. There was no rain in the forecast, and the temperature was mild.

Like the drive from many beach areas inland, the landscape was varied. There were beautiful vistas over the marsh, small old houses handed down from generation to generation of former slaves, and the typical beach area businesses—boat sales, closed used car lots, and the ubiquitous Walgreen's.

Once I made the turn off Folly Road toward Charleston, the view went from varied to spectacular. The marsh, the Ashley River, and the Charleston Marina led my eyes to the awakening, charming city with its international reputation for its history and beauty.

Following Tammy's directions, I followed Lockwood Drive to Chisolm, to South Battery around the edge of the river. The roads were confusing, so I couldn't fully appreciate the extraordinary mansions and stately homes that dotted the latter part of the route.

To my right, in clear view from many of the homes, was a lovely park umbrellaed beneath live oak trees covered with Spanish moss. To add to the beauty, there were a few palmettos with their spiky green fans scattered among the oaks. I drove one block through the park, then turned toward the water. True to Tammy's word, there were several empty parking places against the barrier wall that separated the city from the bay. I grabbed the empty spot closest to our meeting place.

There, I faced my first dilemma of the morning. Do I take my camera? I could only imagine how many excellent photo opportunities I'd have. But I was here to see Tammy. The wise thing to do would be to leave it in the car. I consider myself a wise person, at least part of the time, so I left it. I'd be back, anyway. The houses had been here since before the Civil War, and they'd still be standing two weeks from now.

I climbed the steps and walked along the seawall on a wide, elevated walkway. In the distance was Fort Sumter, known from Civil War fame. Looking back toward the city, I had a panoramic view of Battery Park with its long-silent cannons pointed toward the water, ready for any invader. The view was timeless and peaceful, and a light fog glimmered with sunlight on the horizon.

And there she was—Tammy—walking toward me a full half-hour before we were to meet. Though petite, she carried herself with the confidence of someone much greater in stature. She looked great in white linen slacks and a light green blouse that made me feel underdressed in my dark olive green Dockers, yellow polo shirt, and well-worn shoes. I was still irritated about having to donate my Nunn Bush deck shoes to the police department.

She spotted me, cautiously darted across the lightly-traveled street, vaulted the stairs two at a time, her blond hair bouncing with each bound, and said a bright "good morning!" She then kissed me on the cheek. The kiss surprised me—pleasantly. Very pleasantly. I managed to reply with only a simple, "Hi."

"Welcome to my little corner of the world," she said. Her voice was vibrant and alive. "Did you have any trouble finding this place? Are you up to walking?"

I think I said, "Thanks, no, and yes." I hope in that order.

"The weather's great; I thought you might like a walking tour. You can leave your car here." She swept the area with her arm.

"Most people call this The Battery. The official name of the park is White Point Gardens," she said as we began our walk in the direction from which she'd just come. "We'll go up East Battery toward town, then cut back into the residential streets. As you can imagine, those antebellum, pastel-colored homes belonged to the earliest merchants in the city. Their view is unparalleled."

She was right. The mansions—the only word I could think of to describe them—were huge, and they had fantastic views, but they had dominant stucco, brick, and wrought-iron walls that screamed, STAY OUT!

"This is the kind of house you have in Louisville, isn't it?" she asked. I hope she was teasing, and her smile hinted that she was.

"Yeah, sure," I said. "Not quite; not now, not ever. Actually, I grew up in a very small house—smaller than most of the slave quarters behind these estates."

The houses grew closer together the farther we walked. Many were Georgian style row houses with only the exterior colors separating one from another. We turned away from the water on Longitude Street. (No, I didn't see a Latitude Street cross it anywhere, but then I didn't ask.) As we passed a half-block long stucco fence covered with wisteria, the sweet smells of the vine-like purple flowering shrub were nearly as pleasant as the view. Ivy-covered brick stairs led to the elevated first floor of several of the homes, and liriope and English Ivy covered many of the small front yards. Of course, my bias was for the photo-op view over the sweet smells.

"Tell me about you," she said. "Despite my cunning, reportorial questioning, all I've learned so far is that you're from Louisville, that you're looking for something to buy, and that you're not very fond of having found Mr. Lionetti— slime-sucking prick that he was—on the beach."

I started in wide-eyed surprise at her unrestrained description of the late Lionetti, then when I'd recovered my customary aplomb, said, "Then I guess you won't find it so hard to believe that I've never been comfortable talking about myself. I already know everything that I might say, so it's boring for me. Besides, I enjoy listening to others more than I do talking."

"Makes for an unfair conversation," she said. But there was a smile on her very nice lips.

"Okay," I said, "so here's a block's worth of me. I'm a relatively normal mid-sized city boy who's led a corporate work life. I grew up poor, but didn't realize it at the time because of a couple of wonderful parents. They both worked, often at menial jobs, to keep my younger sister and me in food, clothes, and the basics. I like the beach because the closest thing we ever had to a beachfront vacation was a week in primitive cabins on the Ohio River. No one would confuse the Ohio for the Atlantic. With a couple of small scholarships—athletic, not academic—and working part-time jobs, I was able to go to college, and was the first member of my family to graduate therefrom. Then, *whoops!* We're at the end of the block. That's enough for now."

"That's fine, as long as there's more later," she said.

"Your turn," I probed.

"No, not yet. Let's go another block and enjoy the scenery."

Changing the subject, I observed that almost every house had a stucco, brick, or wrought-iron fence with ornate gates. "Those gates are fantastic," I commented.

Tammy eagerly took up the subject. "In much of Charleston, gates, especially the lacy wrought-iron elaborate ones, are a status symbol. There's an elderly black gentleman, Mr. Simmons, who's world famous for his handcrafted gates. There are hundreds of his in the city alone."

"I'm impressed, not only by the gates, but by your knowledge of Mr. Simmons," I said.

"Don't be. I did a story on him last year. He'd be in his mid-eighties by now."

We continued around the corner and back down Church Street heading toward The Battery. "Are you from Charleston? How did you end up here?"

"I thought we were going to walk and enjoy the scenery," she said.

"I *am* enjoying the scenery, but my ears aren't doing much. You can go ahead and fill them with words."

"You win. My childhood was the opposite of yours. My dad was a successful oil executive, and we had to move every few years with his work. That was until he left Mom in Santa Fe. She was a psychiatrist, so money was never the big problem—no shortage of wealthy people with *issues*. Stability was the variable missing in our home. They divorced when I was five. My mother came back to the East and settled in Virginia.

"Fast forward a bunch of years," she continued while we kept a brisk pace. "After graduating from journalism school, I married a television news 'personality.' I had no desire to be a 'talking head' in front of the camera, so I went into the newspaper business. The money wasn't nearly as good as television, but there's something about seeing your words in print that's gratifying. We moved for his job—money talks, you know—from the smaller markets, to medium markets, to the large markets, until I said 'whoa.' We happened to be in Charleston with me a new reporter for the paper when that happened. That was six years ago—end of story!"

I looked at, smiled, and nodded my appreciation. "I guess it would be hard to get you away from here," I said, not really knowing why.

"You bet." Her shortest answer yet.

"See that house on the right," she said, "the one with the stucco and bronzed gateposts? That's Jim Lionetti's. Or it *was*."

"Wow! Developers make *that* kind of money?"

"Chris, don't you read my stories? The home is his *wife's*. It's been in her family for years."

"Oh," I said. "Sorry. But speaking of Lionetti, any fresh word on who killed him?"

Joking—I think—she said, "The police have worked their way through the alphabet to the Es. He had more enemies than Charleston has one-way streets—and that's a bunch. They're being silent on the investigation. I think they're still taking a close look at the wife, so they don't want to say too much. She's a very influential person in Charleston. The local arts community—remember?"

"I wish they'd hurry-up," I said. "Every day that goes by without an arrest worries me. *You* know I don't know anything that could incriminate him, but unless *he* knows, and believes it … well, I'm worried."

"Enough murder stuff, Chris. Let's get back to you. Wife?"

"Yes, once," I said. "I married my high school sweetheart the second year in college. It lasted twenty years. She came home one day and announced she was tired of me and was leaving."

"That had to be shock," she said.

"I didn't blame her. At that point, I was as tired of myself as she was—maybe tireder—but I was stuck with me. We didn't have children or even any pets to divide. I offered to give her the house, but she declined, requested instead a pot load of money, and moved to Carmel, California. Our only contact after that was the next March when tax time approached—paperwork needed to be clarified and signed. That was it."

"What made you want to live here?" asked Tammy, kindly moving from the unpleasant subject.

"I've visited lots of beach resorts on the east coast and even a couple on the Pacific," I said. "There are some beautiful areas, but I really enjoy the four seasons, and longer summers. Florida doesn't have enough seasonal change. There are some areas north of here I'd consider, but none are near a decent size city. Folly Beach seems to fit the bill. The housing is expensive, but less than in many of the surrounding resort areas. I'm not a spring chicken, so thoughts of retirement have been bouncing around in my head more and more." I gave the passing scene an appreciative look. "I guess this is where I want to be."

"That part, I can identify with," she said, "the seasons and proximity to a city, that is—not the spring chicken comment. Actually, I've no idea what that even means, but farming was never my forte. My chickens come from KFC."

We wove in and out of streets lined with huge, classic houses. Each had a garden that looked like it should be featured on the Home and Garden Cable Channel—in fact, many had been, Tammy told me. She pointed out particular classic gardens and the multi-colored flowers. Most had well-worn brick walks through shrub screens of crepe myrtle and oleander. Climbing roses were everywhere, and plenty of fences and walls for them to cling to. Ornamental grasses grew and cast iron benches sat tucked into corners between wide-open green spaces. Many of the yards boasted statues and fountains. I don't understand much about gardens and yards, but there was no question about the beauty of these here.

"Are you getting hungry," she asked.

I was surprised when I looked at my watch. It was already past noon. The beauty of the area and the charm of my walking mate had moved back the hands of my internal clock several hours. "What did you have in mind?" I said.

"We could head uptown and have lunch on the patio at one of several restaurants."

"You're in charge. Lead the way."

We walked back over to East Battery and north toward town. The name of the road changed to East Bay Street—to confuse tourists, I assumed. The overstated mansions of The Battery area gave way to larger commercial buildings and stores. We continued toward the water and entered a small restaurant overlooking the wharf. The outside dining area was larger than the one inside. We didn't have any trouble finding a table, even though they were in the middle of their lunch rush.

I was hungrier than I'd thought, so I ordered a fish sandwich platter, and Tammy didn't waste too much time choosing the crab cakes. We each ordered a glass of Chardonnay.

"Now tell me the truth," she chided with a smile, "did you order the fish sandwich platter because you really wanted it or because it didn't come with grits?"

I hoped she'd forgotten my anti-grits stand. But that was asking too much.

"Of course not; grits never entered my mind," I said. "I'm sure this restaurant has some of the best grits in South Carolina, maybe in the entire south, maybe even in the world. I just wasn't in the mood."

She actually let me finish saying all that before laughing. A pretty face with bright, inquisitive eyes, and laughter too. Wonderful!

Our wine arrived, but that didn't interrupt her questions. "You mentioned retirement. What do you want to do when you leave the corporate world?"

"Ms. Reporter, that's a good question. I know it's good, because I've been asking myself the very same thing almost every day for the last two years. I guess more than what I *want* to do, I've accumulated a fairly specific list of things I *don't* want to do."

"Will I need my notebook to list the reasons?"

"You take out that notebook, and there is a good chance this drink will end-up in your lap. You're off work, remember?"

"I'll drink to that," she said. "So the glass will be emptier in case my instincts overcome common sense, and I reach for the notebook."

"Okay," I said, "here's my well thought-out answer. The first thing I never want to do is wear a tie. Never knew what they were for, never was comfortable in one. But my world demanded it. A steady paycheck spoke louder than my small protest. I also never want to go to a meeting unless I call it or really am interested in the topic. I don't ever want to go back to work the Monday after I've been on vacation. Monday's are bad enough; those Mondays after vacation are worse than bad. I never want to have to write another report that I know no one will read. At least with your reporting, someone is reading it."

"Actually, I often wonder if anyone is reading my stories," she said. "What else don't you want to do?"

"No. Enough for now. Those are only a few of my never-want-to-do-again's, but you get the point. I was getting bored just telling them; I'll spare you the rest—for now anyway."

"Sometime between collecting your 'nevers,' you must have started a list of what you want to do. Spill it!"

Our food's arrival gave me a brief reprieve. But I knew by now that Tammy wouldn't let it go. I took a couple of bites and continued.

"I know with certainty that I'll have to do *some*thing," I continued. "No way could I just sit around and watch television, or just read, or sit on the porch and rock. I like golf and don't get to play enough now. But if that's all I did, it would become work, and I'd learn to hate it."

"Hate it enough to wear a tie again?" she asked.

"Never! Don't even think of going there. Photography is my passion. I know I'm good enough to take photos that sell. I've done that for several years and love it. Now there—that leads to something I want to try. I'd like to open a small photo gallery somewhere like Folly—or maybe here. Unfortunately, I wouldn't make much money doing that. If I could find a way to simply break-even, I'd pursue it. From a gallery base, I could travel to a few outdoor art shows. There's no greater feeling, in photography anyway, than having someone look at your work and tell you how great it is."

She smiled warmly, leaning slightly forward with interest and eagerness in her eyes.

"It sounds like you have the makings of a plan," she said. "Wouldn't opening a shop be too demanding for a 'retired' person? It seems like the owners of most small shops end up working seven days a week, many hours every day."

"That's why my goal would be only to break even. The first thing I'll do is buy a sign to go on the front door that says, 'Open when I'm here—Closed when I'm not!'"

"That sounds like a better plan." She put down her fork and asked, "When will this life-changing retirement occur?"

"Thirteen months, four days." It must be on my mind more than I want to admit.

"And how many hours?" In her business, accuracy is important.

"Three and a half, but who's counting?"

We both declined dessert, but I wasn't ready to leave the brick-walled patio, and I ordered us another round of wine. She didn't object.

"What about you?" I asked.

"Let's see, thirteen months, four days from now, I'll only be twenty years away from retiring—just around the corner. I won't be as lucky as you and be able to retire before I'm sixty. I work in newspaper; little money, remember? If it still exists, Social Security will play a big role in my retirement. I'm only forty-five."

"You know that's not what I meant. Are you serious about staying in Charleston?" I said.

"In a nutshell, yes. The *Post and Courier* is a fantastic paper. The oldest in the South. They've been more than fair with me, not always the standard in the industry. The roots of my branchless tree are now in the Low Country."

But she wasn't comfortable talking about that, and changed the subject.

"Interesting you mentioned photography," she said. "Yesterday, I spent half an hour calming down one of our photographers. Our paper, like most, is all digital. The photo editor somehow erased the photographer's memory card. He'd just got back with photos of a serious wreck on the interstate. He was screaming something about doubting he could 'stage a bloody wreck to get more pictures.' After the yelling died down, someone realized that with some fancy-dandy software, they could recover the images even though the card *had* been erased. I suspect our photographer gave some thought last night to retiring and opening his own gallery."

We laughed—a really good feeling, and then Tammy asked, "Are you ready to continue our tour?"

An interesting segue.

✳   ✳   ✳   ✳

I didn't realize it, but we were only about five blocks from one of Charleston's major tourist attractions, The Market. According to Tammy, The Old City Market dated back to the mid-1800s and originally sold fresh fish, meats, and vegetables grown or caught in the area. As we walked through the center of the open-air covered building, I didn't see a fish or meat. Vendors by the dozens seemed more intent on selling sunglasses, "I Love Charleston" T-shirts and hats, and countless other things I didn't need. Several ladies were weaving baskets out of the indigenous sweet-grass that looked like straw. I read on a nearby sign that the skill had been handed down from West-African slaves.

The Market was four blocks long and cut across a third of the city. The west end intersected with Meeting Street where up-scale hotels competed with up-scale shopping, and with buildings steeped in history standing proudly while the latest model automobiles zipped through the streets like water bugs on a pond.

The true beginning of the Market was at that corner. A replica of a Roman Temple designed by some famous architect stood like the giant head of a dragon, the rest of the market being the body. It was out of character with the rest of The Market, but had a charm of its own.

"This is drastically different from the genteel Battery and the areas north of here," Tammy said. "To me, the city has four cultures: old money, new money, no money, and tourists. Tourists support the new money and the no money. The old money ignores them all. Charleston has all the characteristics of larger cities. It's just wrapped in a prettier package. I love it!"

Like a proud parent, she continued to show me all the highlights within walking distance. Of course we didn't swim to Fort Sumter!

We stood in a small, very old cemetery behind St. Philip's Church and viewed the drastically different architectural style of the French Huguenot Church a block away. Both were located on aptly named Church Street. In a more secular mood, we walked a few blocks west to King Street, the premiere up-scale retail venue in Charleston. Staid art galleries, fine antique stores, and top-of-the-line clothiers were as prevalent as were the mansions along the Battery. A return to the landmark Old Market completed our walking rectangle.

"I live about two blocks from the market over that way," she said as she pointed northwest. "I'm just a quick drive up the street from work, and a two-minute walk to the the market and the center of town."

*   *   *   *

It's true. Time does fly when you're having a good time—and I was really having a very good time. It was after six, and my feet were telling me that it was much later. My walks around Folly had been nothing compared to the trek that Tammy had taken me on today. So when she suggested we might want to get an early supper, I quickly agreed.

"If you like Irish food, we're about a block from the best Irish pub in town," she said.

I'm not a great Irish pub kind of guy, but the "block away" part sounded good, especially to my feet.

Tommy Condon's Irish Pub and Seafood Restaurant was only a block from The Market, and we found it already crowded. Tammy said it was a local's hangout during the week, and then was overrun with tourists on the weekend. The interior looked like it had been imported directly from Ireland. At least, from the photos I've seen of Irish pubs. For all I know, it could be only a Disney version. The hostess knew Tammy by name, so I deduced that she was one of the "locals." That perception was reinforced when the hostess said she had a table available in the back and one of every five people we passed spoke to her. It was a friendly bunch. I hadn't realized there were so many Irish citizens around.

In keeping with the atmosphere, Tammy ordered Irish ale, but I stuck with my summer drink of choice, a Chardonnay. A gentle roar best describes the noise level in the restaurant. She said there would be live music later and that we'd better get our talking done now when we could hear—although even now, we could hear just barely.

"Do you walk all your guests to death?" I said, leaning toward her so she could hear.

"Not all," she nearly shouted back, "just the ones from Kentucky."

I wondered how many "from Kentucky" there had been.

"So, what do you think of my city?" she asked, again leaning toward me, her eyes full of life and interest in my answer.

"The city is incredible," I said. "Today's only reinforced my decision to find something nearby. But, to tell the truth, the company has been much more enjoyable than the city—and that's saying something."

I'm sure it was my imagination, but I thought I saw a slight blush in her cheeks, "Well thank you, sir," she said. "Your personal Charleston tour guide does wish to please."

That felt good, although the Southern accent in an Irish pub felt a little weak. We weren't very hungry. We split two appetizers and had a second round of drinks, and after a while, I realized that it was as dark outside as it was in the pub.

"I'd love to stay longer, but I've taken your entire day. I need to be getting back to the beach. With all the twists and turns you've taken me on, I have no idea how far I am from my car."

"It's just a little way down Church Street," she said. "I'll walk you back if you'd be kind enough to bring me back to my place before you head out of town."

How could I turn down that offer? What we then did would not meet most people's definition of "a little walk," but I should have known by now that her walking distance must be calculated in the new math. It was a long way.

Being out away from the noise of the crowded restaurant brought a strange peace.

"I love walking down these streets after dark," she said. "Look at the glow of the gaslights."

The gas lamps were everywhere—on gateposts, front porches, and even on some garages, all adding to the quiet peace.

Still, they couldn't compete with the warm glow I felt when she cautiously took my hand. I wondered if she did this when walking all her guests around *her* city.

"See," she exclaimed suddenly, "there's your car—just a little walk from the pub."

Right!

The ride back to her building took much less time than the walk to the car. She lived in a three story brick building that in a previous life had been a warehouse. "I'd invite you up for coffee," she said, "but I know it's late and you want to get home."

I reluctantly agreed with that. But before she got out, she leaned over and gave me a kiss halfway between my cheek and lips. I hoped she'd been trying for the lips.

"You have my number," she said. "Give me a call if you want to see more of the area or if you want me to come over to Folly so you can show me *your* beach—or whatever. And by the way, Chris, I had a great day."

*   *   *   *

On the ride home, I had a slight change of heart about having met Jim Lionetti. I don't think I hated him anymore for ruining my first Monday morning on Folly. In fact, I really appreciate his getting himself killed so I could meet Tammy. Despite what most said, he was after all capable of doing a good deed.

CHAPTER 15

Next morning, a beautiful sunrise greeted the residents of Folly Beach.

I feel sorry for those who sleep past what I consider the best time of day—the moments just before and after sunrise. Many would say that sunset twelve hours or so later is just as pretty and that they don't miss their beauty sleep to see it. But I'd never thought sleeping late could help my beauty. Maybe I should give it a try.

I grabbed my Nikon, got my photo vest and Tilley from the car and headed out to see what the day would bring before it got too hot. I walked to the beach and turned toward the sun. The entire stretch of ocean-washed sand was deserted except for two teen-age girls walking dogs. The tide was out and the gulls were busy scavenging.

That's another advantage of getting-up early—the deserted beach, I mean. A couple of blocks past The Pier, I headed inland. By now, the morning sun was casting strong shadows on the houses. Of course you know, if you've thought about it much, that photography is really about capturing light; its varying degrees and intensities are what make the image. And this morning, even rusty old automobiles and paint-flecked boats that hadn't touched the surf in years stood out like long-abandoned gemstones.

I shouldn't have been, but I was startled when I heard that voice behind me again.

"Morning, Mr. Photo Man!"

I looked back and saw that this morning, Charles was sans bike, wearing his trusty long-sleeve "University of Idaho" sweatshirt, and carrying the borrowed camera. And he had that useless cane tucked under his arm.

"And where are *we* going this morning?" he asked as if we'd scheduled this meeting days ago.

"I'm just out for a walk before it gets too hot," I said. "I'd be honored to have you join me." And I meant it. I was growing fond of this eccentric islander.

His smile said that's what he'd been waiting for. "I could spare a little time," he said. "I do have a busy day—some cleaning later at The Lost Dog. I have to be there by four."

It was only seven-thirty. I told him if we hurried, we could cram about an hour's worth of photo time into the next eight and a half hours. I assumed he caught the humor in my remarks. I've often assumed that about people, and I've often been wrong. Don't they even listen?

"Charles," I said as I cast about for some prize piece of flotsam to photograph, "how is it that you manage to find me? I know the island's small, but it seems I could hide *some*where from you. Have you put some sort of tracking device in my photo vest?"

"Wouldn't know how even if I wanted to," he said. "Really, all I do is try to think where a big city photographer would be on this beautiful island just after sunrise. I walk by your house. If your fancy Lexus ES330, or whatever meaning-less number it is, is there, I know you've gone one of two directions. I take a guess, and here I am! You're really not that hard to spot—hat, vest, and camera held up to your eye. When you're carrying that heavy tripod, you can't get too far. Speaking of getting too far, where were you yesterday? Your car was gone all day."

"I appreciate your concern, but you're not my mother." He looked miffed, so I caved and told him I was in Charleston.

"Oh, did you go to take pictures?"

"No, I didn't. Actually, I went to spend the day with a nice, witty, intelligent lady," I said, slightly smug.

"Well, that leaves out everyone from here. So who was it?"

I told him about her, and a little about how the invitation came about. I also told him how enjoyable I found both the city and the guide.

"Wow! Talk about digging into a pile of shit and finding a pony—or something like that," he said waxing poetic. "Mr. Developerman Lionetti sure did you a favor getting himself killed when he did. You know what John Adams—long dead United States president—had to say about writers?"

"No," I said, "but I have a feeling you're going to tell me."

"Yep, I am. Adams said, 'A pen is certainly an excellent instrument to fix a man's attention and to inflame his ambition.'"

Of course I had no idea what John Adams had said about writers—really no idea what he'd said about anything. But no matter. The lovely writer I'd spent yesterday with had in fact "fixed" my attention.

"Did you take any photos? It was a great day for it."

"No. I didn't even take the camera out of the car. But there are many places I want to go back to shoot. I could see a couple of best sellers with all the gates and details on those incredible homes."

"I could go over with you sometime," he said. "I know a couple of spots in Charleston. I bet the newspaper lady didn't show you those."

He was right, no doubt. "Sure, I'll keep that in mind. So, Charles, what are you interested in taking photos of today?"

But I don't think Charles ever looked at his budding hobby in terms of a planned day.

"Just whatever catches my attention," he said. "What should I be looking for?"

I told him it was really up to him, but a good way to focus on a subject was to give yourself an assignment.

"For example, you could decide you were only going to take photos of bird-houses, or old cars, or unusual fences. It really doesn't matter what the subject is. Deciding on one thing allows you to concentrate better and not go off without a purpose."

"That's interesting," he said. "Maybe I'll look for litter along the road—bottles, cans, boxes, things people threw out of cars or dropped while motorcycling on the streets."

I chuckled. "And I thought my subject matter was unique," I muttered. Then I said, "I forgot to tell you that I went to the city council meeting the other night." Again, I chuckled. "I had no idea what they were talking about some of the time—ordinances, second reading, and setbacks. But what I understood was interesting. I enjoyed the sparring match between two of our candidates for killer—Frank Long and Wynn Stamper."

My friend huffed. "Don't feel bad; I know folks who've gone to those meetings for years and still don't have a clue about what's said. I think that's called 'democracy in action.' What did you think of Long and Stamper?"

"Oh. Well … they both made sense, each in his own way. Stamper has a temper. I thought he was going to clobber Long or anyone else who hinted at being in favor of development. I think he would've re-killed Lionetti if he could."

"No surprise there," said Charles. "I expect the police will come arrest him any day for the murder. As they say on television, he has motive, means, and no visible alibi." But I still like him." He paused. "So, when will you be seeing the reporter-chick again?"

"She's not a 'reporter-chick,' Charles—whatever that is—and I didn't say anything about seeing her again."

"Okay, so that means you're going to see her again. But, enough about your love life. How about teaching me some photography stuff?"

Happy to change the subject, I asked him what he wanted to learn.

"Whatever I need to know."

"That would take years; I only have a couple of weeks left. Let me show you some things about composition." We spent a few blocks—I'm not sure how many classes that would convert to in an academic environment—talking about composition, selective focus, and basic lighting. I'll give Charles credit. He listened and was interested in what I was "teaching."

But he couldn't stay away from the subject that was in the back of everyone's mind—especially mine. "Chris," he said, "I've been thinking. I don't have any idea who offed the developer, but no one's been caught. If I were you, I'd be worried. And I'd be more cautious. I mean, if I were the killer and thought you might know something, and you were wandering around here by yourself, it would be mighty easy to run you down with my Saab. That is, if my Saab were running—which I'm not sure about. Or, I could hide in some of these bushes and shoot you dead before you knew what hit you. I guess I'm saying, be careful. You really don't know who you can trust. Except me, of course. But, you really don't know even that, do you?"

I gave him an uneasy look.

"See what I mean?" he said.

I was touched. What he was saying was true. I wondered if that's why he was appearing out of nowhere so often. "Thanks for your concern, Charles. I'll take that advice."

"Good, cause I have to run. Got a delivery to make and work to do, and I only have five hours to get to my job. See you later."

I didn't want to eat another meal out, so I headed home to fix a gourmet peanut butter and jelly sandwich, download today's photo production, and take a nap. The long day in Charleston yesterday was telling.

Back at the house, eating a peanut butter sandwich not taking much brainpower and concentration, my eyes wandered around the room. The sandwich was half gone with I got a very uneasy feeling. I could have sworn I'd left that pile of photos and fact sheets on the edge of the kitchen table. Why were they on the counter? Was I losing my mind? Did the house have a poltergeist? Had someone been here? If someone *had* been, when? More importantly, *why*?

My new friend's words took on added meaning. The room felt colder; I felt alone. How do you "be careful" in a town full of strangers?

*   *   *   *

It was afternoon as I was taking the photo CD to the car when Bill called to me from his side yard, and I ambled over.

"How about a glass of tea?" he said. "I haven't seen you around the last few days."

I said yes to his offer, we retired to the table beneath his live oak, and he brought out the tea. After we'd exchanged the usual pleasantries, he asked how I was enjoying my stay. I told him the vacation had gone well—except for that first Monday—and I was looking forward to buying a place. I commented on my fascination with the many residents who appeared to be a bit quirky—or just off-center.

"Tell me about it," he said. "Look at me. I'm a black, conservative, Republican, northerner teaching at a mostly white, liberal, Democratic, southern university. And I've chosen to live surrounded by white—or white and sunburned red—folks."

I didn't know whether to try to analyze that, agree that he was one of the quirky ones, or tell him he was the only sane one here, and everyone else was off-center. So I took a sip of tea—a long sip. Then changed the subject.

"Bill, what's the deal with the Morris Island Lighthouse? You said you were involved with a couple of groups determined to save it."

"Well," he began, "the current lighthouse served as the beacon to Charleston from 1875 until the early 1960s when a new lighthouse was built on Sullivan's Island to replace it. In my view, anything as historic as that lighthouse *needs* saving. Unfortunately, the tides around here keep changing the face of the islands, even Folly. When the lighthouse was built, it was nearly three thousand feet inland from the shoreline. Now, as you've seen, it's actually in the water."

He seemed at a natural pause and asked if I wanted more tea. "Sure," I said.

He returned with the tea and continued, "A few years ago, a group was formed called 'Preserve the Past' to raise funds and awareness about the importance of saving the landmark. I don't know how successful the group will be. It has begun building a foundation, literal and figurative, to support the effort. The South

Carolina Department of Natural Resources owns the structure, and it's been declared a National Historic Landmark. There's a small replica of the lighthouse just before entering the old coast guard property."

That took me back a little. Not only had I failed to see Lionetti's car or the murderer's vehicle, I had also missed the lighthouse replica.

"In many ways the lighthouse has become an anti-development symbol," he continued. "Anytime someone wants to develop a part of any of the surrounding islands, folks from the group show up to protest or start a writing campaign to whoever will be making the decisions. That's why we believe Lionetti's killing may be related to our efforts to save the lighthouse.

"I hate to say it, but it could have been someone big in the anti-development community who decided to take the more direct route to stop the man. Not very reasonable, I agree, but it is possible. Anything's possible. After all, *I'm* here."

I nodded, quietly digesting what he'd just said. And then I raised the question that was prying at my mind. "Bill, before I forget, did you see anyone around my house yesterday or last night?"

"No, why?"

"Nothing."

Or was it?

*   *   *   *

Around sunset, I needed a walk on the beach, and I didn't want to lug my tripod, so I left the camera at the house.

My mind was concentrated on the changing colors of the sky as sunset approached, but my heart wanted to focus on Tammy. It had been three years since I had a "serious relationship." That one had ended by mutual agreement. We both had been single for several years and were set in our ways, unwilling to change.

So why was I having feelings for a newspaper reporter nearly seven hundred miles from Louisville? Good question. True, she and I had shared—sort of—a traumatic experience, and that can bring people together. For a time. On the other hand, it could be the romantic setting of quirky Folly and historic, lovely Charleston that was making it happen. That could ignite a spark that I might not experience at home. Or, on the other hand—three hands are better than two, everyone knows that—I really liked her sense of humor, her strong confidence, and her beauty; a beauty she didn't appear to know she had. That is, after all, the best kind.

I wouldn't be able to solve the puzzle tonight. And, the more I thought about the other puzzle ... but maybe I'd moved the papers off the table and simply forgot. So I enjoyed the sunset and cool ocean breeze in my face. That I could do.

CHAPTER 16

The Plum Cruiser arrived at nine sharp. Its master walked toward the porch decked out in a Hawaiian flowery shirt and tan, well-aged shorts to match his pale legs. Even in the off-season, Santa wouldn't be caught dead looking like that.

"Good morning, Bob. Are we going house hunting or to a luau?" I came out and met him halfway.

"The plan's to look for a house," he said. "If we run across any luaus, I'll be ready. Besides, the Island Realty dress code allows for shorts between Memorial and Labor Day."

I looked at him with some amusement. I didn't feel it necessary to point out that this was April; Memorial Day still more than a month away.

"Don't look at me like that," he said. "When you're the number one salesman in the second of three small realty companies, you can extend the summer dress code to any hot day. This one's going to be a scorcher. What are you, anyway? A Seville Row fashion critic or a home buyer?"

Opting for the latter, I climbed in the Realtormobile.

"We have three properties to look at. I took it from last week, you weren't high on the condos, so today we'll concentrate on the single-family houses. Besides, I couldn't get into the condo I wanted to show you. You think it was my pale, white legs?"

We drove several blocks from the center of town and stopped at what looked like a newer house. I'd learned that "newer" in Folly realtorspeak meant post-Hugo.

"We're two blocks from the beach and near The Washout. You recognize that area by the long pile of rocks between East Ashley and the beach. It's one of the best surfing spots on the East Coast ... or so they say. Can you picture me on a surf board, even a Dark Plum one?"

He knew my answer and didn't wait.

"This house is in great shape," he said. "You can tell from the neat, well-manicured yard that the owners take pride in their property."

The inside also reflected that care. There were ceiling fans, one in the living room with those faux Caribbean blades. Built-in dressers were in both the master and the second bedroom. This gave them a larger feel. Nice, soothing, beach art paintings. I'd already begun to like the house when Bob mentioned the nine-twenty asking price. I sighed. There's always got to be a catch.

"It's nice, but I think a little out of my range."

It was a *lot* out of the range, but I have learned to understate things when talking to a realtor—or an IRS agent. We walked back to the car and Bob told me the next house was around the corner. He wanted to drive so I'd have a good first impression of the front; it had good "curb appeal." He said they always taught that in realtor school, so he'd better do it right. I bet he'd forgotten what they taught about convertibles and shorts.

After an exhausting one-block drive, we pulled up in front of a definite pre-Hugo structure. From the outside, it appeared smaller than the first property. It had a rusting tin roof, weathered wood plank siding—cedar according to Bob, much better than pine.

It was only a block farther from the beach that the last house, but this was the part of Folly where the distance between the Atlantic and the Folly River began to narrow, so it was close to the marsh as well.

The inside was a surprise. Photographs were everywhere—many professionally framed, some displayed on the walls, some leaning against the walls; most every surface covered with small to medium size images. I thought I was in a photo gallery—though certainly a cluttered one.

Bob noticed me looking at the photos, especially the large, hanging ones.

"The father of the owner was a lifelong resident and had a studio in Charleston," he said. "He took about every photo you ever see of Folly and the surrounding area. All the black-and-white pictures are his."

From the age of the cars on the streets and along the beach, most had been taken in the 1940s and maybe '50s. There was an amusement park with a large Ferris wheel and a sign in the foreground that said Welcome to Folly's Playground. There was a large covered pier, much larger than the pier that now graced the island.

"Where was all this?" I asked.

"Mostly where the damn Holiday Inn is, and some of it was just east of there. This was a jumpin' town after WWII and through the sixties. In the '40s, cars lined the beach like they do now in Ft. Lauderdale. Residents of Charleston came over and pitched tents. Those better off had those little travel trailers, and the wealthy built small cabins—all to enjoy the beach and cool ocean breezes.

"See that photo of the dance hall pier? In the '50s, that was a regular stop for all the big bands of the day; Tommy and Jimmy Dorsey, Count Basie, The Ink Spots, even one of the best songwriters of all time, Hank Williams Sr. Not his damn worthless rock and roll son *Junior*. There was even a bowling alley. The big pier burned in the late '70s. It's hard to believe now, but not too many years ago, Folly was a much bigger than Myrtle Beach." He paused. "But in case you've forgotten, we're here to look at the house. All this stuff leaves with the seller. By the way, the current owner's also a photographer. I don't think he has a studio. The *color* pictures are his."

"He seems much more interested in photographing people than his dad was," I said.

"I guess he didn't want to compete with his father; who knows?"

Of course, the color photos were much more current, judging from the amount of skin showing on the ladies in bathing suits. I was surprised to find that I recognized some of the people. "Isn't that the mayor, what's his name, with the surfboard?"

Four very happy looking young folks with a surfboard in the sand at their feet were smiling at the camera.

"Yep," said Bob. "Eric Amato prides himself in being a *great* surfer. What I hear, he isn't really very good. Sadly, most are betting he's a better damn surfer than mayor."

In the same photo, I recognized another from the city council meeting—Frank Long.

"But who's this girl, the one on the left beside Amato? She looks familiar."

"She looks familiar because she looks just like her twin brother, one of our fine law enforcement officials, Rod McConnell."

"Oh, I guess so," I said. "I've talked with him a few times. Seems like a nice fellow."

"He is, but his sister's a sad case. She has a long history of being mixed up in the wrong crowd, heavy into drugs, and in-and-out of rehab clinics. I heard she's over in Columbia now, some say attending school, some say drying out. I guess she and Long are—or were—friends. He knows most everyone over here." Bob's impatience with my perusal of the photos was palpable. "Now again," he said, "why are we here?"

The surf shop owner from The Dog was in another frame—standing by a man I didn't recognize.

"Okay, okay, what's the cost of this photo gallery?" I finally asked.

"The owner's asking five seventy. I don't know how firm that is."

That was more like it on the price, but it was hard to see the house for the photos.

Still, it was a real possibility and in my price range. But I said, "Let's check out number three."

*   *   *   *

The third, and I assumed final property of the day was only a block from Center Street on East Erie. Before I even saw the house, I liked the location. Only a two-minute walk to the beach, a one-minute walk to the center of town, and even a shorter walk to a small general store, The Island Food Mart. All plusses.

My first impressions of the house didn't match my enthusiasm for its location. It was a small cottage with a screened-in front porch—part of the weatherworn structure rather than an add-on. The exterior was weathered board in a light blue, faded hue with white trim. The color had once been a strong ocean blue—a long time ago. A nautical rope handrail led to the screen door.

On the other hand, the yard was fairly large and uniquely foliage-free by Folly standards. Only a couple of edging boxwood shrubs grew within the shadow of the tin roof, and a large oak screened part of the large front yard. So large that I almost missed the two junked, rusting Fords resting on pilings of concrete blocks and bricks in the side yard. I did notice the three rotting doghouses in back. Nice size yard, anyway.

As I looked it all over, Bob must have seen the expression on my face.

"Chris," he said, "you know you can't judge a book by its damn cover." He was obviously thinking I'd already decided against the place. "Check out the inside before you make any judgments."

He was right. I was looking for a house, not a book, so I didn't care what the cover held. I gave him the benefit of the doubt and entered the small, well-worn structure, and when I did, was glad I'd trusted him. The interior was a direct contrast to the beach-junk scene outside. The walls were newly painted a crisp white.

The hardwood floors had been traversed by thousands, if not millions, of feet over the years, and they showed their history, but, they were clean and the well-worn paths gave character to the rooms. The kitchen had new laminate on the counters and a new Kenmore refrigerator and stove. The bath, though, was old.

"A young couple bought this place three years ago," said Bob. "They thought they'd be able to come here from Atlanta and start a froufrou, shitty boutique clothing store on Center Street. Anyone could have told them they didn't have a chance in hell of selling anything more expensive than a Folly Beach T-shirt. But they didn't ask.

"They were also big in the Save the Loggerhead Sea Turtles movement. Every year, hundreds of these massive turtles crawl onto the beach—about this time of year, actually—and lay eggs. Something about all those lights on the beachfront properties confuses God's big, ugly creatures, and it screws-up their mothering habits. A bunch of damn brain-addled do-gooders are always fighting folks to turn their lights off, or change the type of lighting overlooking the beach. Shit, I figure if God didn't want us have these lights, he wouldn't have given us electricity. I don't guess I'll be getting any awards from these folks.

"Now where was I?" he continued as we checked-out the backyard. "Oh yeah, the do-gooders' store lasted eight months; their money lasted about six; their creditors—and there was a shit-pot load of them—are still after these two failed entrepreneurs. The State Bank in Charleston owned the house and sold the mortgage to a bank in New Jersey. They want to unload it. All the damn banks want, of course, is money—not houses, boats, or cars. They're asking five thirty-five."

I gazed around, trying to get the feel of the place. "Bob," I said, "I have no idea what turtles have to do with the house. But, from what I think I heard you say, this may be a good option."

"Well," he said, fist on hip while he scratched his forehead, "I don't have anything else to show today. If you want, we could ride around where we haven't looked, and you can tell me if you see anything that catches your fancy. Besides, it'll do your image good just to be seen with me."

We drove west across Center Street and headed to the entrance of Folly Beach County Park.

"That's where the day visitors come to spread out their blankets, cheap beach umbrellas, and get scorched by the damn sun," said Bob, oozing little sympathy—very little. "Best of all, they get to pay a five-dollar parking fee for the privilege. It takes all kinds."

We drove past several houses displaying for sale signs, but nothing jumped out and yelled, "Buy me; I'm exactly what you're looking for!"

"See that house behind the tall fence?" he asked. "In the thirties, that's where George Gershwin stayed when he and DuBose Hayward wrote *Porgy and Bess*. Gershwin spent many summers here. He loved the Low Country, or so they say. I wasn't around then to know for sure, but it makes a damn good story. Besides, that's one of my jobs as top selling realtor; show the customer the important places. I've done that. I think you've seen all the highlights."

I looked at him sitting there behind the wheel, the light in his fuzzy white beard, his slightly bulbous nose faintly red, and I grinned at him. "Bob, have you ever considered starting a Folly Beach tour company? You have such a fondness for the sea turtles, the surfers, the local government, and especially all those Asian tourists. You'd be a natural."

"I'm pretty damn good in the fine art of sarcasm," he said barely glancing my way, "but I think you could teach me a thing or two."

I guessed that, right then, he wasn't being sarcastic.

We were getting close to my place now. I told him I'd think about what we'd seen, and he suggested I call him when I was ready to talk. The ball was in my court. He dropped me at home and headed off in his purple—sorry, Dark Plum—Realtormobile to who knows where.

On the way up the walk, I decided I was being way too wimpy and vowed to take a couple of this afternoon's hours and re-explore the old coast guard site. The sun now would be in a totally different part of the sky than it was that early morning two weeks ago. The light would be different, the shadows in different places. With any luck, I wouldn't find any dead bodies. Beside, I needed to return to the site—my version of getting back on the horse after falling off.

CHAPTER 17

I tempted fate and parked in nearly the identical spot as my last visit, and before getting out, even noticed the miniature replica of the Morris Island Lighthouse that stood watching over the entry to the deserted property. There were more people around today. It was Friday, later in the day, and approaching the tourist season. The police had a car at the dead end of the road to help drivers navigate the turn to get back out. I waved at Officer McConnell who was manning the cruiser. He returned my wave with a salute and a smile. I almost felt like one of the natives.

The path through the sand was much as I remembered. The first time I took this trail it was pre-sunrise, and I hadn't noticed how overgrown the area was. The sea grasses, looking like sagebrush to the uninformed, and sea oats covered the landscape. Small wind-pruned trees dotted the sandy expanse. I knew much more now about the affects of the tides and winds on the low lying beach than before, and was able to appreciate how devastating erosion could be. The natural plants could minimize the damage. I looked for Bob's *beloved* sea turtles, but didn't see any—just more of the ever-present sand fleas. In full daylight, it was plain why this isolated area was such a magnet for artists, photographers, and lighthouse fanatics. And, obviously, murderers also found it appealing.

On my first visit, the huge rocks that haphazardly lined the shore had been backlit, so I hadn't appreciated their strong presence. So now, again using my much dreaded but necessary tripod for stability, I captured several images that should be print-worthy. The place wasn't nearly as unoccupied this afternoon as on that early morning eleven days ago. I had to wait while the occasional tourist—as judged by the pale legs—scampered through my photographic field of view.

When I tried to retrace the steps I'd taken prior to hearing shots, the cold sweat I'd experienced that morning returned. Full daylight made the scene very different from what it had been in the light of dawn, so I had trouble remembering exactly were I'd been. But I thought I was close.

A young couple approached, and the female, much to her significant other's chagrin, asked, "Are you from the newspaper photographing where that guy was killed?"

I often got asked whether I was a professional photographer because of the fairly large camera, tripod, and my photo vest, but I was surprised to hear the reference to the killing.

"No," I replied. "Just shooting the lighthouse and the shore."

"Oh, sorry. You looked like you were taking pictures for the paper or some magazine. My sister works for the sheriff's department. She called last night to tell me they were getting ready to arrest the guy's wife and her boyfriend. They say they know her lover shot him. I thought maybe they had arrested them today."

I stood there mildly stunned. "No, that's the first I've heard that."

They left as quickly as they'd come. Quicker maybe with her being pulled by the elbow. I guessed a lecture on opening her mouth to strangers was in her near future.

Remembering what she'd said, I hoped it was true. Now I had a reason to call Tammy—maybe even give her a "scoop."

After another half hour, I had done all I could do, what with the light and tourists spoiling my shots. Besides I needed to get back to the house, get a glass of wine, and call Tammy with my "anonymous source" information. I could see a Pulitzer in her future. Maybe a date in mine.

*   *   *   *

I caught her on the cell phone—a fairly easy thing to do; she has it to her ear more often than not. From the sound of her voice, she was happy to hear from me. After Wednesday night, I thought she would be, but you never know. I was a little disappointed that she didn't know about any arrests, but she was interested and said she'd follow-up. She had to work all weekend but, if I wanted, she could spend some time with me next week. I'm not sure of my words, but I know I said yes at least three ways. I don't think there were any doubts when she hung up. I leaned back in my chair and laughed right out loud: Friday nights were wonderful!

CHAPTER 18

Thunder and a hard rain on the tin roof woke me at six. I was still half-asleep, but came to the insightful realization that when you're on an extended vacation, Saturday takes on a different meaning from when you work Monday through Friday. It becomes just another day. But, that's okay; it was just another day I didn't have to go to work. I presumed holidays were the same. Did a retired person lose the feeling of pleasant anticipation looking forward to Christmas, Labor Day, and the Fourth of July? And did that balance out the loss of Monday dread? Way too deep a topic for a rainy Saturday morning.

The forecast called for clearing and another perfect day in paradise. The rain appeared to be easing, so I got an early start and headed to The Dog for the latest gossip and a hardy breakfast. That's what we "locals" do.

The restaurant was half-full, and my table by the window was already taken. I really must be a local now; I was irritated that some *tourist* was in my seat. Amber gave me a wink and pointed to an empty booth near the back. I assumed that meant I was to sit there and followed her—a pleasant experience.

When I was seated, she gave me her formal greeting. "Good morning, my favorite Kentuckian," she said with her most radiant smile. "We have the Belgium waffle today, so I went ahead and ordered it for you."

At least I didn't have to decide. With my coffee cup in her left hand, the drink decision was a done deal too. I could start liking this kind of service.

"Will you be photographing our fair island today?" she said. "And if so, which direction will you be heading?"

"I think I'll check out the beach. See what it looks like with the sand and sea oats wet. Then, I don't know where."

She gave me an extra warm smile and leaned both palms on the table, and ...

"You know, doll," she said in a conspiratorial tone, "you can find a lot of nice views right here. I'd be glad to pose. You'll be able to see as much of the scenery as you want; know what I mean?"

I was thinking that I did, and I thanked her for the offer. "You never know; I might take you up on that invitation—good vistas are hard to find!"

"Not to sound too cocky, but you could get better photos than of those sea oats; rain on them or not."

But with that, I ran out of words. Besides, how could I disagree? The coffee was hotter than usual; then again, so was the conversation, and, as I watched her walk away, so was my blood. But I took a deep breath and calmed myself.

Trying to distract myself and still my beating heart, I looked around the room. It was eerie; I recognized most of the diners—the two city council members in their regular places; a lady from the grocery in one of the window seats—not mine. Officers Spencer and McConnell came walking in, and Chief Newman was already seated at a booth. A meeting of the local police department?

I was beginning to see how easy it would be to fall into the *us versus them* mentality. *Us*, of course, being the locals, *them* the tourists. The locals love to see the tourists arrive. More accurately, see their *money* arrive. And love to see them leave. Those tourists—I'm not one of *them* anymore—do nothing but clutter-up streets, take all the good locations on the beach, make *us* have to wait in our favorite restaurants, and, in general, stomp on our day-to-day way of life.

No one will argue about taking the much-needed influx of dollars into the community. Even the blustery and politically incorrect Bob Howard would be out of work if it weren't for the tourists, outsiders, and—perish the thought— "foreigners" he sells houses to.

Amber interrupted my meditation by coming up behind me, asking if I wanted more coffee, and leaning fetchingly against me as she poured.

I swept the room with my gaze. "Are we having a meeting of the entire police department this morning?"

"Not all," she replied, pausing with the half-full carafe in her hand. "The chief's talking about next Saturday's Sun and Sand Festival. It's a big deal. Streets will be blocked; drinking will be allowed outside; and in general, it'll create a big mess. Your buddy Charles hates it, but he makes a bunch of money helping clean the streets when it's over. The local cops also hate it. Traffic's a mess. Last year there was a car fire in the Holiday Inn parking lot, and they couldn't get the fire trucks there—from just three blocks away. To be honest, even if they could have been there in seconds, the car still would've been a goner. The owner got extra riled; I don't think he liked seeing his Beemer become a pile of blackened metal. Who would?"

"And speaking of *hot* things," she continued, lowering her voice. "I hear there was another Chief Newman—Detective Lawson spotting in Charleston the other night."

I was beginning to wonder if Amber's interest in the chief was more than just something to talk about during lulls in the "I'll have scrambled eggs with my bagel" conversations. She sure kept tabs on his alleged love life. Who were her sources? And who really cared what the chief and the detective were doing in Charleston? I guess we *locals* should be concerned. After all, it was our tax money at work. Or, was it at play?

Outside, the sun was breaking through the low rain clouds and the light was casting a pleasant, warm glow on the rain-cleaned streets and surrounding buildings. On my way out, Amber repeated the offer she'd made me earlier this—to give me a personal tour of Folly and to show me and my camera the hidden beauty of the environment. But she needn't have reminded me; I wasn't likely to forget.

*   *   *   *

I got to the beach and walked past the Oceanfront Villas—the site of one of the condos Bob had showed me—toward the more residential portion of the shore. When I began missing shots because there wasn't enough light to hand-hold the camera, I regretted not bringing my tripod. The clouds were quickly moving out of the way, and Mother Nature resolved the light dilemma.

"Hey, Mr. Photo Man, what in the world are you shooting now?"

I no longer had trouble knowing who belonged to that voice. I turned and saw Charles hurrying to catch up to me. When he was along side, he was a little short of breath.

"Charles, I hear you're getting all excited about your favorite event of the year, The Sun and Sand Festival."

"If someone thinks that's my *favorite* event, he either doesn't know me or he's been smoking way too many Follyrettes. I hate, hate, and repeat, *hate* the Sun and Sand Fiasco. Did I mention hate?"

"Actually, that's what Amber said. I hesitated a moment and then said it right out. "Charles, why do you lug around that cane?" He'd attached a sling to it and today had it slung on his back."

"Just because," he said. "Belonged to my aunt."

I eyed him suspiciously then looked ahead and saw something just off the walk that interested me.

"Okay," I said, "now for your photographic lesson of the morning. Look at this flower." We both bent over it while I pointed with my finger. "See the light on the right side and the shiny rain drops on top? That will give the photo a little extra life. Rain and raindrops do great things with the light. Some photographers even carry a spray bottle of water to get that look. Me, I'm too lazy to carry a tripod, much less a bottle of water. But here are the drops ready-made and waiting for us. They work like mirrors and prisms—bending and changing the direction of light, breaking it into colors. Give it a try."

"Yeah, well," he said, pulling the camera out of the water-proof pouch at his side. "I got out with the camera at sunrise, and all I got was rained on. How can you get good pictures when all you're thinking about is keeping the camera dry and not falling in puddles?"

"Sorry," I said, making my best attempt at sarcasm. "I forgot to tell you to stay out of the rain! To get a good sunrise photo, there has to be at least a partial view of the sun. Otherwise all you'll get are just wet, gray shots. Did you take some after the sun came out?"

"Yeah, a bunch, but I ended up pushing the little garbage can *delete* button after looking at many of them," he said. "Even I could tell they were terrible."

"That's progress. Many folks can't tell the difference between a good, or even fairly good, image and a bad one. The next time someone shows you a bunch of vacation photos, notice how many are out of focus, have heads cut off, miss the subject completely, or who knows what? If you delete the bad ones before showing them to anyone, your photos will look much better than most. *Delete* is a great feature of digital photography."

"What happens if you delete a picture and then think about it and decide you want it after all? That'd happen to me."

"Not insurmountable," I said. "There's software that can usually recover photos."

"You mean even after they're erased from the card—what does *delete* mean if it really isn't deleted?"

"Good question," I said. "You need to ask someone more sophisticated in the digital world than I. To me, delete means delete, which means gone, and gone for good. Shows you how little I know." We'd been too long in the same place.

"Charles, you and I could stand out here talking about this for days, and never figure it out. Why don't we delete this conversation and move on?"

We walked and talked for several blocks after leaving the beach. He was taking more time with his shots than before. I still couldn't figure out what he was taking pictures of, but he knew; that's what was important. We talked about composition, lighting, and about Charles. I continued to be amazed how well read he was. Not only did he quote old, dead, obscure United States presidents, he occasionally threw in a quote from Jack London, "Billy" Shakespeare, and Peanuts. He let me know each time who he was quoting. A good thing, because I didn't know the difference. But I didn't tell him that.

"So, Chris," he said, "have you figured out who murdered Mr. Slime?"

Attempting to mirror his serious question with an appropriate response, I said, "Well Charles, no. And, I didn't even know I was supposed to have figured it out. I was hoping the fine folks from the Folly Beach Police Department or the Charleston County sheriff's office were taking care of that."

"I wouldn't be counting on the FBPD for a solution," he said. "You'll see how competent they are next weekend when they totally screw-up the traffic on our fine island during the Festival. Don't get me wrong, the cops here are a bunch of nice, friendly, and helpful folks. But crime solving and traffic control just ain't their thing. Last year, a six-foot alligator decided to crawl ashore near The Washout. No one knows for sure how it got there."

"I bet that was an interesting sight."

"Sure was. Alligators don't hang out in the ocean. Anyway, it'd got lost somehow, or just wanted to sun on our beach. Unfortunately, it did it near a group of tourists. The police put on an exhibition of how *not* to catch an alligator. It wasn't because there was a shortage of cops. The wayward critter was surrounded by three patrol cars and five of our finest. Two of them wanted to shoot it—after all, they had guns and this would be a chance to use them. Two wanted to run— I would have been with *them*. And the other cop wondered if Folly was large enough to start a zoo. A nearby tourist suggested that it would take more than one alligator to support a zoo." Charles chuckled. "Know-it-all tourists."

It was obvious to me that Charles had missed his calling. I'm not certain *what* calling, but whatever it was, storytelling had to be a requisite. I'd learned not to get in the way of one of his tales.

"And as for the sheriff's department," he continued. "We don't get to see those people very often. I guess they do solve crimes occasionally—maybe they'll get lucky this time."

We walked on in silence for a dozen or more steps. Charles broke the quiet. "That's enough crime talk, Chris. What's the latest on your love life? When are you going to be seeing that Cute Reporter Chick again?"

"Whoa, slow down," I said. "I've spent a total of one day and one breakfast— not consecutive, I might add—with Ms. Rogers. That hardly qualifies as a *love life*. She is a very nice person, but let's just call it my *like life!*"

"Whatever you say. But as an expert on other people's love lives, I judge that you passed the *like* stage after you had breakfast with Ms. Reporter Chick. That was days before 'the entire day' part of your story. Trust me on this one."

Trust Charles on the topic of love? Charles? The person with undetermined sexual preference? Charles, who had no visible means of support? Who had never been seen with anyone who could be considered a candidate for his *significant other*, male or female? The jury was still out on the question of whether to trust him or not.

CHAPTER 19

To most Americans, that day—April 15—was "Tax Day." But for the rest of my life, I'll remember it for something else.

I spent most of it with Charles, and at last, my legs told me to go home, fix a gourmet meal of grilled cheese and chips, have a glass or two of fine Piggly Wiggly wine, and enjoy the rest of the day at or near the beach. I know my legs really didn't say all of that, but they told my brain that they were tired. My brain told me the rest. The habitual creature in me said to download the photos from today's extended shoot, burn a CD, put it in the car, and then begin on the meal. The Boy Scout in me obeyed.

*   *   *   *

I was in bed before the ten o'clock news hit the air. I hope I was asleep and dreaming, because I was being chased down Arctic Avenue by an alligator while someone who looked eerily like Charles was taking photos of my plight. The roar of the ocean was in my ears, and Tammy was running alongside taking notes and talking on her phone. Then people suddenly stopped paying attention to the great alligator chase when they noticed smoke coming from the door of a nearby restaurant that looked like The Dog but had a different name.

The dream was very realistic. I even smelled the smoke. When I stopped hearing the roar of the ocean, I knew something was wrong. Somewhere between my sleep and waking state, I realized the silence was because the window air conditioner had stopped. And as I was waking, the smell of the burning restaurant was still in my nostrils.

My dream was over, and my nightmare beginning.

It was then that I opened my eyes and saw smoke illuminated by flames on the wall opposite the bed. This was real! I had to get out, and get out quick.

Smoke was already rolling across the ceiling like waves hitting the shore. It was getting thicker by the second. Flames hadn't reached the door, but they were close. I wasn't anxious to jump from the second floor window, and I wanted to get to my laptop and camera, but they were in the computer room. I grabbed my pants and ducked low to the floor the way they show on television. What you don't get from watching television is the intense heat from above. The air felt like it does when you stick your arm in an oven.

The smell of smoke and burning wood was nearly overpowering. I rushed through the bedroom door, flames coming from all sides, and looked up and saw that the ceiling was beginning to glow; it would ignite any second. The computer room was still untouched except for dark black smoke near the ceiling, so I grabbed the laptop and camera bag. But before I got through the door to the stairs, all hell broke loose.

How could fire be coming from all sides? Flames surrounded the doorframe. A burning part of the ceiling fell on my head. I couldn't tell what hurt worse, the pain from the drywall hitting me or the intense burning sensation on my shoulder. Either way, I had to keep moving. Breathing was almost impossible.

The next thing I remembered was being sprawled out at the bottom of the stairs, my head on the carport floor, my legs still on the second step. The laptop was a foot from my left arm, and I couldn't see the camera bag, but it had to be nearby. My right ankle was twisted and hurting. My shoulder hurt. My head *really* hurt. And then the sounds of the roof collapsing shook me to action. I wasn't out of danger by a long shot. I needed to get away from this rapidly disintegrating house. My first attempt failed miserably; my ankle didn't understand the importance of moving quickly. The burning insulation from the carport ceiling started falling around of me. My lungs were struggling to keep up. Smoke was billowing downward as if sucked by a fan.

Then I thought I heard sirens. I knew someone was yelling, but I couldn't see that anyone was there. In fact, I couldn't see anything; I was enveloped in blackness.

*   *   *   *

"Chris, Chris! Wake up. Can you hear me? Chris, are you there?"

"I think so. Did they catch the alligator?" I opened my eyes. I was lying on my back, and about ten other eyes were smiling down with relief and with a bit of confusion about the alligator question.

"Thank God, you're still among us," said Bill who was standing at my side.

Two more of the eyes belonged to Officer Spencer who, I learned, was an emergency medical technician. He was kneeling beside me with one hand on a portable oxygen tank, the other hand holding the mask inches from my face. "Just be quiet and let me get more oxygen into your system." And he put the mask over my mouth and nose and told me to breathe as deep as I could.

Quiet was okay with me. I noticed another neighbor, someone I'd seen only a couple of times and never spoken to, standing next to Bill. The reflection of flames was flickering off the leaves of the tree whose limbs were spread above me, and off Bill's dark face.

A couple more deep breaths of the pure oxygen gave me enough strength to turn my head toward the house. I'd been moved fifty or so yards—by whom, I had no idea. My house or, what *used* to be my house, looked like a huge, glowing charcoal briquette with tongues and sheets of flames dancing out of it here and there. The structure had completely fallen in, and the only thing standing was the concrete block core—my shower. Geysers of sparks occasionally shot skyward, and I became aware of popping, crackling sounds, and of the rush of water gushing through a fire hose and being played sizzling on the ruins.

The entire Folly Beach fire and police department must have been there, along with at least forty others. Neighbors, and maybe some tourists, obviously wanted to see the best Saturday night show on the island. I felt myself drifting off again, my only thought that I wished I'd been there to see the fire. To photograph it.

"I think he'll be okay," Officer Spencer said to someone standing behind me. "He swallowed too much smoke; his ankle appears to be sprained, his shoulder has a minor burn. He might have a mild concussion."

My eyes popped open at the diagnosis.

"He doesn't sound okay to me," I said. "If you were feeling like I feel, you'd agree."

I heard nervous laughter and recognized the familiar voice of Amber. That's who Spencer was talking to.

"How long have I been out?" I asked. By struggling, I was able to sit-up. I winced at the pain in my leg. I realized that I didn't have a shirt on, but that somehow, I'd gotten into my pants—or somebody else had gotten me into them. I wondered if it had been Amber. Not likely.

"Longer than we wanted you to be," Amber said. She knelt down beside me and with her hand, smoothed back my hair. "Chris," she said, "I'm so sorry this happened to you!" The glimmer of the flames turned her hair a reddish gold and glinted in the tears welling in her eyes. "Your house went from rustic to ruins, and you missed most of it," she said. Then she spoke to Spencer who was still on his knees on the other side of me, oxygen mask still in hand. "Officer," she said, "I'd be glad to take him to the emergency room in Charleston. You think he's okay, but maybe they ought to check."

"I'll be fine," I said, waving off her offer. "Let's wait a little while; if I'm feeling worse, I'll take you up on that." But then my head began to spin. "I think I better lay back down," I said, and Spencer on one side and Amber on the other took my arms and helped me.

"Excuse me, Mr. Landrum, do you feel like answering a few questions?" asked a new voice.

I hadn't noticed that Chief Newman was standing above me at my head. He wasn't in uniform, and even now, for a moment, I didn't recognize him. He must have assumed that my answer was yes, because he knelt down beside Amber, his arms crossed and resting on one bent knee, and the other knee in the grass. "Mr. Landrum," he said, his voice was calm and very earnest, "I'm sorry we have to keep meeting under such unpleasant circumstances. Can you tell me what happened here?"

I rehashed the events. At least those I'd been conscious through. I left out the alligator chase, but mentioned that part of the dream where I'd seen the restaurant on fire, then waking up.

"Did you smell anything strange—other than the smoke and burning wood?"

"I don't think so. What kind of smell?" I glanced around on the orange-lighted faces looking down at me, Bill's, Amber's, and some others.

"We're not sure of anything yet," Newman said, "but my first guys on the scene said there was a faint smell of gasoline, or kerosene. Your neighbor William Hansel said he smelled it too."

Spencer had put the mask back over my nose and told me to breathe deep. When he took it off again, I told Newman, "To be honest, my nose was so full of smoke, I doubt I could have noticed the smell of a skunk if it had been under my bed." I was looking questioningly at him. "Are you thinking it was *set*?"

"We're not sure, but that would account for how quickly it spread. Do you know anyone who'd want to harm you?"

Only one, I thought, but said, "No idea." If he didn't know what I really thought, it wouldn't do any good to tell him.

He sighed and for a long moment chewed on the corner of his lower lip while he gazed at the ground. Then he heaved himself back to his feet. "I won't bother you anymore tonight, Mr. Landrum. But if you think of anything that might help, please give us a call. If you want us to run you to the hospital, just let one of my men know. They'll be around for a while."

My head, shoulder, and ankle still hurt, but my breathing was near normal, and Amber was bathing my brow with a wet cloth Bill had brought to her.

CHAPTER 20

That night when I nearly lost my life was when I learned about the character of Folly Beach and its residents.

Out of nowhere appeared a wooden crutch offered to me by a stranger.

"I hear your ankle's hurt. I had this at the house. It belonged to my grandmother before she passed away. Maybe it'll help," said the middle-aged, heavyset woman wearing a pink housecoat and fuzzy blue slippers. I may have seen her before, but didn't recall. I thanked her as I took it from her hand and held it, a gift of friendship out of the night.

"My husband's bringing coffee," she said. "He'll be here in a minute. Oh, incidentally, I'm Polly, my husband's Lawrence. We live over on Hudson. We saw the flames and heard the commotion."

"Amber," I said, "I want to sit up again. Help me, would you?"

"Chris, don't. You ..."

"No. Please help me." And she did.

Both Officers Robins and McConnell came over to ask how I was and if there was anything they could do to help. They were both out of uniform and, I assumed, off-duty. Sort of—whenever the fire bell rang, no city employee was off duty.

I glanced toward my car. Someone had picked up my laptop and put it on the hood. It was in a hard case, so it might have survived the fire—possibly better than I had.

Then, in his typical style, Charles appeared out of nowhere. "Look what I've got," he said as he lifted my Domke canvas camera bag. Would you believe it? Someone just dragged it out in the yard and left it?"

"Charles," I said. "Thanks for coming." I reached out and took the bag. "And thanks for finding this."

"I heard all the noise from home and headed this way. When I saw it was your house, I was afraid your camera was ruined, and that you'd want to take mine back. If you lived!"

Knowing his sense of humor—if you call it that—and seeing the grin on his face, I knew he was saying he was worried and glad to see me alive. I hoped so, anyway.

The bartender from the Rolling Thunder Roadhouse Café, who I remember seeing once on my second or third day here, pushed his way past Charles and said he'd bring me anything I wanted to eat. And as strong a beverage as I needed. Just give him the word. I thanked him and sat there, stunned not only by what had happened, but also by the sincere kindness of total strangers.

For the first time, I realized that on Folly, no one was a *total* stranger.

I declined the bartender's offer of food, but accepted the offer of clothes from Charles, Bill, and another neighbor I didn't know. Except for my pants and a pair of shoes that I had no idea how and when I'd put on, my laptop, camera bag, and the few items in the car, I had nothing left. Fortunately, my wallet and cell phone were still in the pants, and my Tilley was in the car.

Even though tomorrow—or I guessed it was today now—was Easter, I didn't see any way my house was going to *arise*, so I guessed I needed somewhere to stay.

Folly came through again. Within fifteen minutes, I had four offers of a bed. They ranged from Polly's husband Lawrence, to Charles, to Bill, to Amber. And all seemed disappointed when I said no.

Amber laid her hand on my shoulder. "Do come and stay at my place, Chris. You'll need someone to look after you for at least a couple of days."

I patted her hand. "Amber," I said, "I love you for the offer, but I need to be alone so I can think this through on my own." I was thinking that a night in a predictable, sterile, clean, and neat Holiday Inn sounded like just what the doctor—or an EMT—ordered.

Bill insisted on driving me the few blocks to the hotel. With help, I struggled to my feet, waited a few minutes to gather the donated clothing, kissed Amber on the cheek, hugged Polly, shook Lawrence's hand, and thanked some of the other bystanders and the two police officers who were still looking at the charred, smoking rubble. The firemen were still hosing it down to keep it from flaring up again and spreading.

∗　　　∗　　　∗　　　∗

If someone looking like me had showed-up at my hotel desk at two in the morning, I wouldn't have let him in. But the clerk wasn't that picky; in fact, he was almost chipper as he handed me the keycard.

I wouldn't feel so bad about drinking Holiday Inn coffee in the morning.

∗　　　∗　　　∗　　　∗

I was jarred out of my fitful sleep by the shrill sounds of the phone—not my cell, but the one on the bedside table. The amber readout on the clock said six fifty-eight—I assumed whoever was calling had the wrong number. Only Bill knew where I was, and he'd have no reason to call.

The voice said, "Well, are you ready to go find a place to stay for the next two weeks?"

"Bob, is that you? It's Easter and not even seven in the morning. Are you crazy? Where are we going to find a house to rent at this hour on a holiday?"

"Well shit—excuse my French on Easter—we're not going to find one now, silly boy. I won't be there for another half hour. Get out of bed; wash the smoke smell off your body, and be in the lobby at seven-thirty. Hell, if you want, we can stop at a sunrise service on our way to your next home."

The next sound I heard was the hum of a disconnected line. That meant twenty-nine minutes and counting!

Just shy of my dictated deadline I was standing in front of the complimentary coffee stand, juggling two cups of coffee and a crutch, which wasn't easy. My head hurt and if it weren't for the crutch, I'd have been spread out on the floor. Fortunately, the Holiday Inn folks had thought of most everything (predictable) and had lids.

I hobbled my way to the door, and the Plum Cruiser was sitting under the awning when I struggled out.

"Well, it's about damn time," said my sympathetic realtor. "What took you so long?"

At least with the top down, it was easier to hand him his coffee and sling the crutch into the rear seat.

"No realtor is going to be working on Easter Sunday," I growled, really out of patience with his bluster. "What in the world are you doing here?" I gingerly navigated my way into the front seat.

"I'm not about to let a little fire make you decide you want the luxury of a hotel when you come to the beach. How in the hell am I going to make a commission off that? We've got to find you a ratty old house you can overpay for and keep me in the finer things of life. Now, let's get you away from this hotel."

He gunned the engine and when we shot forward, I winced. The throbbing in my head told me I needed something stronger than coffee. But I just sat and let Bob run things—he would anyway.

"Chris, we don't have a lot of choices. Remember, you're only going to be here a couple more weeks. I've got keys to two rentals. I can sneak you into either. They're vacant until the middle of May. After your track record with the houses here—burning down every one you've stayed in so far—I won't tell the owner who's renting."

The first house was on Forest Avenue, nowhere within walking distance of downtown. Like a good realtor, he showed me that one, knowing I wouldn't be interested. Realtors usually rope you in on the second option. Works for caskets too, but I didn't want to go there. I'd come too close last night.

"You've already seen the second, and, by the way, the only other choice. It's the cute blue house on East Erie that we looked at Friday. Decide that's the place, and we can have you moved in time to have yourself an Easter egg hunt. Your history with fire might make them scrambled eggs."

"I'm impressed with your sympathy," I said. "No need to stop at the house, I'll take it. How much and what do I need to do to move in?"

"Since you only have to rent it for two more weeks, this damn Holiday Inn bland coffee should cover the cost. I'll make sure the utilities are taken care of. Let's get you in so I can go home and play Easter Bunny."

That took me by surprise. Two weeks for a cup of bland coffee. The guy had more heart than he let on; maybe he was Santa Claus after all. We drove another half block, and I asked, "How did you know about last night and where to find me?"

"Your *new* good friends Polly and Lawrence are kin to Louise in our office; distant cousins-in-law on some grand uncle's side of the family. Something like that," he said. "They called her, and she called me. Then Chief Newman called. Incidentally, he told me to tell you he was sorry about the inhospitable welcome you were given two weeks ago. Then Amber called and said she still loves you even if you wouldn't let her take you to the hospital."

"That's sweet," I said.

"Yeah, whatever. After that one, I took the damn phone off the hook—I couldn't talk to everyone on the island if I was going to be over here at the crack of dawn. There must be someone who doesn't know. But for the life of me, I don't know who it could be."

By nine on Easter Sunday, I had checked out of the Holiday Inn. Bob told me to tell them I was never coming back, that I had now moved into my new, uncharred home on East Erie Avenue. The move itself didn't take more than a couple of minutes. All I had was some borrowed clothes, a camera bag, a laptop computer, a folder with fact sheets and notes from the city council meeting that had been in the car, and a headache. Not to mention my sundry other minor injuries.

The cute, blue house did have charm, but the most appealing feature at that moment was the bed. I don't know if it was Freudian, but I dreamt of being on a cruise ship moseying among tall icebergs off Alaska. I remembered sitting on the deck drinking Kahlua in coffee and thinking how great the cool weather felt. My traveling companion agreed. If only I remembered who she was.

∗   ∗   ∗   ∗

For the second time that day, the phone jarred me awake. This time it was the familiar ring of my cellular.

"When in the hell were you going to call me?" A woman's angry voice—or an angry woman's voice—whatever. "Are you okay?" she said. "Where *are* you? What can I do for you? Damn! I can't do anything today. I have to work. I guess I could call in sick." A pause. "Chris, are you there?"

Doesn't anyone around here start a phone conversation with "Hello"?

Not knowing which question to tackle first, I started with, "Happy Easter, Tammy. How are you? Oh, by the way, I'm fine—I'm just on crutches, actually one crutch. I have a splitting headache. Thanks for calling; that was sweet of you. Now, can we start over?"

She sighed a deep sigh. "Sorry. But I was worried, and I had a right to be. Karen Lawson woke me this morning. Remember, the detective from Charleston? She said your house had burned last night, but she didn't know more details. I called the Folly Beach Police Department. All they said was that you were alive, and they didn't think you'd gone to the hospital. The dispatcher said his EMT had to fight off a young woman who wanted to take you—either to the hospital or to her house—but that you didn't go. His final information was that the fire was arson, and that you'd left the ruins in a car with some man. Are you beginning to get the drift as to why I'm worried?"

"I'm sorry," I said. "I thought about calling, but it was the middle of the night before I was alone. Then my realtor had me up before seven looking at houses. We found this one, and I'm already moved in. I was asleep before he drove off."

"That's more like it," she said. "A good apology goes a long way with a girl. I really was worried. I'm thankful you're no worse off than you are." She paused, then said, "I'd be on my way over there now, but I have three assignments. It seems that crime doesn't take weekends off, not even holiday weekends. Could we have supper tomorrow night? I should be off by four and could come over there, or you could come over here if you feel like it. Your choice."

"Why don't I give you a call tomorrow? I should know by then how I feel."

"Okay. If you come here, don't have the woman who wanted to take you home or to the hospital drive you."

I was afraid to go back to sleep. I didn't know if I could take being wakened like that one more time. I also didn't feel like taking a long jog, or even a short one, or a photo-walk around my new neighborhood. My new crutch was still a strange tool that I needed to practice with. So I sat. For that, my head thanked me and my ankle joined in with an Easter hallelujah.

✳   ✳   ✳   ✳

It was a couple of hours later, and I'd been half-sitting, half-lying on the couch, alternately popping ibuprofen and dozing.

"Mr. Photo Man, are you in there and alive?" came Charles's voice from somewhere in the front yard.

I shook my head to clear it, and opened my eyes. "Yes, Charles, I'm both. Just a second and I'll get the door." The second expanded to several before I could maneuver the crutch through the living room and porch.

"Here," he said when I opened the door. "I brought you some food. I would've cooked it myself, but my stove hasn't been turned on since the 1998 baseball season. This came from The Dog—with Amber's love. Said to tell you she wrapped it herself."

I didn't venture to ask how he knew the actual date of the last time his stove was turned on. "Thanks, want to come in?"

"Nah, just wanted to drop this off. I like walking around on Easter afternoons. Everyone's yard looks its best, and lots of folks are outside."

This man never ceased to surprise me. "Have you heard anything about what started the fire?" I asked.

"Sure, everyone knows it was gasoline used as—these days, the technical term is 'an accelerant'—way too fancy for me. And everyone knows it was the developer man's killer. But that's where the opinions begin to go their separate ways. It was someone from Charleston. It was a big city rival. It was his wife's lover. It was some anti-developer people from right here on our fine island. It was a hit man from California. Ain't nobody said it was the butler yet. All I know is that it wasn't me, and I doubt that it was you," he concluded. He gave me a buddy kind of look and laid his hand on my good shoulder.

"Got to run," he said, "it's burning daylight—sorry you're in no condition to walk with me. I'd show you a thing or two about taking pictures."

CHAPTER 21

Monday began unusually windy and cold for mid-April—very much like a Monday two weeks earlier had begun. I'd hoped today would turn out to be better.

My ankle wasn't nearly as sore as yesterday, so I decided to hobble to The Dog. My new home was closer to the restaurant than that pile of ashes, my former residence, had been.

I was beginning to get a better feel for the regulars at The Dog, at least for the early morning group. In fact, the place was feeling just a tiny bit like home. As I hobbled that direction, the crutch was taking some getting used to, but at last, I made it. Pausing just outside, I thought of how in another moment, I'd be a magnet drawing every eye in the place like they were compass needles. I took a deep breath, opened the door, shambled in, and, balanced on one foot and my wooden prop, I looked around. Yep, all heads turned toward me.

Near the back, seated in their regular booth, were the two city council members, easy to spot since most who enter The Dog either nod or talk to them. Officers McConnell and Spencer were also seated at a table near the back, laughing and having much too good a time for this early in the morning. Then there was the guy from the surf shop across the street, an usually friendly sort who had the look of having just stepped out of the 1960s—it was his clothing and slightly crooked grin. He reminded me of Arlo Guthrie, but his name was Jim Sloan, "Cool Dude" to his friends.

Joining the regulars this morning was a table of tourists. From their clothes, I'd put money on their heading over to one of the expensive golf courses around Kiawah Island. In spite of their high-priced Calloway golf shirts and Nike caps, they were trying to fit into the crowd, succeeding about as well as Shriners at an Amish funeral.

Playing the regular, I nodded to the council members, who, I suspected, had no idea who I was, except that I was the fellow who nearly died in that spectacular house fire. I spoke to the two police officers and waved at the surf shop owner. I ignored the *tourists*.

Amber saw me immediately. There was a young couple ahead of me, but she rushed over and took my arm and escorted me to a nearby table.

"This is where you need to be," she said. "You can stretch your leg out better. Let me take your crutch. And, oh yeah … how do you feel?"

I adjusted myself on the chair, stretched my leg out, and handed her my crutch. "Thanks. I'm much better. My ankle is on the mend. I really don't need the crutch now; brought it in case it starts hurting." Which was, of course, a bit of a lie.

"I've been worried about you," she said. She was looking down at me with her best Florence Nightingale expression. "You should have let me take you to the hospital. I really wanted to, you know."

"I appreciate the offer, Amber. But I needed just to get to a bed and sleep. If we'd gone to the emergency room, it would've taken hours, and they wouldn't have done anything more than what the EMT did."

She said, very sweetly, I thought, "Well, I could have taken care of the bed too." I felt my face heating up in what must have been a deep blush.

I didn't ask how that would have worked with her son being there. I awkwardly changed the subject by ordering, asking her about the weather forecast, and what the latest gossip was. Predicting the weather was not Amber's greatest skill, but she was fantastic with gossip. She'd missed out on a career as a hairdresser.

"Most of the talk's about you," she said. "Actually, about the fire, the killer, and then you. People were just beginning to feel that the killing was in the past—that whoever did it was long gone. Nobody's going to miss that awful developer—good riddance, really—and life on the island was back to normal, at least normal for Folly. Now you've gone and screwed that all up again."

Frankly, I was tired of being the center of attention, and now, even worse, I had their pity. I sighed and looked up at her. "So what're they saying?"

"Let's put it this way," she said. "I doubt many folks will be inviting you to stay at their house. That is, unless it's over-insured and they want to build a new home. I don't think people blame you. A couple of 'em are saying you brought this trouble over with you. But they're just kidding … I think."

She continued without pause. "Our two crack law enforcement officers," she nodded toward Spencer and McConnell, "just told me that the chief has them on overtime to keep an eye on you. To be honest, I think they're worried about your safety."

I huffed and shook my head. "I guess killing tourists isn't good for vacation rentals," I said.

It was Amber's turn to shrug. "We don't know *what* you are. Not a tourist for sure, but I don't think most are ready to accept you as a card-carrying resident. But everyone agrees that you sure know how to liven things up! Officer Spencer asked how long you were staying and what you were really doing here. I asked him how he thought I'd know. That I doubted you'd be telling me if you had some strange, mysterious reason for being here."

"Good, I guess my secret's safe." Did she catch the sarcasm? If she did, it didn't register on her face, and she just went right on talking. In fact, she changed the subject—Amber's mind worked that way.

"Then Rod began telling me about his latest, greatest harebrained scheme. Something about being in the middle of a great deal that'll change the look of Folly. More likely he's just interested in changing the bank balance of Officer McConnell. Maybe it's a timeshare office building. Who knows with him?"

"Look, Amber," I said. "Thanks for sharing, but I'm hungry."

"Oh!" She straightened, surprised she'd forgotten what she was there for. "So what will it be?" she said. "The Belgian waffle, or ..."

"Yeah, yeah, that's good," I said impatiently. "Just the waffle and trimmings."

"She laid her hand on my shoulder and squeezed. "Be right back, hon."

I watched her go, thinking of how she turned movement into poetry and what a bundle of information she was. I wondered how much of the information was accurate. Instant fame wasn't something I wanted. The closest I'd ever been to so much mayhem was on the thirty-six inch screen of my television set. Maybe this island wasn't the place for me after all. I sat drinking the coffee—which this morning was a little stronger than usual—and lost in thought. Then there she was again. This time she'd come in from behind me with the food.

"Any closer to buying a house?" Amber asked as she set the plate in front of me. "I don't know where you're looking, but it better be within walking distance of here."

*   *   *   *

A while later, I left The Dog for a short walk to test my ankle; the crutch had to go. And I'd thought the *tripod* was a problem. The first block was encouraging.

There was little pain and I felt I could go farther. Instead, I thought better of it and headed home. It was time to test the cameras and laptop to see if they had fared better than I. I'd avoided it for fear of what I'd find, but couldn't put it off any longer.

Finally, a clump of positives. Both cameras performed perfectly, and the laptop appeared to be as good as before the fire.

With that streak of good luck, it was time to revisit my former home. I grabbed the camera and walked, or limped, sans crutch, three blocks to the charcoal pile. I was surprised to see Officers McConnell and Spencer standing in the drive watching two official looking gentlemen in white coveralls sifting through the still-hot ruins.

"Good, I'm glad you're here," said Spencer. "Those two guys are from the Charleston Explosive Devices Unit. They want to talk to you."

"If it's an Explosive Devices Unit, I'm not sure I want to talk to them. Not here anyway."

The Folly officers found that humorous. "Don't worry, I don't think they're looking for unexploded devices," said McConnell. "They investigate all potential arson cases. Most of the time, they're busy disarming unexploded Civil War shells. You'd be amazed how many there are around here."

Spencer introduced me. The Charlestonians had just a few questions. Mainly, had I smelled anything before I discovered the fire? I said smoke. I don't think that's what they had in mind. I walked them through the events, and they appeared satisfied that I didn't have much to offer. They expressed their condolences that I'd lost most everything.

It was then I spotted among the tangle of blackened debris about twenty feet from where we stood the charred, melted, blob that had once been my printer—it looked especially sad. I told the four I was pleased that I'd saved my cameras and laptop. Everything else could be replaced.

There was nothing I could do standing there except be depressed. I took the good adult approach and walked away.

*   *   *   *

The sun finally broke through the clouds and the day was warming nicely. I walked, almost without a limp, to the pier and sat on one of the many benches. The view looking back toward land was fantastic. To my left was the beginning of the county park. To the right, I could only see as far as The Washout. The mix of buildings—old and new, dilapidated and McMansions, and a handful of vacant lots—reflected the mix of people, attitudes, and charm of this barrier island. Focusing on where the pier meets land, I tried to picture how it had looked in the 1950s—its heyday. Why hadn't I sat here before? Then I felt somewhere deep inside the impact of all I'd been through the last couple of days, and knew that, with the rhythm of the waves in my ears, if I gave in to temptation, I'll fall asleep right here in the warming sun. I resisted.

The temperature must have been in the upper seventies or low eighties, but now, thinking of it all, suddenly, I was chilled. Until two days ago, I had merely stumbled on a murder. I hadn't seen anything other than an already dead body; I hadn't heard anything other than gunshots. I didn't have a clue who murdered Lionetti. And that's what, from the very get-go, I'd told everyone who would listen.

Now something had changed. For some reason—God only knows what—I was now a target. It appeared to my non-crime fighting mind that it could be one of only two things. Someone thinks I know something. Or, I knew something and didn't know what it was and didn't know that I knew it. All I'd ever admitted to seeing was something blue, and that could've been anything. Nothing that had anything to do with the killing. Frustrating and scary. Scary now that I thought again about someone being in my house and going through my papers. And no telling what else.

What I knew for certain was that this was now personal. I couldn't just sit by and let myself be killed. Sure, there were kind, caring folks who were doing what they could to offer me assistance and, to a minor degree, some protection. But the cold, clear reality was that I'd known none of these people for more than two weeks. How could I know who to trust? I was really alone and feeling it.

So now I understood some realities. Other than packing up my car and leaving, what could I do? I was stubborn enough to eliminate leaving. That stubbornness had brought me a lot of professional success over the years, and there was no reason to change now. My decades in marketing and human resources had taught me to make a realistic appraisal of the problem, challenge the problem, and then attack its weaknesses and the needs of the prospective client—or in this case, the enemy.

With all the names I'd heard bandied about, how could I possibly figure out who the killer was? After all, the professionals hadn't managed to do it.

The general consensus was that the wife and someone else—her lover, I guess—were guilty. According to Tammy and the young lady at the beach, that was what the police believed.

Then there was Wynn Stamper, the anti-development fanatic. He had motive, opportunity, and I'd seen his temper. That had been in a room full of people including the police and the entire city council. What would he do if provoked on a deserted corner of Folly Beach? He was *my* choice, but no one appeared to be pursuing him. Was I wrong?

And Frank Long. He had a good alibi, but he could be working with someone. I didn't know a lot about the island's development policies and politics, but he was a local developer, and Lionetti had been an interloper.

No one had mentioned the possibility, but I wouldn't rule out Chief Newman. Everyone around here said he had a hidden side. He disappeared on a regular basis. His secret military background was suspect. He was having some kind of relationship with the detective in Charleston. And, now that I think about it, he was always late at the scene. He never seemed to be on duty.

Then there was me. Had I not known better, I'd have considered me a suspect too. After all, I was there; no one around knew a thing about me, and I'd arrived only a couple of days before the murder.

Maybe I should ask Amber's son Jason. His guess was as good as any. Besides, the thought that it was an exotic killer from some far away country gave me a sense of adventure.

From watching television mysteries, I could even add the SODDI candidate. I think it meant, "some other dude did it." That's the one I hoped they were after—some *other dude* who was now far away.

Why did I even have to think about this? All I wanted to do was have a nice vacation and try to find a second home I could use as often as I liked in retirement. Wasn't life supposed to get easier with age?

But I had no chance of figuring anything out while sitting here. So I pulled out my cell phone, called Tammy, and made a date—there I'd said it—for tonight. I'd meet her at the Charleston Crab House. I wouldn't have to drive all the way to Charleston, and she could get there quickly after work. Besides, she said it had a great outside deck on the Intracoastal Waterway.

*   *   *   *

When I showed up a little before six thirty, she was waiting. Showing deference to my leg, she stood and gave me a big hug and a kiss on the lips. At that, I forgot all my aches and pains; I should have called this woman the night of the fire. A bottle of Chardonnay was already opened, and I didn't waste any time offering myself a glass. A lady shouldn't have to drink alone.

"I'm glad you could make it," she said. "I wanted to see you, but work was in my way. Fortunately, I don't have to be back until noon tomorrow." She touched my hand.

After the last few days, it was a relief to see Tammy and be relaxing here in such an idyllic setting where I finally felt somewhat safe. We sat and watched three large cabin cruisers slowly working their way down the Intracoastal.

She shared some about her last two days. She covers many general assignments but specializes in crime reporting. That made her work schedule unpredictable. She had regular shifts, but if she began working a crime, she had to follow through with updates.

"I love the work and wouldn't want it any other way—except maybe for more time off," she added.

We both ordered salad and the seafood platter. The menu said "fresh southern seafood." I think that meant fried fish—not fish with an accent. That's fine with me; after all, I'm southern.

"So," she said earnestly, "tell me what in hell happened! How did you escape the fire? And your injuries,"—she laid her hand on mine—"how *are* you? Isn't this whole thing driving you crazy?" She was looking into my eyes, and I saw genuine concern.

When I'd given her a full report and she seemed satisfied, we chatted a while, and then she said, "Chris, tell me more about yourself. I know most of what's been happening the last two weeks. Even the list of the things you don't want to do again. But what about your first fifty-something years? What do you like and dislike? What do you read? What's your favorite music? What irritates the heck out of you, and what do you love?"

Talk about not knowing where to begin.

"Well, Tammy … you already know that I'm a very private person. I'd rather listen than talk. I've already given you the *CliffsNotes* version of my life. Your question about what I like reminds me of the old country song, something about loving pick-up trucks, slow moving trains, and rain … among other things. I have no problem with trucks, or rain, but when I get caught at a railroad crossing by a 'slow-moving train,' the word *love* never passes my lips. The reason the song came to mind is that I share its sentiments. I like, or maybe even love, the small things in life. Sunrise is my favorite time of day."

She lifted her eyebrows and smiled, an invitation to go on.

"It's a new beginning," I continued. "The past is over; a new day's dawning—to steal someone's phrase. That's also why I like rain. In addition to washing away some of the pollen that's constantly affecting my allergies, the rain is a turning point. It's another chance to start over. To continue with my own song, I also love grass, just after it's been cut; a car, just after it leaves the carwash; and, laughter, especially if it follows something I've said."

She laughed.

"You see? Like that." And I laughed with her. "What about you," I asked.

She modestly averted her gaze. "I like country music. So I know the song you mean. I guess more accurately, I like the traditional country and not the new junk-rock-country that's popular. My age must be showing."

She continued, "I'd rather dress in jeans or shorts than dresses or the more formal pant suits the paper prefers. From our day in Charleston, you can tell I like to walk. And, I guess it goes back to my journalism background, I appreciate, or maybe you could say love, honesty. I don't get to experience it often. Most people like to put a positive spin on what they tell me. I'd rather they'd be honest, even if it hurts, than sugarcoat their words." She paused. "And speaking of honesty, Chris, you must have a bundle of strong feelings inside you after the last couple of weeks. Can you tell me about those?"

"That sounds way too much like a newspaper interview question, Reporter Rogers."

Another laugh.

"Then let me preface it with this; I told my editor I wasn't going to do any more follow-up stories on you or have any further professional contact. I said I didn't think I could remain objective. He said sometimes he hates my honesty, but appreciated the warning. With that said, I'm simply a woman who likes the person who's sitting across the table from her. I'm concerned about him."

"That's better, but does this mean I'll have to break in another reporter if something else happens to me in the *friendly* city of Folly Beach?"

"You're such an optimist," she said. "Now, back to my question, how are you—really?"

"To be honest—and after what you said, I guess I'd better be honest—I'm extremely frustrated and more than a little scared. I've given some thought to leaving and going back to my safe cocoon. I'm frustrated because it appears the police aren't doing anything. I'm annoyed because someone thinks I know something. And I don't know what they think I know. All this is foreign to me. Sure, I've had serious challenges in the workplace; marketing is really one battle after another. Even in HR, I had to deal with conflicts and conflict resolution. But, I've never experienced anything like this."

"You know, Chris," she said, "the police really are doing everything possible. Unlike many crimes where they can identify one suspect, usually without much work, in this case, there is no shortage of suspects. That takes more time. I think the police are still focusing on the grieving spouse. Maybe they'll have an announcement soon."

The sun had begun to set. The temperature was perfect. The food—even fried, fried, and fried again—couldn't have tasted better. The company of a beautiful and charming woman spoke for itself. Had it not been for the small matter of someone trying to kill me, I could easily have gotten used to being here from now on. And I was hoping the "from now on" would be many, many years.

"Tammy," I said, "at the risk of sounding trite, you're even more contagious than the charm of Folly."

When her self-conscious laughter subsided, but not the redness of her cheeks, she said, "Clearly you don't make a living crafting words. But unless you say otherwise, I'll take that as a compliment."

"What I'm trying to say is, it feels like I've known you for years. I feel comfortable around you. I'm not sure where that falls in this concoction of emotions I've felt since arriving. I've gotten fairly comfortable being by myself over the years. Whatever issues I've had to deal with, I've confronted alone. To simplify, I really like you too. And, I hope another reporter doesn't have to cover my demise. Unless it's when I'm a hundred and twenty-three years old and get run over jaywalking across Center Street."

"Maybe you should be a writer after all; you have quite an imagination."

At some point during the second bottle of Chardonnay, she said that if I felt up to it, we could share a cup of after-dinner coffee, a warm bed, and a bowl of cereal for breakfast at her place.

In a way, I wasn't surprised, and yet … in a moment of stupidity, I declined.

It wasn't because I didn't want to share the warm bed with her. But I didn't think my battered and sprained body was ready. I could've handled the coffee and cereal, but. She said she understood, but looked disappointed. I took that as a good sign.

"Will you be off this weekend?" I ventured. "I missed the World Grits Festival, so I just couldn't live with myself if I had to miss Folly's Sea and Sand Festival Saturday. I'd love for you to be my guest. Part of the package is a one-night, all-expense-paid stay at Folly's newest *local's* house."

"Let's put it this way," she said, her eyes shining again, "I'll be off this weekend. And if I'm called in to work, I already feel a bad sore throat coming on!"

Our evening ended in the parking lot at Tammy's little, bright yellow Mini Cooper with black racing stripes on the hood that reminded me of a bumblebee.

We shared a nice goodnight hug that evolved into a very warm and passionate extended goodnight kiss.

I loved this part of the country!

During the ride home, I had a chilling thought. Would I be alive this weekend to entertain Ms. Rogers?

CHAPTER 22

Tuesday's forecast called for a "picture perfect" day—high puffy clouds, temperatures in the mid-seventies. A week or so ago, during one of my complimentary coffee stops at the Holiday Inn, I'd picked up a brochure on plantations in the area, and was surprised how many there were. One of the largest and most attractive, at least from the photos, was Middleton Place about fifteen miles northwest of Charleston. If my ankle was up to it, today would be a great day to step, gingerly, into the past.

I threw my borrowed crutch in the corner and headed around the block on a test run, or test *walk*. I'd already covered the first block toward the beach before hearing the voice I'd come to expect.

"Hey, Mr. Photo Man, you're moving pretty good!" My shadow had arrived, and this time he was on his vintage Schwinn. The blue paint shining as though he'd just taken a chamois to it. No packages in the basket this morning.

"I'm heading over to Middleton Place to take some photos. Want to go?"

"I think I can free up my calendar," he said as he rolled up beside me. "Besides, you'll need someone to help pick you up when your ankle gives out. When're we leaving?"

"As soon as I get my camera and tripod." I almost added photo vest, but then I remembered it was part of the rubble at my former abode.

"Give me a minute to roll home and get my stuff," Charles said. "Could you pick me up there?"

I agreed and he wheeled away in a u-turn that would have done credit to a junior high boy. I watched after him, smiling at his complete disregard for convention. Charles was one of a kind.

I plodded home—without pain, I should add—and loaded everything up and headed to Sandbar Lane and to the Fowler residence where I found Charles sitting on a log that served as a bumper stop in front of the apartment. As warm as it already was, he was still wearing his long sleeve "University of Maryland Terrapins" sweatshirt. Jeans and hiking boots completed his wardrobe. I was in dark green shorts and a white Hilfiger golf shirt and tennis shoes. We looked like we'd just met in an airport—he off a flight from Alaska and I on one from Cancun.

"You haven't seen my fine ride have you?" he said and pointed to an aged Saab convertible parked half on the gravel drive and half in the grass. "That's my eucalyptus green, 1988 Saab 900T classic—a beaut ain't she?"

From the thick coating of gravel dust and rust around the wheel wells, I wasn't sure if it should be classified as a stationary piece of art or a car that appeared not to have been driven since the beginning of the twenty-first century. I questioned whether the paint color experts from Sweden would still call it eucalyptus green. My guess was that it was closer to something like *gravel tan, rust brown, or dirt-seasoned pate de foie gras.*

"Does it run?" I said, probably with too much doubt in the tone of my voice.

"Of course! I just had it out the Fourth of July, or maybe that was Memorial Day—one of those holidays."

I'm no whiz at math, but that would have been at least nine months ago. But no matter. I was driving, so I wasn't worried whether his *classic* had the ability to get us anywhere.

But, he wasn't ready to change the subject. "Clearly you don't appreciate the significance of this fine example of Swedish engineering," he said. His own tone was testy.

Clearly, he was right. To me, it looked like an old foreign car going to rust on American soil.

"I'll have you know," he said. "Saab makes the best convertible in the universe. This is their most famous, classic style. Saab prostituted itself to General Motors a few years ago and now makes one of those generics that you can't tell from any other cute convertible. This, however, is the *classic.*"

Seeing no reason to argue, I agreed. As soon as he started telling me the luggage capacity (10.7 cubic feet if you're interested), I said it was time to go.

*   *   *   *

The ride up Folly Road was becoming quite familiar. We stopped at a McDonald's and had a McBoring Breakfast and coffee before heading northwest of the city. This was uncharted territory, but I enjoyed the mix of businesses and residential areas. Once we hit the more rural stretches, the vegetation changed drastically, and I felt the years slipping backward. Live oaks with moss dangling precariously from branches lined the streets. At one point on Highway 61, the branches met in an arch over the roadway. We should have been in a horse drawn carriage rather than a car.

The Middleton Place plantation was on the banks of the Ashley River. I was glad to see that there were only a handful of cars in the gravel visitor's lot between the museum shop and the entry gate.

"Charles," I told him, "I'm going to pay your way in. Admission won't be cheap and didn't want you hyperventilating at the gate. I owe you."

We exchanged glances, but he didn't say anything.

I debated carrying the tripod. I could use it as a crutch if necessary.

The first views of the property made the trip worthwhile. I'm not big on history but could appreciate the beauty and care that went into the grounds. A calm reflecting pool with a gaggle of floating swans welcomed us. (Or is *gaggle* just for geese? Never mind; that's close enough.) An English garden featuring precisely planted rows of shrubs and small trees flanked the pool. The brochure said the gardens had taken a hundred slaves ten years to complete.

To the right stretched a large rectangular turf-covered lawn that Charles so eloquently referred to as "one hell of a front yard." It must have been the size of two football fields. Grazing on the field were sheep and cattle. There must have been a shortage of Lawn-Boy mowers.

I took a couple dozen photos before we got to the first structure. Charles must have taken a hundred. I questioned his subject matter but admired his concentration. I'm sure a museum somewhere would covet his photo of a cow patty.

Once we'd walked up six steps and opened a simple wrought-iron gate and crossed the old brick fence line, the views went from nice to spectacular. We walked toward the rear of the property where from the fence we could see the beautifully manicured, tiered lawn flanked by rectangular flower gardens that angled down toward the river and a scattering of ponds. The only house on the property that had survived the Civil War was an odd-faceted brick structure with black trim. The brochure said it had been built as gentleman's quarters—whatever that is.

We sat on one of the many brick walls and overlooked a large, motionless pond. The walls, in various states of repair, divided the property by function—gardens, walkways, pasture, and now, parking. The lawn gently sloped down to the water. But even the peaceful feel was deceiving. Two alligators, slowly swimming, were crossing over, only their heads visible. The ducks and geese knew the danger that moved slowly around them, and they seemed to play a game with it. "The enemy's getting closer, we'll move now." People could learn a lot from that. But we won't.

To the few tourists wondering the grounds, we must have seemed quite a pair. Charles with his cane—always that cane. Me with a limp, no cane, but a heavy-duty tripod.

There was a winding path around the pond, and we followed it. Charles stopped us atop an arched wooden bridge crossing a narrow part of the water and bent to use the railing to steady his camera. He was learning after all.

I was standing to one side, watching as he peered through the viewfinder, slowly adjusting this and that, when, out of nowhere, he quietly said, "Chris. I'm not gay."

I thought I'd misunderstood him. "What did you say, Charles?"

He snapped the picture, stood and looked me right in the eyes.

"I said, I'm not gay."

"Oh, well. That's …"

"In fact, I really like women—a lot! But I can barely afford even my *lavish-less* life style. I can't imagine adding another person on my budget."

He started on across the bridge, me standing a moment before following behind. I had no idea what to say. I really wasn't surprised with what he'd said, and I was pleased he chose to stray a bit out of character to say it. Prone to resort to humor when in doubt, or to an attempt at humor, when I was beside him again, I said, "That's a relief. I've been practicing ways to reject your advances. Of course, if you'd found me appealing, I would've understood."

"Dream on, Mr. Photo Man! I just feel sorry for you." He stopped and turned to me. "Here you are," punching the air with his finger, "stranded on a desert island, or barrier island, whatever, and someone is trying to kill you. You need someone to look out for you. Today I'm taking my shift."

He didn't offer more, and I took the opportunity to practice silence. We stopped at a tiny, simple wooden chapel overlooking the pond where we entered and sat on the small, low bench near the back wall. I framed a couple of photos while Charles studied a cane bottom chair sitting in the corner. The room was Quaker-simple with whitewashed walls and was lightly furnished—only a chair, two benches, and a small table in front. The atmosphere encouraged silence and pensive meditation. But not with Charles around!

"This plantation," he said, "especially early in the morning, sure is a place for photographers, painters, writers, and poets."

"That's an astute observation," I said. "I can agree about the photographers and painters. I don't know about the poets and writers."

"Well Chris, 'You will never be alone with a poet in your pocket'—old dead United States president John Adams."

I chuckled. "I think you made that one up—but I really don't want to take time to find out."

It felt good to give my ankle a rest. It wasn't happy about all the walking.

"That's enough of this peacefulness, Mr. Photo Man. Let's walk."

We completed the meandering loop, walked by a tall stand of bamboo, and rounded the corner approaching the main house.

Abruptly, Charles stopped, held up the camera, and said, "Mr. Photo Man, you were holding out on me. You didn't tell me this magic digital camera'll take movies. I had to read it in the instruction manual. You'd be amazed how much is in that small white book."

I was surprised. "Charles, I don't think I knew the camera could do that! It took me long enough to figure out the features I needed. I've never had any interest in movies. Have you tried it?"

"Yep," he said, "and it's neat. You can shoot as long as a three-minute movie—the quality's not so great. Shorter ones are better."

Amazing what you learn if you read manuals—en*tire* manuals.

"Charles, I'm impressed. By your reading all that, and impressed because this multi-thousand dollar outfit I'm carrying *won't* take movies."

"And something just as impressive, Mr. Photo Man," he said as we walked on, "I convinced Sam Edgars, the head of the library, to buy a better photo software program and install it on two computers. What's there was crap. The new one won't be as good as your high-falootin' Photoshop, but I can still do cropping, lightening and darkening the picture, and a bunch of other things I don't understand—yet. He even bought a card reader and said I could store my downloaded pictures on the library's hard drive. My photos are now in a library." He raised an eyebrow. "Are any of yours?"

"I must admit, Charles, I don't have any photos in a library. Congratulations!"

After another hour of shooting in the expansive garden area, my ankle was at its limit. On the way home, I called Bob Howard to see if we could meet in the morning to ride by the houses I'd seen and possibly come to some decision. He said we could if I promised no one would torch his fine Realtormobile. I couldn't make that promise, but I told him I'd help him put it out if they did. He agreed to pick me up anyway.

∗   ∗   ∗   ∗

On the way home, we stopped for an early supper at The Anchor Restaurant. I stuck with my traditional fish and chips, and, to my surprise, so did Charles. I'd expected him to order something more exotic—raw oysters and liver or something worse. We talked about everything from how to shoot a sunset, to modern jazz, to his eight *miserable* years working at Ford, to surfing at Folly. Enlightening, to say the least.

Charles couldn't compete with Amber in the looks department, but was pretty good at gossip. I learned all sorts of things about the sex lives of people I knew and many I'd never heard of. Rumors of affairs between a local waiter and one of the richest men on Folly; between Frank Long and a drug addict from out of town; between the mayor and a "surfer chick who's a close friend" of young Officer Spencer. He seemed to be hinting at a threesome there. I was afraid to ask.

He knew more than anyone should about the corners cut by some of the contractors who built or remodeled houses on the island, and even rumors about people in Charleston who'd never set foot on Folly.

Charles was entertaining, but the evening wasn't as pleasant as my lunch with Tammy on that same deck overlooking Oak Island Creek had been.

When we approached Sandbar Lane, he said, "Mr. Photo Man, this has been the best day I've had in many a year. And, don't think you were putting anything over on me when you paid the admission to the plantation and supper at The Anchor. I know how much both cost. I owe you big time; you don't owe me a thing."

CHAPTER 23

On time as usual, the Plum Cruiser and the best realtor in the second largest of three small realty firms pulled up in front of my most recent residence. I'd had a shower, edited a couple of photos from yesterday's shoot, and walked around the block to check on the condition of my lower limbs, so I was ready to go.

Sitting in his car with top down—thankfully the car's, not his—he greeted me with, "Well, sir, are you ready to buy yourself a house?"

Bob was dressed in shorts more wrinkled than last week's model and a T-shirt bearing the classy, motivational phrase "I'm with stupid!"

I was trusting my home buying future to this man?

Before opening the passenger side door, I stood there looking at him over the car. "Is that me you're referring to on your shirt? If it is, could we stop at the store so I can get one that says something like "I'm with more stupid, and more fat, and more ugly?"

"Mr. Landrum, the sentiments expressed by this shirt do not reflect the feelings, beliefs, and opinions of the wearer. In fact, I didn't realize which shirt I had on. My wife and I gave this and one that says "Stupid!" to each other for our anniversary. We love romantic gifts. Besides, everyone on Folly knows I should be wearing the other one—only it's too small for my sturdy frame. Now, I repeat, are you ready to buy yourself a damn house today?"

"Maybe, maybe not," I said. "I'd like to ride by each of the houses we've seen one more time. Are there any others we should look at?"

"Nothing new, at least nothing different from what you've already seen. There are a few, but they're in poorer condition, the same money or more, and in worse locations."

"Then where do you suggest we begin," I asked.

"Well, not to belabor the obvious, I *suggest* you turn around and look at the house you just left. Now, get in, and let's check out the others."

There was a light drizzle in the air, but it didn't seem to influence the placement of PT's top—it remained down. My Tilley would be my part-time umbrella. As we rode with the windshield wipers on, Bob sat there behind the wheel, oblivious to the precipitation, while it plastered his hair to his forehead and made his white beard drip. About the citizens around here, have I used the word *eccentric*?

We headed toward the beach and turned on Arctic Avenue, from which Bob turned into the parking area of the Charleston Oceanfront Villas. We parked under the four-story building so as to "stay dry." Talk of shutting the barn door after the horse is gone.

As we sat there, both Bob and my Tilley still dripping, I looked around. The development was almost within sight of my formerly cute, now charcoal-broiled residence. I'd had many chances over the last two weeks to walk through these grounds and contemplate living here. It had everything one could want, two nice pools, a fantastic view of the beach, ocean, and the pier, large units with ocean views from the living area and the master bedroom, solid construction. It had everything but character.

I had suspected during my first visit five years ago, and now knew it, that Folly Beach was *about* character. For me to stray from that would be to reject the island's heart, its quintessential nature, its very spirit. Plus, I couldn't afford it.

"Bob, this simply isn't what I want. It's fantastic, but just not where I want to be."

He said he understood; I believed him, and we pulled out from under the protection of the complex and headed to West Cooper. The rain—or heavy drizzle—had eased.

We sat in the car in front of the West Cooper house, and I gave the place another once over. It had personality. The wrap-around screened-in porch was a must during the summer. Mosquitoes and other flying irritants were also fans of Folly. The biggest drawback to this place was the seven hundred fifty thousand dollar price tag.

"Bob, I don't guess they would cut—oh let's say—a quarter of a million off the price, would they?"

"I'm good, really damn good, often even damn better than good. But I'm no miracle worker. I can talk them down a little, but not the price of a whole handful of your Lexuses."

Not quite understanding what my car had to do with it, I said, "Then why are we sitting here? Let's move on."

Fortunately, the rain had completely stopped for our ride to the two houses on the other end of the island. I was pretty sure before even seeing the first house that the cost would eliminate it from contention. But it wouldn't hurt to see it again.

Bob hadn't even put the Plum Cruiser in park before I said, "Keep moving." The next house was just a block away. The price was in my range, but all I could remember about the interior were the hundreds of photos that covered every vertical surface. The black-and-white history of Folly had left a strong impression on my photo-oriented mind. As stupid as it sounded, I didn't want to be the person to displace history. I knew someone would do it, but it wasn't going to be me.

Besides, this house was not within easy walking distance of town. Amber's reminder was speaking to me.

"Bob, I don't think this is it."

"You're the boss. But while we're here, let me show you one just past The Washout. I don't have access. A family is renting it for two weeks. But, if you're interested, I'll get you in."

We drove about a half mile east on Ashley Avenue—the road to the old coast guard property where I had found Jim Lionetti's body. Coming back to look at houses here felt ... well, unpleasant.

"See those three houses on the right? They're on ground that was owned by Raleigh Sims. He made his money in the early days of the stock market and bought almost three hundred feet of oceanfront property adjacent to the land where the coast guard station was built. Old Raleigh had five kids—three they say he liked, two he disowned. Before he died a decade or so ago, he divided the property and gave his three favorite kids a third each. A year ago, they began seeing dollar signs bigger than ocean waves, and sold the properties to your *good buddy*, Jim Lionetti."

I humphed at the thought of Lionetti. "I assume Lionetti didn't want to give those nice oceanfront houses to *his* three children—if he had three, that is." I said. "And don't call him my *buddy*."

"Lionetti didn't give a rat's ass about those houses," replied Bob, articulate as ever. "The purchase of the three properties was contingent upon his getting the damn planning commission and city council to allow him to consolidate the properties and build a large condo complex. The development would be about two-thirds the size of the Oceanfront Villas. They approved it for sixty-four condos—starting price of each, one point two mil. If you haven't calculated it in your head, that's a shitload of millions of dollars."

With such a quick mathematical mind, no wonder Mr. Howard was such a good realtor. He now gave a vocal imitation of Gomer Pyle.

"Surprise! Surprise! Many of the citizens were up in arms. Your reaction to the Oceanfront Villas—no character—is the same as they had to Lionetti's plan. Unfortunately, the planning commission and the city council had their hands tied. Lionetti's high-paid Charleston lawyers argued that the Sims property had never been legally divided for Hewey, Dewey, and Louie—or whatever his three fair-haired kids are named. So the three hundred feet of priceless oceanfront property is still intact. In the real world, a few high-paid Charleston lawyers plus one sleazy developer will always defeat two thousand residents. No match. Fuckin' Lionetti won."

"So what'll happen with him gone? Will his wife continue with the plan?"

"I doubt it. She already has more money than God. From what I hear, she couldn't care less about her worthless husband's business. Someone will step in and build the development—as long as there are high-paid Charleston lawyers out there. I just don't know who. But whoever it is, he better not take any early morning walks on the damn coast guard property. That would not be a healthy thing to do. I don't have to tell you that, do I?"

Without further comment, we made a u-turn and and headed back toward town.

"The next house is just ahead on the right," he said. "It may be too much, nine seventy-five, but it has a great view of the beach, and it does have character."

The raised house did have a fantastic view. It was just off the road and from the elevated porch had a clear panorama of the ocean. As we gazed at it, the sun finally broke through the rain clouds, and its rays gave the house a bright, cheerful look. It appeared to be post-Hugo construction. Now if I could just win the lottery and we could move the house closer to town, it would be a great choice.

"Sorry Bob, just too much and too far from town."

"Shit, don't be sorry. I knew it was too much before bringing you out here. I just wanted to show you something out of your reach before showing you the house you're going to buy."

I laughed. "What are we waiting for?"

With that, the Plum Cruiser head back with us in it, and on Erie Avenue, we stopped in front of a very familiar property—my rental.

Bob sat back, one hand still on the steering while with the other he brushed something or other out of his still wet beard, and said, "Well, what do you think?"

"I think I've been tricked. You've driven me around the entire island in the rain, jabbering on-and-on about the advantages of the other houses, knowing full well that we'd end up here."

"Chris, Chris, *Chris*! *You're* the one who said you wanted to revisit all those places. I was just being your humble, accommodating servant. So, are we going to make an offer on this damn shack, or have you wasted my morning?"

"Gosh, I don't want to be responsible for wasting your morning! Let's talk about what I should offer on this 'run down, badly in need of repair, shack.'"

"Spare me the 'ain't it terrible, they ought to give it to me before it falls down argument.' I'm on your side. We know the couple paid five forty for it. The bank's asking five thirty-five. Banks aren't in the real estate business. They buy and sell money. They don't want to own *things*. Your crack realtor also knows the couple paid ten percent down and had a mortgage of only four eighty-six. State Bank financed it originally but sold the mortgage to a large mortgage bank in New Jersey. They ended-up repossessing it. No one from the bank has ever seen the house. They really don't know what it's worth. If it were me, I'd make an offer of four ninety. They won't accept, but I'd guess you can get it for just over five. That'd be a win for the bank and a great deal for you."

I looked at his self-satisfied smirk, and said incredulously, "Bob, how long did it take you to figure all that out?"

"Since you called yesterday."

Okay, now I was convinced that he really *was* a great realtor. "Write it up. How long do you think it'll take before we know?"

"With anyone local, a day or two, but with these damn large out-of-state money mongers, it'll be at least a week."

We were done by noon, and Bob promised to fax it to the bank before the end of the day. He left, and I stood watching the Plum Cruiser pull away from the curb. Stood watching from the porch of my new resort home. I hoped.

I had done many things this morning, but eating was not one of them. The weather had warmed nicely, and it appeared the rain was out of the picture. Lunch on the deck at the Crab Shack sounded good. A little she-crab soup, flounder, coleslaw, wine, and Jimmy Buffett would hit the spot. And it would remind me of the day I met Charles, which was also the day Tammy asked if she could interview me about having found a body. That was less than two weeks ago but seemed like months. In hindsight, that had been a very, very good day.

✳   ✳   ✳   ✳

A nap to sleep off all the excitement rounded out the afternoon.

For some reason, I woke up thinking about Dr. William Hansel. I hadn't seen him since the night of the fire. I missed his friendly waves. Besides he was the second person, if you count *Aunt* Louise, I'd met when I arrived.

I knew he didn't have classes today and guessed he'd be home—most likely working in his yard. On a whim, I'd pick up a couple of bottles of wine and pay him a social call. We could relive old-times, and I could tell him about my venture into home ownership in South Carolina.

Instead of driving to Piggly Wiggly, my usual source of *fine wines by the jug*, I walked to 11 Center Street Wine and Gourmet, which was no more than two minutes from the house and had a tremendous selection of wines from around the world. They had been open only a short time and were more up-scale than most of the businesses and restaurants on Folly Beach. The cashier told me the building used to be the Island Grocery, and I told her I hoped it would be a success in its new incarnation.

I bought two bottles of an imported Chardonnay, a cheese ball, and some rye crackers. A little after six o'clock, I packed the wine and cheese and walked to my pile of ashes and Bill's house next door.

"Well, well, if it isn't my former neighbor," he said as I walked around the side of the house. "You didn't forget and go to the wrong house did you?" He appeared to be doing a little carpentry repair to a screen window that lay across two sawhorses.

"No, I missed your friendly smile and wave, so I thought I'd just drop by in a neighborly sort of way—or former neighbor sort of way. Interested in sharing a glass of wine and some cheese with me?" I held up the bag.

"I'd be delighted," he said, folding up his carpenter's rule. "I've missed seeing you around with your camera and stuff. How's life treating you on the other side of Center?"

"Great," I said as I took the wine out and set it on his table in the shade of a live oak. Then I began unwrapping the cheese.

He said he'd get a corkscrew and put the second bottle in the refrigerator. "Unless you think we'll drink both bottles tonight?" It was obviously a question.

"I'd have no problem with that—I have no where to drive. Do you have a big night planned?"

"I do now." He untied his cloth tool apron and draped it across one of the sawhorses. "I'll be right back."

He returned with a large pitcher of ice to set the opened bottle of wine in, a tray with two glasses of ice, and another pitcher of water, two unmatched wine glasses, and a roll of paper towels.

"So what's happened since I saw you Saturday, Chris? You looked in much worse shape then. You're not hobbling."

"I'm much better—nothing big wrong. I'm feeling lucky to be alive."

"You certainly are," he said. "I checked with the police each day to see if they knew how you were. They always said everything was fine."

I was touched by his concern but a slight bit irritated that my medical condition was such common knowledge.

"How're things at the college," I asked.

"About the same. At the oldest institution of higher education in the state, things don't change quickly. Tradition is hard to mess with."

After two glasses of wine, his remarks about work were not so generous. His bottom line was simply, I have tenure and will do as I please. My years in the corporate world had taught me it was not the exception but the norm to feel resentment toward one's employers. I could have told him some stories about my employer, but I wasn't on vacation to think about work, so I didn't.

"I have some of those little hot doggy things you eat with a toothpick," Bill said, "If you want, I'll get them and we can make this a full-fledged picnic."

While he was in the house, a Folly Beach police cruiser pulled into the drive of my former residence. I recognized Officer Spencer and waved as he got out of the car.

"I thought I recognized you," he said, standing just outside his car, the door still open—obviously he didn't plan to stay long. "How's your leg?" he asked.

"Feels much better; thanks for asking. My former neighbor Dr. Hansel and I were having a picnic and looking at my former abode."

Behind me, I heard the screen slam and Bill asking, "So, Officer Spencer, what brings you to this part of the island?"

"Oh, hi, Doc. I was on patrol and saw your picnic mate and thought I'd check to see how he was doing. Also to tell him that the sheriff's department has put a warrant out on Mrs. Lionetti's friend. They have enough to tie him to the murder."

"That's great," said Bill.

"Unfortunately, he may have already left the state," continued Spencer. "No one's seen him for a week. I hope they're right about his being gone. It'll finally get this burden off Folly's shoulders." He looked directly at me. "And I suspect you'll be relieved, Mr. Landrum."

I laughed a mirthless laugh. "That would be an understatement, Officer. A monumental understatement!"

"Got to go stop crime," he said. "Good to see you, Mr. Landrum, Doc." He ducked back into his cruiser, backed out, and was gone.

I breathed a deep sigh of relief. "Well, Bill, I said. Now you and I really do have something to celebrate! Pass the wine." As a second thought, I said, "You should feel better now that your lighthouse group is off the hook."

"Yes indeed," he said quietly, settling down in his chair, freshened glass of wine in his hand. "Some of us were becoming paranoid about it. Rumors about someone or other we all knew being involved. Just being rumors, we hadn't narrowed down the suspects, but our last meeting was especially interesting. I kept looking around waiting for someone to raise a hand and say, 'I killed that sorry devil—do I get an award?'"

I laughed. "I don't guess anyone confessed. Why did they think someone on the inside was involved?"

Bill continued in that low, self-possessed tone of his. "Because we have such a strong interest in the lighthouse. To us, the beach at the end of the old coast guard property—where that son of a bitch met his nemesis—is where we physically and symbolically look out for the lighthouse. Also, the general feeling is that the killer had to have more than a passing knowledge of the area. Especially for you not to have seen him and for him to know where to hide a car so no one would notice it." He looked at me with a faint smile. "There was a minority opinion that said you did it, but most of us disregarded that one."

I didn't know whether to be complimented or insulted. So I took another drink—from the second bottle. In the back of my mind, something Bill said kept ringing true. Not the comment that I had done it, but something about the logic of some outsider's coming to that isolated spot. What kept bothering me wasn't why the old coast guard property had been chosen for the murder, but the absence of a logical reason for Jim Lionetti's coming there in the first place.

"Chris," Bill said, "did you know the word 'Folly' is Old English for an area of dense foliage?" He crossed an ankle over a knee and gestured with an outstretched hand as though he could see the island from shore to shore and end to end. "This entire body of land was once covered with some of the greenest plants, shrubs, and trees in the entire country."

I'd heard that somewhere, but I was silently wondering what it had to do with anything.

"As I tell my students, 'he who fails to learn from the past is condemned to repeat it.' Being in an academic environment, I'm also quick to attribute that quote to some famous philosopher whose name I would've remembered three glasses of wine ago. I think it starts with a *G*. But whoever said it, it's true.

"So the history of this island is not only interesting, but also important," he continued. "When the first settlers arrived in the 1600s, they found the Bohickets, an Indian tribe, and of course, ran them off. Two hundred years later, the first shots of the Civil War were fired just over on Morris Island, and all hell broke out. So there's another piece of the island's history. They say bootlegging was big in the '20s, and the law be damned. Only nine families lived on the island full-time in the early '30s, so they *were* the law. And even during our adult lives, this place has been a bohemian hangout. Adherence to the law, the mores of the state, and the convention of the established system sort of go by the way once you cross that bridge. Painters, poets, and photographers—none as straight-laced as you—have gravitated here for decades. Frankly, I think the aura of the dense foliage carries over from ages gone by and clouds the sensibilities of many of our residents."

Wow! A little history, a little philosophy, and some metaphysical mumbo-jumbo from the professor. I wondered, are his students enchanted by his lectures or bored out of their minds? I wondered what they really learned about hospitality management. I wondered how he could remember the name of an obscure Indian tribe and forget the name of the philosopher? And, I wondered if I'd had too much wine! But I dared to ask him what was on my mind. "With that said, what's it have to do with Lionetti, the lighthouse, or the price of gas in Canada?"

Again, softly and with a quiet, restraining gesture, "No, no. Not so fast. I can't tie it to the price of gas, but as far as the others are concerned, sometimes we can't see the forest for the trees," he said.

Another attempt, "Is there something in all those words that I need to know?"

"Chris, you're just like my students. Always wanting me to *dumb down* my lectures."

I was beginning to understand their need.

"No, I'm sure your message is quite clear. But maybe I've had a wee bit too much wine, and my thinking isn't as clear as it needs to be to understand."

"That makes more sense," he said. "All I'm saying is, if I were you, I wouldn't let down my guard. Not everything here is as it appears. Occasionally people see without knowing what they're seeing. And see things that no one else ever will."

He roused his tall frame out of the chair, and as he went up the steps, said back over his shoulder, "I've got a third bottle of wine in here, all chilled and available for a special occasion."

I wasn't thinking too clearly, but I said sure, and while he was gone, thought that I liked Officer Spencer's news better than Bill's. Of course, I didn't really see what Bill was saying!

When he returned, I told him we could toast to my making an offer on a house and my hopes that I was about to become a landowner. That was my first mention of the transaction, and he expressed disappointment that I wouldn't be his neighbor. But, we both agreed that my former residence wouldn't take on vertical, livable status for a long time. And even when it was rebuilt, I wouldn't be able to afford it.

We enjoyed each other's company until well past sunset—in fact, well past ten or so. With both three bottles of wine and conversation depleted, it was time to head home. If Bill would only point me in the right direction.

As I left, he yelled after me. "Chris, did you know Folly Beach banned palm reading in 1964?"

I must admit, he got me on that one. I'd have to remember later to ask him the significance of that factoid.

Thinking about my new home, the current definition of the word *folly* made more sense than the Old English translation.

CHAPTER 24

Today began in a way that was the very opposite of yesterday's beginning. There wasn't a cloud in the sky, the predawn glow was dimming the view of the stars, and rain was nowhere in the forecast until the weekend.

This was the day to go to Charleston and photograph the things I'd missed during Tammy's whirlwind tour.

Despite a slight … okay, not so slight … overabundant consumption of the grape last night, I managed to be at The Dog when it opened. Amber continued to amaze me with her early-morning smile and enthusiasm.

"Happy Thursday morning, Chris! The usual? You're out mighty early."

I said yes to *the usual* and told her I was heading to Charleston to take photos.

"Have you been over to the old Seabrook property yet?" she asked.

"No, but I heard about it from Charles."

"The reason I mentioned it is they say it's where you can get the best view of the sunset. I thought you, being a professional photographer and all, might be interested. I'd be glad to show it to you; we could go over there some evening."

I thanked her and said I'd keep it in mind. I was trying to keep conversation to a minimum; I wanted to get to Charleston.

I waved at one of the two council members; I assumed he was waiting for his colleague, and said hello to Officer McConnell who was entering as I was leaving. It was nice to be noticed.

On the walk back to the house, I almost wanted my bicycle-riding shadow to appear. He'd enjoy a day of photo taking, but I had several shots in mind, and he might have been a distraction. I made it home without hearing "Mr. Photo Man ..."

✳   ✳   ✳   ✳

In Charleston, I headed directly to my parking place on The Battery, put on my Tilley, missed my photo vest, and filled my pockets with an extra battery, two memory cards, and crammed in the wide-angle lens. I had to get a new photo vest soon! I slung the Nikon's strap on my shoulder, grabbed my much-hated but necessary tripod, and headed out to find those yet unrecorded, award-winning images.

With the sun still low to the horizon, I headed around East Battery where the sun's rays were just beginning to hit the facades and barrier fences of the stately homes. Other than a few joggers and the ever-present dog walkers, the sidewalks were deserted. I loved this time of day. The houses, gardens, and even the fences were beautiful and photogenic. Before walking a block, I had taken forty shots.

Following a path similar to what Tammy and I had taken, I headed away from the water. The most impressive thing about this area is the sheer quantity of fantastic residences and gardens. Most cities have places that contain a few mansions and picture-perfect garden spots, but South Charleston has hundreds. Each property is more beautiful than its neighbor. *House & Garden*, *House Beautiful*, and *Southern Accents* would be honored to have any of these gardens gracing their covers. The purple flowered wisteria were in full bloom and covered many of the stucco walls and wrought-iron fences.

My flower vocabulary is limited, and I wouldn't even venture to guess the names of the many blooming plants. So I did what I do best—I photographed them. I could already visualize many of these images hanging in my display. The beauty may be common here, but in Kentucky, it would be exotic.

I was struck by how many work trucks there were once I got away from the perimeter of The Battery. Most had the word *gardener* or *remodeler* stenciled on the side. It seemed every third or fourth house had workers scurrying around, watering flowers, weeding gardens, or climbing a ladder with paintbrush or hammer. The sweet fragrances competed with the strong smells of hot motor oil from the aging construction vehicles.

Affording one of these beautiful, historic homes would be only the beginning; the cost of upkeep must be more than I make in a year. I felt like writing a thank-you note to some of these homeowners for allowing the rest of us to take in the beauty. Of course I wouldn't.

When I came to the James Lionetti house, I slowed my walk. The yard and house were immaculate, but I had a feeling that everything inside wasn't quite as perfect. I pictured the police dragging Mrs. Lionetti in handcuffs out the front door.

I still couldn't imagine her and her lover being the least bit concerned about me. I couldn't possibly know anything tying them to the crime. So why would *they* break into my house and try to roast me like a hog on a spit?

A couple of houses south of the Lionetti mansion, I paused to talk to one of the gardeners, the unsung heroes of the "Charleston look." He'd returned to his truck for bags of pine needle mulch, and I quickly found out he was talkative. I made the mistake of asking if there were a lot of palm trees in the yards.

"Palms are a problem around here," he said. "They really need a more tropical environment; can't take the cold of Charleston winters. Reality doesn't stop many of these *common senseless* owners from having them planted, though. Most of the trees you see around here that look like palms are really Palmettos—that's the sub-tropical state tree of South Carolina."

"I've been walking around most all morning," I said, "amazed at how beautiful the gardens are. It must keep you busy."

"Yeah, me and a thousand other guys. The folks in these houses have two ways to show their wealth. They're all rich, but they want to keep letting the others know how rich. They try to *outparty* their neighbors; you should see the catering trucks in the evenings. And they try to *outgarden* their neighbors. I'm not complaining, mind you; it keeps food in the mouths of my three kids."

I asked if he had a garden at home.

"Are you kidding? If I could, I'd concrete my entire yard. The wife won't let me do that, so we have a tiny, tiny area of grass and two damn rose bushes. She takes care of both the grass and roses."

Time to move on.

Looking at my watch, I was surprised to see that it was now after eleven. Tammy was working today, but I chanced calling to see if she was available for lunch. She sounded glad to hear from me and pleased I was retracing our steps, but unfortunately, she was covering a double murder about sixty miles away in Georgetown. Her description of Georgetown, a picturesque seaport village on the Waccamaw River, and double murder didn't go well together. She wouldn't be home until late. I told her what Officer Spencer said last night and asked her if she'd heard anything about the arrest of Mrs. Lionetti's lover.

"I know there's a warrant," she said. "But my sources say there's no hard evidence connecting him with the crime. They're basing the warrant on their being involved in an affair. He couldn't account for his whereabouts at the time of the murder, and he hasn't been seen for more than a week. Unless they do better than that, a good defense attorney will have him out on bail before his fingerprint ink dries."

"Hardly what I wanted to hear."

"My sources could be wrong. Is that better? Sorry about lunch. But nothing's keeping me away from Folly Saturday. So get ready!"

I told her that I also hoped her sources were wrong, was sorry about lunch, and wondered what *get ready* meant.

✳   ✳   ✳   ✳

Tammy or not, I was hungry. I was nearer to my car than a restaurant, so I gave up my valued parking spot and drove up Meeting Street toward The Market where I parked in a bank's garage and walked a short distance to a sandwich shop overlooking the busy market. I had a sub sandwich and ice tea—I wasn't ready for wine again. Way too close to last night.

After lunch I walked the short distance to King Street and checked out some antique shops, most of which specialized in high priced European furniture that I doubted would look good in my new home at the beach.

I left King Street, and back at The Market, took one more quick walk through the covered shopping area, then returned to my car. The entire time, I was thinking how much more fun this had all been with Tammy at my side.

CHAPTER 25

On the ride back, I was surprised to find myself thinking of Folly as being as much my home as Louisville. Maybe I'd made the correct decision.

As I passed *The Boat*, I smiled. Even the slight traffic jam on Center Street caused by some heavy equipment working on storm drainage pipes didn't upset me. As I pulled up in front of my current, and, hopefully, future home, I felt a tinge of pride.

I went briskly up the walk, opened the door, and what I saw wiped the smile off my face. The fragmented remains of my laptop were strewn across the living room. It would have fared better if someone had taken a baseball bat to it. The screen was shattered and separated from the innards and keyboard.

Without thinking, and chilled with fear, I asked as loudly as I could muster, "Is someone here?" I prayed I would not receive an answer. I didn't. I tentatively stepped back out the front door, called 911, and was comforted to hear, "Folly Beach Police Department. How may I help you?"

After giving my name and address and being assured someone was on the way, I reached the car and sat down before my shaking legs gave out. I heard a siren. The patrol car started at the station less than two blocks away, and pulled in my drive almost before I could get back out of the car.

Officers Legend and McConnell were immediately out and asking what had happened. They told me to stand behind my car until they said it was okay to come in. Officer Legend took the front door, McConnell the rear. I thought it frightening that in less than three weeks, I knew the names of most, if not all, of the officers in the police department. I was willing to bet that some folks had lived here a lifetime and couldn't make that claim.

They had been in the house only a brief time when Officer Legend opened the screen door and waved me in. "The good news is there's nobody in here; the bad news—everything's a mess."

Officer McConnell met me at the door. "If you don't mind, Mr. Landrum, please go through each room and tell us if you notice anything missing. If possible, don't touch anything."

The inspection didn't take long; I didn't have that much to begin with. The fire had seriously reduced my personal belongings. But that hadn't stopped someone from making a colossal mess. My clothes were thrown about the bedroom. Some were cut and torn. A few folders I'd used to organize my house search were thrown in the kitchen sink and soaked. The fact sheets on the properties I'd visited were spread across two rooms and some were missing. The television that came with the house was on the floor, and I didn't know if it would ever show another rerun of Lost! The laptop didn't look any better the second time I examined it.

"They came through the back door," said McConnell. "The glass in one of the panes is broken. The lock was easy to reach from outside." We'll take a few prints, but I don't think they'll tell us much."

"Could we ask a few questions?" asked Officer Legend. "When did you leave the house, and where have you been since then?"

I related my day's events, and Officer McConnell reinforced the account by saying that he'd seen me in The Dog early this morning.

"How much longer do you plan to be on Folly?" chimed in McConnell. "It looks like you've looked at several houses," he said as he picked up a couple of the fact sheets from the floor.

I answered the best I could.

Chief Newman walked in though the front room. "Mr. Landrum, you're slipping. The house is still standing, and there are no dead bodies around."

He smiled as he said it, but I didn't smile back. I didn't like being reminded of my encounters with the unusual.

"Well, Chief," I said, my voice heavy with weariness, "I'm sorry to present you with such a boring crime this time. I would say I'll do better on the next round, but I'm not anxious for a next round."

"Boys, what's it look like?" he asked as he turned to his colleagues.

"Random vandalism," said Legend. "We've had a couple of these on West Beach Court and Clam Drive the last few months."

"Most likely you're right. Mr. Landrum, have you found anything missing—cash, computer equipment, any of your photo stuff, cell phone, anything?"

I told the chief that everything appeared to be here—just in a lot worse shape than when I left.

"There's nothing else we can do here," said Newman. "Officer Legend, contact Larry at Pewter Hardware and see if he'll send someone over to replace that glass in the door. That's the least we can do for Mr. Landrum. I think he's beginning to believe we're an inhospitable bunch."

*   *   *   *

The police cars left with less fanfare than when they arrived. I picked things up and sat down on the couch to "count my blessings" and try to figure something—anything—out.

Before I could start counting, there was a knock on the front door. Larry, from the hardware store was there to fix the window. Maybe if there were other emergencies, I should call Larry. Although he was no taller than a jockey, he was quicker than the police and fire department.

He said he'd been hearing about me for weeks and was glad to finally have a chance for us to meet. I didn't ask what he'd heard.

When Larry had the glass fixed and left, I got back to my blessing counting. The house was still standing—that was an improvement. I wasn't harmed—physically anyway. I'd be able to get a new laptop if my insurance agent was still speaking to me after the fire. That one was a real stretch. And whoever broke in had been kind enough to leave a bottle of wine unharmed in the refrigerator. Those were the blessings.

Now it got complicated. What in the world was going on? I didn't believe for a second that this was a "random act of vandalism"—no way! Did the police really believe that?

I reached no conclusions that made sense, so I looked through everything again to make sure nothing else was missing. I was right, only about half the fact sheets from my house hunting were here. Why would anyone want those? Just as strange, I had had notes taken at the city council meeting. They were here yesterday, folded and in a magazine I was reading. I remember because I'd almost thrown them out. The packrat in me had won; the papers had even survived the fire by being in a folder in the car that fateful night. Now they were gone.

For the second time in ten minutes, I said out loud, "What in the world is going on?"

Another full day of walking and disruption. I was exhausted. It wasn't really time for bed, but the sun was going down. I thought about how the sunset would look from the Seabrook property, at least how it would look from Amber's perspective. Then I took advantage of the spared bottle of wine and slept soundly.

CHAPTER 26

Like a steel marble rolling toward a magnet, I was drawn to The Dog—after all, regulars do regular things. I wasn't there as early as usual. I'd needed the ten-hour sleep.

The just-after-opening crowd was already gone. Officer McConnell was among that group, so Amber—and I suspect everyone else in The Dog, with the possible exception of the tourists—had already heard about my messy housekeeping.

"And a happy Friday," said Amber. "I hear your housekeeper got her orders confused while you were in Charleston. Want me to *scramble* your eggs today? They'll remind you of home."

I was really feeling like I belonged; receiving abuse with the best of them. "Good morning, Amber. And thanks for asking. I'm just fine. If you want, you can just throw my eggs on the floor. I'll clean them up—practice makes perfect."

On a less acerbic note, she continued, "Rod said it was vandals. Did they get anything valuable?"

"About all they did was totally destroy my laptop. I don't suppose there's any-where on Folly I can get a new one?"

"Do you think the surf shop or the T-shirt shop would be the best?" she said, knowing full well there wasn't. "I'm not the computer type, but I'll ask around."

Halfway through breakfast, she reported back.

"George over there says the best place to get a computer is Office Depot. It's about thirteen miles from here. Head toward Charleston, but don't turn on Highway 30. Keep going and turn on St. Andrews Boulevard, then right on Sam Rittenberg Boulevard. You can't miss it—that's what George said. Me? I could miss it."

I thanked her, and then said, "Before I forget—when I was in yesterday, I told you I was going to Charleston. Do you remember telling anyone?"

"Let's see, you were in early, and everyone kept asking about you. I think I said something to Wynn Stamper; he came in just after you left. I may have mentioned it to the police, and I remember telling Charles Fowler. He came in asking if I knew where you were. He said he hadn't seen you and was a little worried. Oh yeah, I almost forgot, Mayor Amato made one of his rare visits. He was standing with Stamper, so he may have heard."

I buried my face in my hands. "Amber, it's easy to see why Folly doesn't need a newspaper."

I couldn't get it through my head that the ransacking was vandalism—too big a coincidence. It would have been a big risk, breaking in with me on the island. Knowing I was in Charleston would have made the task both easier and safer.

*   *   *   *

With a plan in mind, I walked to the house, got in the car, and headed to Office Depot.

George was right on both counts; Office Depot would have been hard to miss, and it sold two well-known national brands.

The sales clerk, about the age of my deck shoes, convinced me to go with the IBM ThinkPad. The screen was the same size as my old laptop, and with the word "think" in its name, it could help me do better work. It also had the mobile technology I wanted, plus twenty-five or so other features the clerk was excited about. They sounded like gibberish to me. *Frontside bus, 512M PC2-4200, DDR2 SDRAM, Media Accelerator 900*—how could I possibly get by without them!

Thanks to my friendly neighborhood arsonist, I also needed a printer. I opted to go with the same model that now sat as an amorphous plastic lump among gray ashes. I had extra ink cartridges, and most importantly, a new one was sitting there waiting for me to take home.

My credit card was already getting a workout, so I added a little more and bought a data-recovery software package. The software, DataBack, was under a hundred dollars—hardly anything on top of the other three thousand I was donating to Office Depot's increasing profitability.

*   *   *   *

I was close, and it was early afternoon, so I decided to go back to Charleston for more photos. Like yesterday, I parked in the bank's parking garage and walked around the downtown area. The Market was a big tourist attraction, but within a few blocks, there were several historic and majestic churches. With my wide-angle lens, I captured the somber tombstones and the steeples reaching for the sky in the same image. This was the kind of view I like, even though I knew it would never sell.

I returned to the parking garage and noticed how cool it was inside—a drastic difference from the sweltering heat of the downtown area. The security guards even wore lightweight jackets.

I drove a few blocks north through the College of Charleston, wondering where Bill's classes were held on the sprawling downtown campus. I'd ask when I saw him next.

As I headed home, something was nagging at me. The garage … what was it about the garage? It'd felt strange being in such a cool environment after the heat, but there was something else.

As I approached *The Boat*, I once again felt I was where I needed to be. Traffic was worse than yesterday; a Folly Beach City Works truck was blocking traffic while four workers removed barricades from the bed and placed them at each intersection. I guessed to make them handy when they closed the streets for tomorrow's festival. Some of the stores had already put tables on the sidewalk to hawk their wares to the unsuspecting tourists. Good plan, we *locals* need to bleed those *tourists* dry!

I pulled into my drive, and as I walked up the front steps, I wondered what condition my house would be in now. Thank God, it was untouched. But, what else could it be? I didn't have anything worth anything left.

But now I had work to do—to get the house ready for company, and to get the new computer up and running.

The laptop came with several software programs, so I had everything I needed, except Photoshop. My copy was in the car, so it was safe. I loaded the DataBack software and fiddled for a few minutes trying to get online, and failed miserably.

Always a frustrating process for me. So I put it aside for another day. Why not? I had no one to e-mail.

Setting up the new printer proved to be much easier. I guess because I had done it just last year when I got my first one—the currently artistically melted blob of plastic. I wondered if Charles had photographed it yet.

Now to get the house looking good. That shouldn't be too big a challenge; it was almost empty. But for me, not the world's best housekeeper, it wasn't that easy. But I got it done—not ready for an *Architectural Digest* photo shoot, but good enough to entertain a beautiful reporter from Charleston.

CHAPTER 27

April twenty-second means little to most citizens of the world, but to those in the know around Folly Beach, South Carolina, it's Sea and Sand Festival day. Still, the Chamber of Commerce was not going to be happy; a cold front had brought heavy early morning showers and much cooler temperatures. The forecast called for the rain to be breaking up late morning, but it might discourage some off-island folks from attending. I hoped not. I especially hoped it wouldn't discourage one particular Charlestonian.

Rain or not, this was to be a busy day. It would begin at eight with a 5K Run/Walk and a 5K skate. I left the house at six sharp, knowing The Dog would already be full, so I headed to one of my other homes away from home—the Holiday Inn—for some coffee and possibly breakfast, depending on the crowd in its restaurant. Even for that short walk, I took along my umbrella and Tilley.

As I walked, I was remembering earlier comments about the traffic problems during the festival. I should call Tammy and tell her how to avoid the blockades.

The restaurant was half full, or half empty, depending on your perspective. I was in a half-full mood because I had no trouble getting a table.

It was a relief sitting and reading the morning paper without having to entertain, or be entertained by, the waitress or to talk to the regulars. That was an advantage of the large chain hotel; it wasn't frequented so much by locals. The first thing I looked for in the paper was Tammy's byline, and there it was.

It was strange reading her follow-up story of the double murder in Georgetown. Her writing style was direct and convincing. Yet she communicated a warmth and concern for the victims that I seldom saw in the papers. Was it possible that I was biased? Naaa. She was just a great reporter.

By half past seven, I was finished with the paper, my breakfast, and the desire to be in the Holiday Inn. The rain looked like it could pick up again any moment. But I was well covered with the umbrella and rain-resistant Tilley, so I ventured up the main drag to watch the runners, walkers, and skaters as they ran, walked, and skated by. A little rain didn't stop these athletes.

No—rain or shine, Folly was ready. The barricades were in place blocking the downtown area off to motorized traffic. Balloons were tied to stop signs. Many tables that had been outside yesterday were inside the stores now, just waiting for the weather to clear. You have to make sure those with money have a chance to spend it with ease.

On Center Street, kids in dance tights and martial arts uniforms were running from one store canopy to the next, trying to miss the raindrops.

Indeed, this was a big day for the city of Folly Beach.

I called Tammy before the parade and did my best to explain how she could wiggle around on the side streets to avoid having to wait. I hoped no one overheard my conversation, because I told her she could "… turn either east or west on East or West Indian Avenue, then south on whatever the next street is, then west on East Erie …" It didn't take either her or me long to realize I was the blind leading the blind, and at last, I said, when you get on the island, park wherever you can, call me, and I'll meet you. We could figure out the final flight plan to my place later. Nothing like good planning!

The Sea and Sand Festival's official opening began with a parade down Center Street, the rain just a drizzle by the time the fire engine announced its arrival with sirens blasting. The engine was followed by five convertibles—a vintage red Corvette with Mayor Amato sitting on the trunk behind the passenger's seat, two jeeps carrying two city council members each. And two newer model Chryslers carrying two people I swear I'd never seen before rounded out the convertible brigade. I was disappointed not to see Mr. Howard's Plum Cruiser.

Three young baton twirlers no older than twelve led the Folly Beach Community Band in a medley of The Beach Boy's best. I knew it was the Folly Beach Community Band because two elderly gentlemen in the middle were carrying a banner proudly announcing the name.

"Hey, Mister, I remember you."

I looked down toward the sound of a high-pitched voice coming from a young boy. He was not more than a foot from me and looked familiar.

"You do," I said as I searched my memory bank for clues to who he was.

"I saw you taking pictures of 'Old Blue' a while back," he said as he leaned against the tall trash can on the sidewalk. His gaze alternated between the parade and me, his jaws ferociously attacking a piece of gum.

"Sure, I remember," I said, figuratively kicking myself for not remembering him at first. "Enjoying the parade, Samuel?"

"Yep," he said, "sure beats watching nothing."

I couldn't find fault with that.

He waved at a girl about twice his age in the community band—she must have been an ancient twenty—and without taking his eyes off her, said, "You found the shot-up body, didn't you?"

"Where'd you hear that, Samuel?"

"I heard a strange photographer found him. I thought of you."

I hoped he meant a *photographer who was a stranger*, but who knows. His attention was now transfixed on the two police cruisers moving at a snail's pace a short distance behind the band.

"I'm afraid it was me," I said. "It was a tragic thing."

"I figure the killer's from right here," said Samuel as he turned his attention back in my direction.

Finally, somebody agreed with me. It was nice to know we ten-year-olds could agree!

"What makes you think that?" I asked with more, much more, than a passing interest.

"Had to be," he said, oozing confidence. "He knew too much about over here. Heck, I bet he's here right now."

I hadn't thought of it that way, but he could easily be right.

"I bought myself some red Christmas lights to put on 'Old Blue,'" said Samuel who was getting bored with the murder talk. "Got them seventy percent off over at Wal-Mart. Dad said I could string um on the tree if Mr. Black says it's okay." After a pause and a couple of more chews on the gum, he added, "I'm going to wait closer to Christmas to ask."

"I think that's a smart idea," I said, hoping some day I'd be able to see his creation.

"Gotta go mister; see ya."

He disappeared into the growing crowd before I could respond.

The parade had just ended—or, more accurately, passed where I was standing—when I felt my cell phone vibrate. It was Tammy. She was parked near the post office behind the Baptist Church. I told her to hang tight, that I'd be there in five minutes.

I made it in four. I hadn't realized how very excited I was to see her. And there she was, standing by her car and looking radiant. She could have been on the summer cover of the most prestigious of glamour magazines. Light blue linen blouse, navy shorts, a lightweight tan jacket draped over her arm. I greeted her with a huge hug and a big kiss—I didn't want any misinterpretation. I was thrilled to see her. Her return kiss told me the message was received.

"Well, are you ready for a day of Sea and Sand?" I asked.

"I'm not sure what that means, but if you are, I am."

Good enough. "Just lock your car and leave it. I don't think your being with me will get it burned, shot or vandalized."

We walked arm and arm the half block back to Center Street, and then left toward the beach and the activities of the day. Tammy had brightened my day just by appearing, but the sun was also contributing. The Chamber of Commerce must have some connections; the rain was gone.

The festival covered only six square blocks, so it wasn't difficult to take in all the activities—several times if one were so inclined. We talked, but mainly just enjoyed each other's company.

Those who knew me appeared to take a keen interest in my walking mate. I wanted to introduce Tammy to Amber, but with the long line out the door of The Dog, that could wait.

When I heard "Hey, Mr. Photo Man ..." from behind a group of tourists, I knew there was one introduction I couldn't delay.

Charles, using his cane as a shield, wove his way though the crowd, wearing a tattered "University of Washington Huskies" purple and gold long sleeve sweatshirt and a big smile. Pants and shoes, too, of course. Under the image of a husky, the sweatshirt said "2005 Women's Volleyball Championship." I didn't want to know where he got it.

"Excuse me, I mean Mr. Photo Man *and* Ms. Hot-Shot Newspaper Reporter."

"I see you know my companion," I said. And then, "Tammy, this is my friend Charles Fowler."

"Nice to meet you, Charles. Chris has told me some nice things about you."

"Well, if you put it that way, it's a pleasure to meet you, *Ms. Rogers*. Your friend's told me some things about you—and even what he didn't tell seems very nice—if you catch my drift."

"Tammy," I said, "if you catch his drift, I'm going to worry. He drifts to the beat of a different drifter!"

"Ms. Rogers, will you be heading back to the big city this afternoon or joining us for sunrise?" Ever so subtle, my friend Charles.

"It's Tammy, and my plan is to enjoy the beautiful sunrise over the Atlantic. Thanks for asking."

"Good," said Charles. Then he turned and walked away—throwing a wave in our direction over his shoulder.

We stood there watching him disappear into the crowd, a little stunned at his unconventional departure, and laughing with delight. We then headed toward the corner of Center and Arctic, the hub of activity. The hula hoop competition was already underway. There must have been an age limit; the contestants were all in their early teens. A DJ had his sound system in the middle of the street, and at least twenty-five kids were swirling their hoops to beach music from the sixties. I was amused and surprised to hear music that was popular during my own youth, happy that it was alive and well and popular with the ten-year-olds. We watched.

At a table overlooking the Holiday Inn parking lot—the scene of more fun and games—we sat down with two gourmet all-meat (*kind* of meat unspecified) hot dogs and soft drinks. I was in the middle of my first bite, anticipating a slush of mustard on my chin, when, before I knew what she was doing, Tammy quickly stood and approached Frank Long and a lady I assumed to be his wife. They weren't far away, and I heard most of the conversation.

"Mr. Long, we haven't met," Tammy said. "I interviewed you by phone a few weeks ago about James Lionetti's murder. I'm Tammy Rogers with the *Post and Courier*."

"Yes, I remember," Long answered. I couldn't read the expression on his face, but was a little worried—he might not welcome a conversation with a reporter. "This is my wife, Sue. Are you on an assignment or just over for the festival?"

"Hello, Mrs. Long. No assignment. I'm visiting a friend and enjoying the festivities. I'm glad the weather's improved over this morning. Well … I didn't want to bother you, only to let you know I appreciated your comments about Mr. Lionetti."

"It's good to meet you in person, Ms. Rogers. Have a great day."

When Tammy rejoined me, I couldn't help tease her about coming over here just to scope out stories. She feigned shock, and I didn't buy it. But looking over her shoulder, I noticed Long looking back to see who Tammy's *friend* was. I guess he didn't know yet that I'm one of his fellow locals.

The temperature was still cool, but with the rain clouds having disappeared out over the ocean, the merriment took on new excitement, and the beer was flowing as much as the tide. This was Folly's day to celebrate the beginning of summer without the huge influx of tourists that was still a few weeks away. The natives were here and jubilant, and the open container law waiver was working.

As the day wore on, Tammy and I talked about our childhoods and the small and large festivals, carnivals, and church picnics we'd attended during those years. We tried to figure out exactly where the old Folly Pier, amusement park, Ferris wheel, and even the bowling alley used to be. I thought we were close, but, as they say, no cigar.

Chief Newman was leaning against the meaningless stop sign at the pedestrian-filled corner of Center and Arctic Avenue.

"Afternoon, Chief," said Tammy.

"Good afternoon to you as well, Ms. Rogers, and Mr. Landrum. What brings you to our festive little city?" I assume he was asking Tammy.

"I thought I'd come over and see what all the buzz was about," she said. "I've heard about the festival for years and wanted to be part of it."

"Oh good! So you're not investigating corruption and graft in the local police department," said Newman. "Any new murders I need to know about?"

"No murders," she said. "Is there corruption *I* should know about?"

"Always the reporter," he said, laughing. "I don't think so. About the hardest thing our department is doing today is trying to control the flow of cars. As has become a tradition, we're failing. Too many cars, too little space. That's normal during tourist season, but we make it worse today by closing the main streets. Oh well. Citizens will complain to the city council. The council will complain to me. We'll say we will do better next year. Then we won't!"

"Can I quote you on that chief?"

He laughed and said no more about it.

On a topic nearer and dearer to my heart than traffic patterns, I thanked him for keeping me informed on the status of the Lionetti case, and asked if any arrests had been made.

"No, but I suspect Ms. Lionetti's lover and alleged killer is long gone by now," he said. "He's from somewhere in southern California. Most likely he's now sunning himself on a beach somewhere on the left coast. I hear that Mrs. Lionetti is playing the grieving widow role to the hilt."

As long as the killer being long gone part was correct, that was fine with me. I didn't care what she played. But, Samuel's words kept resonating in my head.

A dance contest was just about to begin on "center stage," usually known as the Holiday Inn parking lot. We wished the chief good luck with his traffic and walked over.

Thirty-five couples participated, most made up of young children and a parent or the nearest grown-up sucker they could snatch out of the crowd. Some couples looked just this side of wheelchair age. The rest were in between. Actually, it was much more fun to watch than the morning's parade.

I was amazed how well the contestants did—especially the kids—and impressed that I knew the words to many of the songs. And so did Tammy. The ones she knew were newer songs than mine. My musical taste must have been more mature than hers. Nothing to do with age, I'm sure.

I wanted to see the surfing, but was too lazy to walk to The Washout.

By late afternoon, the crowd was thinning, so it was a good time to get Tammy's car to the house. On our way back up Center Street, I noticed she was getting looks from the locals. Many knew who she was, and I suspect they were leery to have a big city reporter in their midst. Or, maybe they were just happy to see me with someone. Yeah, that was it!

We drove the roads less traveled, and, with even the residential streets lined with parked cars, were pleasantly surprised to find an open space in front of my house. Tammy grabbed up an overnight bag from the trunk and a small hang-up bag from the back seat.

"Lead me to your abode," she commanded. As we went hand in hand up the walk, she said, "This is cute—it looks so like Folly Beach." Of course she couldn't let it go as a compliment. "It has a nice large yard so if someone torches it, the fire won't spread to your neighbors."

"You're such a romantic," I replied as I opened the door for her. "Welcome to what I hope will become my retirement cottage."

The tour of porch, kitchen, living room, computer room, and bath took about five minutes. The stop in the master bedroom, two hours. Neither of us had misunderstood the other's intentions.

I had thought she looked fantastic this morning when I saw her in her light blue linen blouse and navy shorts. But she looked even better with blouse and shorts strewn on the chair by the bed. With some giggles and much awkwardness, it was clear we were a bit rusty in the fine art of lovemaking. But both of us were intelligent, healthy people, so we adjusted quickly. To make sure we improved, we practiced some more.

Afterward, curled together beneath a single sheet, we rested, Tammy's head cradled in the hollow of my shoulder, my arm around her, and her arm lying across my chest. It seemed a thousand years since I had felt as I did in that moment. And so we slept.

When we awoke an hour later, we smiled and accused each other of snoring. We touched and teased, but we were hungry—for food. Tammy showered and we walked back to a vendor stand for a healthy dose of hamburger, French fries, and coleslaw.

By that time, the community dance was in full swing. Unlike the day's earlier events, a live band blared music written all the way from the sixties through the present. Some sounded harsh, without purpose, and flat-out loud. I assumed those were the hits of today. We danced for a while, and then ambled through the crowd.

The weather was much cooler now, and we were glad she'd brought a jacket.

I introduced Tammy to a few of the folks from The Dog. She was impressed that I knew so many of the police officers. I said it was a curse.

When I'd taken all the *music* I could stand and suggested a walk on the beach, I got no argument. The ocean breeze was even cooler at the water's edge. That worked out well; we had to wrap our arms around each other to stay warm. The beach never felt better. Sharing it made the difference.

It was then, right in the middle of that exquisite, unlikely moment as we strolled in the moonlight, that it hit me—the thing that had been in the back of my mind since I saw the guard at the parking garage in Charleston. What an idiot I'd been! Where was my memory?

On that horrible Monday, the last day of Jim Lionetti's life, I had seen an *emblem*, a patch on the navy blue object I told the police about. I had no idea whether it said police, security, fire, or anything at all. But, I'd seen it, and I knew that it belonged to the killer. Why else would I continue to be a target?

Tammy sensed it, raised her head from my shoulder and looked up at me. "What is it, Chris?"

Not wanting to ruin the mood, I tried to fight down the emotion. "Nothing," I said.

"Chris, it's *some*thing."

"You're right," I said, "something I just remembered. I have no idea what it means. Let me think about it, and then I'll tell you."

It was true. I didn't know what the patch said. I didn't have a photograph of it. If it was on the blue thing I'd photographed, the emblem wasn't visible. We walked another hundred or so yards in silence before she suggested we head back to the house. She said we might need a little more practice with our amorous pursuits. I agreed—quickly.

CHAPTER 28

Sunday was glorious. The sun was spreading a golden glow over the beautiful island of Folly. The birds were singing cheerful tunes for all to hear, and the temperature was perfect.

That's how I viewed the world as I woke beside the beautiful, charming, funny, and talented Tammy Rogers. The sun wasn't even up yet, and I couldn't hear the birds for the air conditioner, and, I had no idea whether it was cool or hot outside. It didn't matter—it was a glorious day.

Tammy slept until eight, and I tried to be as quiet as possible as I prepared for the day. If the shower bothered her, she didn't let on. Not trusting my coffee pot, I snuck out and got two cups from the Holiday Inn. In addition to the usual good morning comments, I received an extra knowing smile from the desk clerk as I exited with twice the usual number of cups.

Tammy was in the shower when I got back. To my pleasure and relief, I could tell she had no regrets about yesterday—especially last night. Dressed only in a wet towel and a big smile, she walked over, gave me a huge hug, and said good morning. She also said, "Thanks for the coffee, but where're we going to eat? It's grits time!"

* * * *

There was no time like the present to bring the two women in my life together. Secretly hoping it was Amber's day off, I suggested The Lost Dog Café.

With Tammy's short hair and lips and skin that needed little make-up, she was ready in fifteen minutes.

I wasn't used to arriving at The Dog this late, so waited impatiently for the first available table. Amber was there, and I know she saw us. She hid it well. After a fifteen-minute wait, Carolyn, one of the other waitresses took us to a booth that had come open.

Amber acknowledged our presence with a nod, and then came over, but not with her usual greeting.

"So," she said, "I finally get to meet the lady you escorted around town all day yesterday." Then focusing on Tammy, "Hi, I'm Amber, and you are?"

"Hello, Amber, I'm Tammy. Chris has told me all about you, that you're one of his best friends. I'm so glad to finally meet you." Then with the faintest pause, "How's your son?"

Ohhh, I thought. She's good—*really* good!

"Tammy's a reporter for the Charleston paper," I said. "She came over for the festival."

"I *know* what she is. At least five people told me yesterday and last night. Two already this morning. You can see, Tammy, that we don't really need a newspaper here; word travels much faster than in that rag of yours."

"Amber," I said, trying to get on task as quickly as possible. "We're a little hungry—any specials today?"

Belgium waffles, and of course I ordered one. Tammy requested two eggs scrambled with bacon, toast, and *two* orders of cheese grits. "One for me, and one for my friend," she said.

Amber faked one more smile and left to place our order.

"Chris," Tammy said, "to my highly trained journalistic eye, I can safely say, that young lady is seriously smitten. Actually, I believe a blind stalk of asparagus would see the same thing. Will you take a bite of my food when it arrives so I can see if you live?"

I sighed. "I know. I've tried not to lead her on; but she is fun and a pleasant sight for tired eyes in the morning. Anyway, I think most of her flirting just comes with the job."

"For someone who's fairly bright, you have a stupid streak," she said.

"Thanks. You really know how to make a guy feel good. Now drink your coffee, and ignore the stares from my fellow citizens."

When she appeared with our breakfasts, Amber appeared to be in a more forgiving mood.

"Tammy, do you mind if I watch him eat those grits?" she said. "They're are the first he's ordered—correction, ordered *for* him—since he's been here."

"My pleasure. I'm anxious to see it myself. He pretends to be a southerner, but his eating habits say otherwise."

Amber laughed—more sincerely, I believed—as she left the table to take care of other customers.

The table on each side of our booth was empty, so we could talk without being overheard. I looked at Tammy and smiled.

"Tammy, I'm having a great time with you; almost too good, in fact. But I need to tell you something. Hopefully you'll be able to shed some light on the situation."

"You aren't going to tell me you have a wife and seven kids in Louisville, are you? And wondering if we could all live happily ever after in your house here?"

"The good news," I said, "is absolutely not. The bad news is, I believe Jim Lionetti's killer is still out there—and nearby. If Mrs. Lionetti's musician, actor, or whatever he is, lover's flown the coop as the police think he has, there'd be no one around to burn my house or break in and steal who knows what. Someone believes I know something that could land them in jail. And now, I believe I know what that something is."

She listened eagerly as I told her about my nagging feeling and the revelation that had come to me last night. Before I got very far into the story, she suggested we leave and take a walk or go back to my place where we could talk with no chance of being overheard. I agreed and left a generous guilt tip for Amber.

There weren't many people on the pier, so with shoes in hand, we took a short barefoot walk and settled on one of the benches about halfway to the pier's end. The tide was out, and the sandpipers were scavenging the foam as it rushed in and receded, rushed in and receded.

"Okay, who do you suspect?" she asked. "Just say what's on your mind; we can analyze it later."

I slipped my arm around her and began, her face very close to mine. She was caressing my ankle with a bare foot.

"My bottom candidate is the grieving widow," I said, "for the reasons I gave you. I'd put Wynn Stamper at or near the top of the list. He's the anti-growth, long-time resident. I told you about him getting in an argument with a developer at the city council meeting. Many people think he did it. From what I understand, he doesn't have an alibi, hates developers, and knows the island backward and forward. Honestly, I don't know why the police haven't been looking at him more closely."

"Don't assume they haven't," she said quietly. "Detective Lawson and her folks are very good. Their not saying anything doesn't mean they aren't working on it."

For a moment I watched a gull hover on stiff wings just a few feet above us. Then suddenly it caught the wind and veered away. I touched my lips to Tammy's forehead.

"Okay," I said. "Point taken. The second candidate on my list is Frank Long. I didn't even think much about him until Wednesday. My realtor, Crazy Bob, told me Long was trying to get permission from the planning commission and the city council to take over the development plans and permissions secured by Lionetti. He's trying to develop an up-scale, large, condo complex adjacent to the coast guard property. With Lionetti gone, Long could be sitting on a gold mine. And didn't you say, 'follow the money or love'? Sounds to me like money."

"Wasn't Frank Long out of town?"

"Yes, in Columbia," I said, very, very conscious of her bare thigh against mine. "If he's involved, he's got to have had an accomplice. The person who believes I know something I didn't know until last night. I still can't prove anything." Looking down, I gave her a weak smile. "See why I'm confused?"

"A couple of points," she offered. "You've narrowed it to two candidates just because they're all you know who might have a motive. There could be any number of others who'd have as good a reason. You just don't know who they are. Also, Stamper might sound like a good suspect to you because you saw him in action against a developer. Sure, he might benefit a little if he can keep his rental houses full, but they aren't really in competition with a mega-million dollar condo complex. I don't see the money motive. Hate is related to love, but usually not enough to kill for. If Stamper is against all development, Lionetti is just another person in the enemy camp. Again, not enough reason to kill."

I sighed, leaned forward, and rested my elbows on my own knees. I was a little stung by Tammy's having so easily riddled my suspicions. "Okay, again," I said. "But what about Long?"

"Other than interviewing him the day of the murder and talking to him and his wife yesterday," Tammy said, "I don't know anything about him. The money motive is there …" and her voice trailed off. Then, "Let's talk about the patch or whatever it is you remember seeing." She was leaning forward now, her shoulder against mine.

"That's where it gets scary," I said. My mind was divided, and I reached up and stroked her cheek, then leaned back and drew her to me.

"Scary?" she said, laying her head in the hollow of my shoulder.

"Yeah, scary. If the patch is what I think it is, the jacket could belong to one of the members of the local department—the chief himself, a member of the Charleston sheriff's department, any of the hundreds of cops in the area, a firefighter from here or anywhere nearby, EMTs, security officers, on and on. I think it's someone local who knew the coast guard property, but really, it could be anyone with a uniform jacket. All the local police own a jacket that same color."

"Mmm," she said, obviously thinking. The wind was blowing her blond hair about, and she fingered a strand back over an ear. She looked up at me, her blue eyes searching out my thoughts. "Go on," she said.

"For the longest time, I thought all the police attention I was receiving was out of concern. After all, it wouldn't help tourism if they let a tourist get killed right before the season. But now, I'm not sure. They could as easily be keeping an eye on me because of what they think I know." I looked down at her earnestly. "Have you got it figured out yet?"

She shook her head. "No, but one thing I have figured. If it wasn't Mrs. Lionetti, and the killer is still in the area, you can't trust anyone. Except me, that is." She reached up and kissed me full on the lips—a long, lingering kiss. "But speaking of me," she whispered, "I have to leave in less than two hours. An important interview." She kissed me again, and her tongue touched my lips. Her breathing was uneven as she said, "And another thing I have figured out."

"What's that?" I said.

"That we can't do here what I'd like to do. Why don't we go back to your house and discuss this further in the bedroom?"

"Could we discuss it in silence?" I said.

＊   ＊   ＊   ＊

I had mixed feelings when Tammy left. I felt great; her visit had made the weekend complete. Not only did I now have a dream about living here; I also glimpsed myself sharing this house with someone—a thought I hadn't had before. But I also felt more fearful than any time in the last three weeks.

The possibility of danger seemed more real knowing that I really did hold the key, even if I had no idea what that key unlocked. And, as with most vacations, I dreaded the end of this one. In just a week, I'd be back at my desk with only memories of my April on the beach.

In the late afternoon, I set out on foot again. A long walk along the shore didn't bring closure to any of these emotions I'd struggled with, but it felt good. The soothing Atlantic sea breeze, the smell of saltwater in the air, the late day sun, and the feel of the sand under my bare feet—all reminded me why I wanted to be here.

A fitful night followed. I couldn't sleep. I tossed and turned, imagined hearing someone trying to break in or start a fire, imagined someone watching every move I made. Finally I did drop off, and sunshine peeked through the window before I awoke. This was the latest I had slept on Folly Beach.

A quick shower helped me wake up, but not much. I wasn't ready to face Amber and the others at The Dog, so I walked to the Holiday Inn instead. A little predictability would be a good thing. I imagined I was in another Holiday Inn in another city far away, but that wasn't what I wanted either. I asked if I could have a table by the window.

I remembered exactly three weeks earlier, sitting at this same table, hearing from the waitress how long the pier was and how many benches there were. Numbers I'd promptly forgot. I fondly remembered the strong impression Tammy made as she purposefully walked toward my table for our first conversation—cell phone at her ear, smile on her face. And it frightened me to think how close I'd come to refusing to talk with her about the murder.

But she wasn't here now, so I didn't order grits. I stuck to my Kentucky breakfast of two eggs, burnt bacon, hash browns and toast.

The quality of the food and the atmosphere was a given. What I knew about the crime wasn't. I needed to go back to the house and start over. Look through each of the images from that morning. Try, and try again to determine what I could prove that was of so much interest. It was clear to me now that my life depended on it.

I looked at the images from April 3; the second time I'd gone through this exercise, and I didn't really expect to find anything.

I looked at the shots of the Morris Island Lighthouse standing precariously perched off shore, the waves breaking on the rocky terrain, the sea oats bending under the dew. I scanned the images of the low windswept trees and deserted foundations of what had been a thriving coast guard station in years gone by. I looked again at an enlarged, blurry image of what now appeared to be a jacket. Of the seventy or so images from that day, nothing even remotely looked like the patch I thought I remembered seeing.

Then I noticed it. The camera always gives each image a number to be used for identification. The numbers were consecutive and remained attached to the digital photo. Anyone wanting to print an image could identify it by number.

The images from April 3 had gaps in the numbering. I had deleted five photos that morning. Maybe when I was on location, maybe after I returned and downloaded them to the computer. I often looked at an image immediately after taking it. If it was out of focus or I simply didn't like it, I deleted it on the spot. No sense in looking at it again.

Three of the deleted numbers were sandwiched between photos of the lighthouse. The remaining two were just before I had inadvertently photographed the mysterious object. Could I have taken a photo of the patch and not known it? A photo that I had deleted?

A sinking feeling overwhelmed me. I could have kicked myself for deleting the potentially incriminating images. I got up from the chair and paced the room. I went out and stood on the porch, leaning against a column with my arms crossed over my chest in frustration.

There was no way to retrieve the images from the memory card.... or was there? With the new DataBack software, maybe. I went back in. I had brought five cards with me. I had rotated them but hadn't planned to reformat any of the cards until I needed them again. The Boy Scout in me reemerged. If I had reformatted the first card, I was already out of luck.

I was literally shaking as I went out to the car to get the cards I had numbered one through five. I grabbed the case and tried to walk nonchalantly back to the house, but by the time I reached the porch, I was running. I felt like everyone in Charleston County was watching. Including the person who was after whatever it was that I had. Paranoia at its best.

The first memory card I'd used was intact. I hadn't used the DataBack software before, so being unfamiliar with it, I made two failed attempts before getting the card and the software to feel comfortable with each other. My shaking fingers didn't help. But I waited, and it seemed like an eternity before the software worked its magic.

I was sitting at my laptop—blinds closed, more paranoia—looking at the five missing images. Three of the five were worthless—but the other two were priceless.

In the first three images, I'd tried to capture the shadows of the scraggly, wind-bent trees in the maritime forest with the lighthouse in the background. No luck. In the other two, I'd focused on a clump of sea oats gracefully reaching above three rocks about the size of large watermelons. The sun was just rising and, unfortunately for my photo, the light hadn't quite conveyed what I wanted. I could see why I had deleted these images. I had used my new wide-angle lens and hadn't seen the sleeve of a navy blue jacket protruding slightly from another rock in the lower left corner of the frame.

Excited

Excited now, at last on the verge of something that might solve this puzzle, I saved both underexposed images in Photoshop. Now my fingers were trembling even more, and sweat was running down into the corners of my eyes.

I worked on manipulating the light in the shadow areas, at least enough to be able to see the sleeve more clearly. Photoshop was busy working wonders. And there it was—the patch as clear as day, and what it said—"City of Folly Beach" on top of the crest, "Police Department" on the bottom. I must have held my breath for thirty seconds. Here I was, a tourist looking for a beach house, now looking at what appeared to be a critical piece of evidence in a major murder case.

I grabbed three blank CDs and made copies of the two images before the computer could explode, someone shoots me, or the house burns. I put one in my suitcase and took another one to the car along with the original group of memory cards. I'd mail the third copy home in case something happened to me.

Now what do I do? I thought. Who could I tell?

Would it be safe to show the photo to the Folly Beach police? Absolutely not! I had no idea who I could trust there. To be honest, I didn't know if the photo would even prove anything. It didn't show who killed Lionetti. The jacket could be years old and given to Goodwill for all I knew. If it belonged to a member of the police department, what motive would there be for the killing? Did he or she act alone? Back to Tammy's question, "for love or money?"

Should I take this photo to the *sheriff's* department? With the connection between Chief Newman and Detective Lawson, it would be foolish to go to them.

I could take it directly to the public through Tammy. But what would that achieve? I could hear the Folly Beach police responding to a reporter's question about the jacket with statements like, "Yes, we have jackets like that. We've bought dozens over the years. There's no way to track down each one. That one could have been discarded or lost years ago. We'll investigate." A dead end.

I didn't know what to do.

The rest of my day was as fitful as last night—just with sunny, warmer weather. I walked on the beach, sat on a log along the sea oats, stared at an erosion fence along the dunes, walked some more, and resolved absolutely nothing.

Then about eight o'clock, Tammy called. She was in her car on the way back to the office from her interview and sounded pleased.

"I didn't really get to say it when I left," she purred, "but I want you to know how great a time I had. I can't remember ever having such a nice weekend."

I took that as a very good sign, and told her I agreed. When she asked how I was, I said a little depressed with this being my last week. I already missed Folly, and I especially missed her. She said she didn't know what her work schedule would be like the rest of the week, but that she'd find some way to get over, or maybe I could visit beautiful, historic Charleston—and this time, her not-so-historic apartment.

I didn't tell her anything about the lost images and my dilemma. Again, I didn't want to ruin the mood.

I'm sure I slept some, but it didn't feel like sleep.

CHAPTER 29

The thing I was sure of when I woke Tuesday morning was that I needed to have breakfast at The Dog. Not because of the fine culinary fare, but to talk to Amber. She'd been a good friend since I arrived. I knew she was hurt and that I shouldn't have sprung Tammy on her the way I did. So I wanted to get there as close to opening as possible so it would be fairly empty. I hoped it wasn't her day off.

There was a little drizzle, but it looked like the sun would be breaking through the low clouds rather quickly. The cool ocean breeze gave a refreshing bite to the air.

When I walked through the door of The Dog, Amber was standing behind the counter waiting for my entry.

"Good morning," she said, "will there be two of you today?"

I told her no, and with a grin she seated me at my favorite window table.

"Your regular or grits?"

"Just the regular."

Only the two city council members had made it in before me. Now everyone else who entered would be waving or speaking to me instead of the other way around.

Amber returned with water and said the rest would be up shortly. My turn to speak.

"When Tammy got here Saturday I came by to introduce her. It was almost eleven, and you had customers standing out the door. I knew you were busy. I didn't want you to hear she was with me from someone else. Sorry."

"So that means you don't want me to give you the personal tour of Folly?" Direct has always been her style.

"I guess not right now," I said. "I really don't know where Tammy and I are headed. I don't even know when I'll be back after this week. I really like you. I want to keep you as a friend. That may not be what you want to hear, but it's true. I hope you understand."

She nodded and headed to the kitchen, and I, sitting there, felt like a heel.

I ate in silence, except when I briefly spoke to Officers Spencer and Robins who came in for their morning coffee and gossip. And my nodding buddy, "Cool Dude" from the surf shop, nodded but didn't speak.

I paid Amber, and before I left, she said, "I know I don't have nearly as much to offer as Ms. Rogers. You deserve the best; you're a great person, and I've really enjoyed our conversations." She paused, and then with a smile said, "I'd be honored to have you for a friend."

Now I felt like *both* heels. Especially when I noticed the tears behind her words.

From there, I walked to my thinking spot—the pier. As I had thought it would, the sun had won out over the low clouds and drizzle. The day was going to be nice. Being Tuesday and still early, I had my choice of benches, so I chose one as far from the beach as I could go. I wanted to distance myself from land.

I didn't know what my secret photo said. It didn't directly implicate anyone, but someone thought something about it could cause serious grief. It was common knowledge that I was leaving Friday, so if he or they wanted to get to me, there wasn't much time. Would I be safe even back home in Louisville? I didn't think so.

I had to bring this to a head. So far I'd just been reacting. I needed to take control. Easily said, but how?

I needed help. I couldn't go one-on-one with a killer. That kind of thing only happened in cheap novels and the movies—mild-mannered common-person took on gang and won. Sure!

The answer came to me almost like a revelation. A revelation in the form of a distant figure that was this moment ambling down the beach—that ever present useless cane in hand, borrowed camera slung over his shoulder.

I pondered for only a moment. Charles was loyal, fairly athletic, and seemed to know how to take care of himself. And from the day I met him, okay, maybe the second day, I'd known I could trust him totally.

A more important question was, would it be fair to subject him to potential danger? Before I finished asking myself, I knew the answer. The Charles—not

Charlie—Fowler I knew would be angrier if I didn't ask for help. So, who was I to let down a friend?

I practically leapt from the bench.

Waving my arm in the air as I ran along the peer, my shoes beating a loud rhythm on the boards, I yelled, "Charles! Hey, Charles!"

This morning, he was sporting a green on gray light sweatshirt with "University of Hawaii Rainbow Warriors" emblazoned on the front—long sleeve, of course.

"Hey yourself, Mr. Photo Man. Where the hell have you been all day? I've been looking all over for you. Got a whole wheelbarrow full of questions about what you've been doing since Ms. Reporter Lady showed up on Saturday. Are ya'll hitched yet? Is she pregnant? What does she think of me? Where are you two going to live? Are you gonna get a dog?"

By the time I reached him, I was short of breath, and stood with my hands on my waist, gasping and laughing at the same time. "Whoa!" I said. "If you're real nice and walk with me, I'll answer any polite, courteous question you ask." I paused to breathe. "The first one being, no to a dog. And to some, that's none of your business. But, most importantly, how could she not like you?"

That slowed him a bit; a small bit. "She has good taste," he said. "Okay, now that you have your breath back—at least so you don't sound like an asthmatic—let's walk. By the way, she seems really nice, especially if she likes me."

I nodded my head and caught one more deep breath. "Let's walk toward your apartment and the Seabrook property," I said. "Amber said that would be a good place to photograph the sunset. Have you explored it much?"

"Heck, yes. It's in my neck of the woods, you know. I've spent a fair amount of time walking through it. That bunch of high-priced houses messes things up, but there are a few unspoiled acres and trails left. They're sort of off-limits, of course, but that doesn't stop yours truly and an occasional bird watcher, and today, a stray photographer from Kentucky."

Where Indian Avenue met the woods, it was like walking into an unspoiled forest. The scrubby, windswept trees that covered much of the island gave way to massive oaks, pines, palmettos, cedars, and others I didn't recognize. It felt like we were in the 1800s. The path also led through a marshy ground, and then opened onto the Folly River. Now we were facing west, and I imagined the sun disappearing over the river and the marsh. Amber was right, the view of the sunset from here would be terrific.

By now, I had told Charles about the deleted images. Not only was he fascinated by the technology, he listened closely to the details of what was on the two photos that showed the jacket.

"You know, finding that jacket doesn't mean much," he said. "I bet there are lots of those unaccounted for. Each guy on the force has a couple, and they've gone through many cops since I've been here. Pay ain't the greatest. The best leave for better jobs. And knowing some of the guys, they've lost a bunch of jackets over the years. I remember about four years back, one of the cops—no longer here—even lost his gun. Never did find it. We joked about it for months—how he had *disacquired* his firearm."

Standing there on the river's edge, I looked down, shaking my head in mild discouragement and nudging the soft ground with the toe of my shoe. "Charles, you're right. That's why we're here. The jacket doesn't mean much, but I have a hunch who killed Lionetti, and I think I know why. I can't prove it. The police still think it's the wife and her lover. I don't. I think it's local, and I intend to do something about it. If you're willing, I need your help. Let me tell you my theory and how I think we can prove it."

"Well, for pity's sake, stop wasting my time by staring at the river! Who did it and what's the plan? I think I can work some crime solving into my busy schedule."

We sat on a rock ledge overlooking the river while I shared my thoughts and theory. We debated the best way to go about this, and together found ways to fill in the gaps. We looked at options, debated details, and hatched a plan.

And in his own inimitable way, Charles summed it up. "'One cool judgment is worth a thousand hasty counsels. The thing to do is supply the light and not heat.' Woodrow Wilson, long-dead United States president." Charles's tone was positive, almost cheery.

I was wishing I had his confidence.

CHAPTER 30

The first thing on our agenda was to have lunch at The Lost Dog Café, Center Street, Folly Beach, South Carolina. Hatching a plan to catch a killer can make one hungry.

"Twice in one day and accompanied by one of our strangest residents? What've we done to deserve such an honor?" asked Amber.

"You're just living right, Ms. Amber," replied Charles before I had a chance to add to the banter. "And I might add, you're looking radiant today." I'd never before heard that tone in his voice or seen that light in his eyes. As he spoke, his gaze swept Amber from her feet to her face.

Shaking off the surprise, I told her I was treating him, since this was my last week here. We were early for the lunch crowd, so Amber was able to sit down and chat for little while. We talked and laughed about how I first ran into Charles—or more accurately, how he'd run into me—and how he was driving people crazy with his rejuvenated interest in photography. He said he didn't understand why more people weren't interested in photos of crushed soft drink cans. And how anyone could not be fascinated by an out of focus photo of a McDonald's coffee cup that had been run over by a half dozen cars.

"True art's so unappreciated," he lamented.

She and I agreed—with a faintly detectable lack of sincerity.

"Amber," I said, "I'm finally taking your advice."

She looked at me quizzically.

"I'm going to photograph a sunset from the shore of the Folly River at the Seabrook property. It's supposed to rain tonight, so I may have to wait until tomorrow," I said.

This time she didn't offer to accompany me. Neither did Charles. He said he had work to do tomorrow for one of the other restaurants. He'd be available tonight, though, if the rain held off.

Amber was obviously pleased that I remembered her suggestion about sunset at the Seabrook riverside. Our luncheon conversation was light, pleasant, and void of the sexual innuendo she had formerly specialized in. We were just three old friends having a pleasurable conversation. It felt good.

Charles would have been content to spend the rest of the day in The Dog if they'd let him. He was at ease with Amber and, of course, spoke to everyone who came in. Counting breakfast and lunch, I'd already spent four hours there. And now I needed to do more walking and thinking, so I paid and said I'd catch up with them later.

*   *   *   *

The seeds were now planted, and I was confident that a good crop of gossip would grow and be harvested by the intended parties.

I spent a couple more hours doing what I'd spent hundreds of hours doing over the last twenty-five days. I walked and took photos. Today I was more sensitive than ever to where I walked. I stayed on the more heavily traveled roads and on the beach where vacationers were sunning every so many yards.

On the outside, the rest of the afternoon was uneventful. But inside, my emotions, thoughts, and heartburn said otherwise. At the thought of ending my vacation, I was sinking deeper into depression by the minute. The month off had been great, but had made the ending much harder than a shorter respite would have.

Thoughts of Tammy and our weekend together competed with my gloominess. Did we really have a future? Is that what I wanted? This sunny afternoon, I answered yes. But what would my thoughts be when I returned to the real world? I didn't know.

I was amazed how many wonderful people I'd met in my short time here. Thoughts of each one gave me a warm feeling.

I also thought about how I'd met one, and maybe two, far less than wonderful folks. If my theory was correct, I had more than *met* a killer—I had *talked* with him. That sent a chill down my spine.

I was so deep in thought, it was a minute or so before I noticed the rain dripping off the brim of my hat. I was probably the only person on the beach who was happy to see the rain; it was key to the success of *our plan*.

I went home, hung my still dripping Tilley on a peg by the front door, and before drifting off into another night of erratic sleep, sat down at my new computer and wrote Tammy a detailed note describing my theory and the killer's motive. I gave her as much evidence as I had, told her where it could be found, and briefly described the plan. I felt a tightness in my chest when I realized that if she ever read the note, it meant that I wouldn't be around. I ended with *I love you*. Then deleted it. What did I really feel? I typed it in again. And stopped—two out of three must mean something.

CHAPTER 31

My sleepy mind told me the alarm was going off. I looked at the clock; it said 6:18. I also noticed it didn't even *have* an alarm. That's when my slightly more alert mind said it was my *phone* ringing. I couldn't understand how the phone could be ringing at 6:18 AM. I picked it up and quickly understood.

"Chris, how the hell are you?" my cheerful realtor asked. "I know you're awake; you're an early riser," he *assumed*—erroneously today.

"I have two questions. First, why the hell did I have to hear from three Folly Beach residents that you were squiring around a lovely—in fact, too pretty for you—newspaper reporter all day Saturday and most of Sunday? And second, the damn bean counters from that northern bank countered your offer. Want to hear it?"

At that, both riveted and irritated, I lifted myself on one elbow, and with undisguised annoyance, said, "Good morning. It's good to hear from you too." I hope he grasped my tone. I doubted it. "Let's talk about your second question first. Of course I want to hear their offer," I almost shouted.

"Well, my friend, you'll have to open your damn door. A professional realtor of my caliber never discusses offers over the phone—Real Estate Etiquette 201, I believe."

I groaned. The clown was sitting right outside. "Give me five minutes," I sighed, "and I'll be out—I assume your smiling face and my favorite Realtormobile are out front."

"That's a 10-4, good buddy!"

I opened my door seven minutes later, walked out, and leaned my palms against his door top. He was, of course, sitting in the Purple Cruiser, its top down, and from the look of his sweat-stained, smelly "Virginia is for Lovers" T-shirt and the dark bags under his eyes, he was on his way home and not just getting started. Regardless, we met his criteria from Real Estate Etiquette 201 and were face-to-face. I should have known he wouldn't let me do this over the phone.

"Well, my young studly friend, tell me all about your weekend. Or better yet, forget most of it. I just want to hear about the sex."

When he saw my stubborn stare, he knew he wasn't going to get much juicy information, and tried a different tact.

"Okay, forget all that mushy, gooey, sweaty, sex stuff. What I really need to know, are you going to need a bigger house with plenty of room for kiddies, dogs, and a damn swing set?"

What was the deal with dogs here?

"I think this house will do. Are the bankers going to make that possible?"

"You're no damn fun—business, business, business. Get in and I'll show you what we've got."

So I sat, and he opened his folder and handed me some papers.

"So here's where we are. The bank's bean counters came back with a counter of five twenty. By law that's all I can tell you, period!"

"But—" I said.

He raised his meaty hand and signaled me to slow down. "Patience. Patience. If you were to go around in front of my talking car and asked *it* nicely—promising a quart of oil as a peace offering—I think it would tell you the bankers said they'd take five oh five. They love money, hate things."

"Things like houses?" I asked.

"You got it. Now, Mr. Sex Machine, seducer of one *helpless* local southern reporter, would you like to make another offer on this lovely piece of real estate on fabled Folly Beach, South Carolina?"

"I'll tell you what, Mr. Savvy Realtor, I believe I'd like to make an offer of five hundred five thousand dollars."

"A damn fine offer, if you ask me! Let's get it written-up, and I'll fax it to those big-city bankers before they open their teller windows this morning. My trusty Cruiser has a hunch that we can have this wrapped-up before you head home. Since the bank's out of state, we'll be able to complete the closing without you having to come back." He chuckled as he said, "I love getting my commission in the mail."

Such a caring realtor. I wondered if Folly actually *bred* quirky characters or if they simply gravitated here.

He said he hoped I lived long enough to close on the house. You can see how he really cared. He told me if I wanted to rent out the house to vacationers, he could recommend a fine real estate firm to handle the details—for a percentage of course.

"After I take possession of this fine example of Folly Beach's vernacular style, in addition to myself, there'll be only one person permitted to stay."

He fired up the engine of his trusty talking Realtormobile to depart. "Thanks," he said, "I consider it an honor to be that person."

I *thought* he was teasing. As I watched him drive away, I noticed black smoke swirling from the tail pipe. Hmm, I thought, the thing really *does* need oil.

On my way back up the walk, I felt like a marine—I'd accomplished more before breakfast than most did in an entire day. Had it hit me yet? I'd just spent more on a semi-dilapidated wooden beach house without a view of the ocean than I would ever get from my two-story, traditional, relatively large two story house in a forested, high status, section of Louisville. Location, location, location! Or more correctly, location, location, location—plus an ocean!

Anyway, buying an overpriced property on one of the world's strangest islands while surrounded by a real-life murder mystery had made me hungry. My Folly Beach life had begun in the Holiday Inn, so it seemed appropriate to spend part of today—God forbid, maybe my last day on earth—there.

Weather-wise, today was predicted to be all I hoped for. The rain moving out to sea with a mostly sunny day and early evening on tap. A great day to photograph a sunset.

Sitting in the restaurant, I couldn't help thinking about my first visit five years ago. I asked myself, "Had I known then what I know now, would I be here today?" Good question. If I could get past that elephant in the closet, the answer would be a resounding *Yes.*

Maybe by the end of the day, I'd be able to slay that elephant. My life depended on it, after all.

CHAPTER 32

I thought late afternoon would never arrive. Sunset would be around eight, so at half past six, I got ready. Getting ready didn't amount to much—gathering my camera, tripod, and the other little stuff I take. I added a small flashlight, a light jacket, my hat, and headed toward the sunset.

Charles and I had walked this path yesterday, so I had a good idea where I'd be setting up. I wanted to get the sun going down with one of the windswept, short trees silhouetted in the foreground. Here I had an open view out over the river. The earth, soft from the rains, made a sharp, low bank, the water swirling past it in little eddies. Perfect, I thought, and began what ordinarily would be a routine procedure, but I couldn't have been more nervous. I fumbled with the dials on the camera, adjustments I'd made without trouble a thousand times. I was barely able to screw in the shutter release cord. All because either the sunset would be the target or I would be. As perverted as it may seem now, I hoped it would be me.

With the remote shutter release in place, camera securely attached to the tripod, and adjustments set, I was ready for show time.

Now to wait—and to feel extraordinarily vulnerable.

The sinking sun was casting shadows across the river and the trees. A dozen yards upstream, a turtle slipped soundlessly into the dark water and disappeared. When a frog jumped with a *yike* and a splash, I almost knocked the tripod over.

Real or imagined, I kept hearing noises from the woods behind me. Somewhere, an owl hooted, and from close by came the chittering of a squirrel—and a crack like the breaking of a twig underfoot. Why hadn't I simply gone home to

Louisville and let the chips fall where they may? But Louisville seemed a million miles away.

This was the stupidest idea I'd ever had.

I was concentrating so on my stupidity that I failed to notice movement just to my right. The same instant that I became aware of a presence, I heard a familiar voice and looked up to see Officer Rod McConnell. He was standing there in jeans, a casual shirt, with his right hand in the pocket of his police jacket that displayed the emblem of the "City of Folly Beach Police Department" on its sleeve. No surprise; I'd seen that emblem before.

"Good evening, Mr. Landrum," he said quietly. "You know, you really shouldn't be on this restricted property. Especially alone. It could be dangerous."

Confirmed!

I stood up straight and smiled, trying to look surprised. But I wasn't. "Rod! You startled me. What brings you out here?" As if I didn't know.

He drew himself up to his full height, both hands in his jacket pockets, chest swelled out a little, a short man trying to look tall, and paused. "Mr. Landrum ... Chris, let me answer with a story. You'll find it interesting." He motioned to a place down the path a little way. "Let's have a seat over there."

We walked fifteen yards down a gravel path to a log that someone had placed there to sit on and view the sunset. It had been there many years from the looks of the moss and weeds growing around it. And all those years of folks watching sunsets had worn the bark away, so we sat down on smooth, weathered wood.

The temperature was cool, but I was sweating.

McConnell made himself comfortable, pulled a piece of long, fresh grass from its stem, and began to toy with it. "I think you already know most of this story, but I'll tell it anyway. I have a twin sister, Rhonda. You haven't seen her, because she's in a drug rehab center in Columbia. A few years ago, she made the mistake of falling in love with one of our leading citizens. He, of course, was married and had no intention of divorcing his successful wife. I'm not saying he was responsible for her drug addiction. He wasn't. She's had drug and alcohol problems since high school." He paused. "You're an observant fellow, Chris. I think you know who she fell in love with."

His voice was so calm that I didn't know whether to relax or run. But there was no sense playing dumb. "Frank Long," I said.

He compressed his lips and nodded. "I knew you'd figured it out. During your house hunt, you toured the one with a zillion photos. One of those photos being of Rhonda and Mr. Long, the mayor and one of my sister's friends. I bet you noticed. You knew who Long and the mayor were, and Rhonda looks so much like me it's not even funny. Your seeing that picture gave me a problem.

"Mr. Long and me had got close when Rhonda and him were hot and heavy. I knew about them; he knew I knew. That was two good reasons for him to be nice to me. He was in development, and I had a big interest in getting into it too. He told me if anything big ever came along over here, he'd bring me in. Sis and Mr. Long went their separate ways a couple years ago, her drug situation out of control. She didn't know what she wanted. I think he was glad she broke it off."

Tension had built inside me until I blurted, "Okay, Rod. That's interesting, but what's it got to do with you showing up here tonight? You didn't come just to see the sunset."

"I'm afraid you're right, Chris. I like you ... I really do. The problem is you're too smart. You know too much—whether you know you know it is another thing. But if you haven't figured it out, you will."

"It," he'd said. And I knew what "it" was. We looked each other straight in the eyes; his were calm and cold. And mine? I didn't know, but my heart was pounding in my ears.

We understood each other perfectly. Then I said, "I don't suspect you came out here to turn yourself in, and I don't imagine you have any intention of letting me leave alive. Were I to guess, I'd say your right hand's on a gun. But since you haven't shot me yet, your plan must be to make my untimely death appear to be an accident. Maybe drowning."

In a foolhardy display of bravado, I pulled my gaze away from his and looked out over the water, darkening as the sun sank beyond the oaks on the far side. "This can be a fairly deep river I hear," and then I turned my eyes back to his.

He just stared at me. I took that as agreement.

I continued, "Then why don't you tell me about Lionetti?"

He looked at me with those dark eyes as if to say, "And why would I want to do that?"

So I said, "I realized just yesterday that I have photos proving you were within a few feet of Lionetti when he was killed. It wouldn't be hard to convict."

Announcing *proof* was a major exaggeration, but he didn't know it. As far as he could tell, I had a photo of him with the lighthouse in the background and the date and time stamped on the image. A sheen of sweat broke out on his forehead.

"All right," he said, "I'll tell you. Jim Lionetti found out about three properties out by the old coast guard station and conned the owners into selling him the entire tract. He promised them the moon, tons of money, condos in his development in Mt. Pleasant, and no telling what else. He told them that they'd just as well sell, because nothing big could ever be built there since it would violate code. But the shit *forgot* to tell them that the properties had never been legally divided, so that some of those codes didn't apply. He could put whatever he wanted on that ground. His lawyers would have the planning commission and the city council over a barrel, because he'd have the law on his side."

"Ahh," I said. "So, basically, he outsmarted everyone—except Long. Long saw his chance and told you he would bring you into the development if you helped him eliminate Lionetti. Long was local, and with Lionetti gone, he could buy the land from Lionetti's widow, transfer the approvals, and make a mint. He couldn't do it himself because that would point the finger at him. He needed an airtight alibi. Does that sum it up?"

"Yeah," McConnell said. His sharp little eyes never left me as he went back in his mind. "That morning, you got there before Lionetti, so you never saw his car, and you were off the path when he came walking in. I never saw you until right after I shot him. It never entered my mind anyone would be there at sunrise. I was damn lucky you didn't see me then. I almost broke my leg diving behind the scrub trees. But then later, when I'd thought about it, I knew you had to be shooting pictures near where I'd had my sleeping bag and jacket. And I knew you would've seen the picture with my sister and Long. And, knowing how gossip travels—especially with as much time as you were spending with Amber—someone would've told you about their affair and maybe even my interest in becoming a developer. Like I said, Chris, you know too much."

"Yeah," I said. "Too much. My tough luck. So you set the fire, broke into my house twice, and maybe did stuff I don't even know about. All to get rid of me or find out what I knew."

Again, silence—his dark eyes fixed on mine—his way of saying yes.

"I guess it's not dark enough yet for you to speed my demise," I said, sounding more relaxed than the knots in my stomach indicated. "Tell me one more thing, Rod. How did you get Lionetti to such a deserted spot at that time of day? How did *you* get there? That's bothered me from day one."

"Well ... Mr. Long followed me over to Charleston the day before. I left my car a few blocks from The Market, and he took me out to the old coast guard property before sunset. I slept there so I'd be ready whenever Lionetti got there— damn mosquitoes almost ate me alive. Lionetti visited his construction sites early each morning. That was one of the arrogant bastard's quirks; always had to be hands-on—no secret there. Mr. Long bought one of those disposable cell phones so the number couldn't be traced, and called Lionetti just after seven when Lionetti was sure to already be on the road, but wouldn't likely talk to anybody about where he was going or who he'd talked to. Mr. Long's smart like that. Lionetti had the one small construction site near the end of Ashley, so Mr. Long asked him to meet him at the point overlooking the lighthouse at Lighthouse Inlet."

So that was it, I thought. A nice, tidy bundle, with me tied right in the middle of it—all by accident. But the moment of truth was close now, and I was watching McConnell like my life depended on it. I saw in his eyes that he was ready.

McConnell took a deep breath and pulled what appeared to be a hand towel from his hip pocket.

"Chris," he said, getting to his feet, "stand up and put both hands behind your back."

This wasn't exactly part of *our plan*. I glared at him. "And what makes you think I'll do that?"

"This," he said, and he took out the gun I'd all along suspected was in his jacket pocket.

Now, lest you think I gave in too easily, let me explain. I'd never looked down the barrel of a revolver before, and this one was pointed right at my left eye. Instantly I again saw Lionetti's empty eye socket, and the seawater washing in and out. What a surprise that a black hole thirty-eight hundredths inch wide could look as big as a well! Besides, McConnell having used it on one man, if he thought he had to, would use it on me. So without any more resistance, I did what he said.

When I stood, he wrapped the towel around my wrists, took out three black plastic ties that contractors use to secure electric wires and hooked them together. And the next thing I knew, he was putting the ties around the towels and pulling them tight against my wrists. No marks—smart!

He yanked them tighter. "Good," he said. "I don't think you'll be going anywhere. Now sit. I'm not done."

He pushed me and with a yell, I fell awkwardly back and hit the ground so hard it knocked the wind out of me. I'd never felt so helpless.

He knelt beside my feet, and through my gasps for breath, I managed to brokenly ask, "Why would Lionetti ... even consider meeting Long ... at such a strange place at sunrise. Or ... any other time?"

"Simple," he said, his hands working rapidly with what looked through my bleary eyes like another towel and length of nylon rope. "He was a damn greedy, sneaky, son of a bitch. Mr. Long told him he had information that would make Lionetti's development even bigger than he hoped. That information in return for a small part in the expanded project. Long told him that what he had to say would be worth at least five million dollars. That's all it took. Long told Lionetti that he wanted to meet at the deserted beach; it was important no one saw the two together." McConnell chuckled. "It was greed brought Lionetti there."

By now he had fastened one end of the rope to my right ankle and snugged it tight. I was mad now. "At the risk of sounding impolite, what's that rope for?" And in return, he gave me a look I will never forget. It was a dark leer combined with a smile, and his slow-spoken words chilled me.

"So the river won't take you away from me, Chris," he said.

And then, still kneeling, still looking me right in the eyes, he continued, "You've heard most of the story; now you'd just as well hear the rest of it. Mr. Long was also smart enough to tell Lionetti that if he wasn't there when Lionetti arrived, he should follow the path to the end of the beach. This way no one would see them together. The rest was easy. Except for you. Lionetti arrived and no one else was in sight. He did as Mr. Long said and walked the quarter of a mile or so to where you found him. I just walked right up behind him, said his name. He whirled, and I shot him twice.

"I was taking his car keys out of his jacket when you showed up out of nowhere," he said. "So I ducked quick as I could, circled back behind you, got my sleeping bag and jacket, then got the hell out of there. I took his Mercedes and drove to Charleston and stowed it away in the one of the big parking garages on Meeting Street. I left the car, walked back to mine, and drove home. End of story."

I think the thing that was making me sick—and mad—was the pride McConnell took in his story. At last I asked, "So what next?"

He got to his feet and reached down and lifted me to mine. "Next? Next you get to walk slow like to the edge of the river. There's a nice easy slope just over there. We'll walk in and you'll get on your knees. I'll help you stay underwater a while. All your problems will be over." He said this while giving me one of his strange salutes. "It won't matter much to you, but I'll cut off those straps and unwind the towel, and then the rope, and let you float wherever the current takes you. Thanks to your shooting off you mouth in The Dog, by now, half the town knows where you are. When you don't show up tomorrow, some of your buddies will start looking and will find your camera stuff. They may, or may not, find your body. I'll be over here looking with the rest of the concerned citizens. A sad ending to a vacation at the beach."

By now I thought I'd made one tragic, final mistake, that this thing hadn't a chance in hell of turning out according to *our plan*. I'd always wondered how a man going to the electric chair could make his feet move. I still didn't know.

When he saw that I was going nowhere, McConnell got a death grip on my right arm and forced me.

Now we stood on the shore looking at the sky as the sun receded below the marsh. The dark water was swirling past my feet and my head was spinning. His grip had cut off the blood flow to my arm, and he gave me one last shove forward.

And then, just as I felt the warm water around my knees, I heard a scream so loud and close it nearly split my eardrums, and with the scream, a moan. I felt the grip on my arm go slack and his hand fall away.

I was to my knees in the river, hands bound behind my back, and didn't dare look around for fear of losing my footing. So I didn't see what was going on behind me. And then I felt a steadying grip on my shoulder and myself being helped onto dry ground. It was then that I saw something that made a beautiful sunset boring.

Charles—not Charlie—Fowler.

He had that useless cane gripped in one hand like a batter who'd just hit a homerun. His camera was draped over his right shoulder; there was a huge smile on his face and a "University of Rhode Island Rams" mascot was staring at me from the front of his long-sleeve blue and white sweatshirt.

"Hello, Mr. Photo Man," he said with a grin. "Enjoying the sunset?"

I exploded. "What in the blazing hell took you so long? He could have killed me five times over!"

"Why, Mr. Photo Man, you always told me to wait for the photo I *wanted*. I wasn't too worried about composition. I wanted to get a good confession and a *who done it* on this handy-dandy video feature in my ... I mean your ... camera. He kept jabbering through his story, and I had to wait until he'd said all the important things. Besides, he wasn't going to kill you yet. He was too interested in hearing himself talk."

"Cut this thing off my wrists," I almost screamed.

"Only if you promise you won't hug me for saving your ass," he said.

I didn't promise, but said I really didn't want to hug him. That was good enough. He cut the ties and removed the towels.

"McConnell will be coming around any time," he said. "We should call the police."

"Charles, remember our story."

"Of course. I was out for a walk. Everyone who knows me will believe that. Amber and I knew you were coming out here, so I walked over. I came upon the two of you. I didn't think it was quite normal for you to be standing here with your arms tied behind your back. I hid and photographed some of the conversation. When I thought the evil police officer was about to harm an innocent tourist, I hit him with my trusty cane. That's it." He paused for effect, grabbed up the cane from where he'd stuck its point in the mud and brandished it. "By the way," he said, "did I ever tell you that this cane is loaded with lead?"

"Lead!" I was rubbing my wrist, trying to get some circulation back, and he handed it to me. I nearly dropped it. The thing weighed five times what it ought to weigh.

"Sure, lead. Why do you think I carry it? To *walk* with?"

"Charles Fowler," I said with new respect. "You're a … you're I don't know what!"

"Quit blathering and call the police," he said.

I called the number on the card Detective Lawson gave me when we met at the coast guard property, hoping upon hope that she'd pick up. My prayer was answered. I nervously told her who I was and why I'd called. I told her I would have normally called the local police, but under the circumstances wasn't sure I could trust them.

She said I could trust Chief Newman and told me to call him as soon as I hung up. I was surprised when she gave me his cell number and said she was on her way over. The hardest part was giving her directions to this spot on the river.

Before I called the chief, I noticed that McConnell was moving.

"Charles, help me tie his arms before he's awake enough to disagree."

Charles had planned for this and brought a six foot rope from one of the boats near his house. And there was the rope still tied to my right ankle. I noticed right away how much better it felt to have McConnell's hands tied than mine.

The chief answered on the second ring and sounded surprised to hear my voice. It was as if he were expecting someone else. I told him where I'd got his number and the reason I was calling. Reluctantly, I told him why I'd called him direct instead of at the police department. He said he'd be here in ten minutes.

Only moments later, the wail of sirens filled the still, cool, evening air. It sounded like they were coming from all directions. But with only two ways in, the sounds must have been echoing off the trees. We were a couple of hundred yards or more from any road, and the wails stopped well short of us.

I was pleased to see Chief Newman coming through the brush first. In the back of my mind, I feared that some of the other officers were in cahoots with McConnell. If they were, their arrival first would mean nothing but trouble. The chief was closely followed by Officer Spencer, then by Robins. Already there were rubberneckers converging.

When Newman saw Charles and me standing over one of Folly Beach Police Department's finest with his hands tied behind his back, he seemed ill at ease to say the least. I guess he was somewhere between arresting us for assault, being embarrassed that one of his underlings was hog-tied on the ground, and simply not knowing what to do.

But his years of military experience kicked in, and he took command. He told Officer Robins to guard the fallen officer. Just then, Detective Lawson broke into the clearing, and she and Newman took us away from the growing crowd.

"Okay, guys," Newman growled, "what the hell's going on?"

"Rather than trying to explain, Chief," I said. "Let us show you a video that your local resident Charles here took just a little while ago." I made a flourish with my recently tied right hand. "Charles, it's all yours."

There in the gathering dusk, we three gathered around Charles as he held up the Nikon. Charles was fumbling to get it to work.

"Now, the movie isn't very good," he warned. "Chris hasn't taught me how to shoot a video yet. I kept shaking the whole time, but if you listen carefully, you'll hear the important stuff."

The four of us watched what I thought was the most beautiful, enlightening, life-saving three minutes in video history. The quality stank. I didn't care. The experts would enhance the images to get a clear view of Officer McConnell.

Even with the poor quality, we recognized him. The audio was weak, but the words were powerful. Beyond a shadow of doubt, we heard Officer Rodney McConnell say he'd killed James Lionetti. And that he had worked with one Frank Long of Folly Beach, South Carolina. Exclamation point, period!

I never felt better.

The crowd was getting larger. Two EMTs arrived. An additional two officers from the sheriff's department, including formerly Detective No Name, now Braden, were looking at each other, wondering what to do. A crew from one of Charleston's television stations was shooting footage of this bunch of official looking people standing around like they were lost. Not very captivating video. Not nearly as good as what Charles had taken.

Not much unlike a few weeks earlier, I had to tell my story to the different police agencies. This was a longer story then the one in which I'd done nothing more than find James Lionetti's body.

Again and again, in the hushed chatter of the crowd, I heard Charles telling anyone and everyone who would listen how lucky it was that he'd walked onto the Seabrook property and come upon this dramatic event. I'm not sure how convincing he was. But no matter—the result was the capture of a murderer.

It was now too dark to see beyond the end of your arm, so those with flash-lights looked like mother hens leading the lesser-prepared police *ducklings* out of the woods. Only Charles, Detective Lawson, Chief Newman, and I remained.

"Chris," said Detective Lawson, "now that I've heard your *public* story on what happened, could we go somewhere where we can see? I've got a feeling that you have a private story that will shed more light on this than you have so far. How about your house? I'd rather stay out of the Folly Police Department head-quarters for now."

"That's fine," I said. Actually, it was more than fine. My legs were still quiver-ing under me, and I needed a place to sit down. I added, "I'd like to have Charles there."

"I don't see anything wrong with that," she said. "Chief, is that a problem for you?"

And of course, it wasn't.

＊   ＊   ＊   ＊

I hadn't prepared to have a party, but I did have enough chairs for the four of us to sit around the fine, old oak dining table. I fired up the coffee pot and got out mugs and spoons and napkins. Appetizers, however, were out of the question.

We sat, Lawson across from me and the chief to my right. Charles sat to my left and laid his hand carved cane on the table in front of him.

"First, Chris," Detective Lawson said, "what made you think you were so much smarter than the police? And second, what on God's green earth made you do something as stupid, foolhardy, and dangerous as you did tonight?" Though tonight the detective was dressed in jeans and sweatshirt, her voice had lost none of its command.

Two good questions, I thought as I desperately searched my mind for the answers. She was obviously onto the fact that Charles and I had set the whole thing up. Now, humility seemed the most promising way to begin.

"Well," I admitted, "the most detective work I'd ever done was with sexual harassment claims at work. Outside of that, my investigative skills are taxed to their maximum just trying to find the reading glasses that I constantly misplace. In answer to your first question—it wasn't a matter of being smart. It was luck—both good and bad luck—that provided me with a little more information than you folks appeared to have access to. I was able to put information received from several people together. And as it turned out, I guessed correctly."

"For example?" asked Chief Newman in that calm, gruff voice.

"For example, I learned that Mrs. Lionetti was the main suspect, but that didn't make sense. A week or so ago, I was having supper with Tammy Rogers, a reporter with the Charleston newspaper. As you would imagine, the murder was one of the main topics of our conversation. She told me that you were convinced Mrs. Lionetti and her lover were responsible, but that the only fact you seemed to have was that the lover had disappeared. I *wanted* that to be the case. With him gone, I'd be safe."

My eyes were on Charles' cane. Twice as we talked, I'd picked it up and examined it, hefted it. There were flecks of blood on the shaft, but Charles and I seemed the only ones to notice.

"But that just didn't compute. Someone tried to kill me in a fire; someone broke into the old house looking for I don't know what; then someone ransacked this house and destroyed my laptop, and even took notes I'd made at a city council meeting. There was no chance that all that was random vandalism. And I couldn't see how I could possibly know anything or have anything that would tie Mrs. Lionetti or her friend to the murder. So it didn't make sense."

"Then," said an impatient chief of police.

Just then the coffee maker quit groaning and making all those weird noises coffee makers make. I got up for the cream and sugar and spoons, and brought the carafe back to the table and poured. That gave me a little more time to think.

"When I was looking at houses, one of them had a photo on a table," I said. "The girl in the photo looked familiar, but I couldn't place her. I asked my realtor, Bob Howard, if he knew who she was. It turned out that the reason she looked familiar was that she was Officer McConnell's twin sister. I recognized one of the men in the photo as Frank Long; I had seen him at the council meeting. Another familiar face in the photo was your Mayor Amato. I didn't know who was connected to whom, but connections there had to be."

I sat again and took a long draw on my coffee, set the mug down, and continued. "Another day, Amber, over at The Lost Dog Café, told me about a rumor that McConnell's sister and Long had had an affair a few years earlier. I remembered that Long was a developer and had been quoted in the paper the day after Mr. Lionetti's murder. Amber told me that Officer McConnell was always coming up with ideas on how to strike it rich. Some of them involved strange business deals."

Charles had been uncharacteristically quiet. Now he spoke up. "Like the ice cream parlor, coffee shop, summer and winter restaurant time-share," he said.

"That's the one Amber mentioned," I continued. "I hadn't even thought of anyone specifically, not until he came to my house to investigate the burglary. He was intent on convincing me it was vandals. And that made me think of the time two weeks earlier when I called your office, Chief, to say I might have seen something at the scene of the murder. McConnell was one of the officers who came. Once he knew I didn't really have hard evidence to share, he kept looking at my computer and everything else sitting around. I thought that was strange."

No one commented, so I continued, "A week ago, I was meeting with my realtor to write up an offer to buy this house. He mentioned that Mr. Long had just gone to the planning commission to get them to allow him to assume Lionetti's permits to develop what promised to be a multi-million dollar project over by the coast guard property. What a fortunate situation for Long, I thought.

"Finally, that piece of information reminded me of a conversation I'd had with Amber just a couple of days earlier. She'd told me McConnell had just told her how he was going to be part of a huge project that would change the face of Folly and make him rich."

The chief exchanged long looks with Detective Lawson, set his coffee cup down and shook his head. I could see by his expression that he found all this less than reasonable.

"Those are a lot of unrelated pieces of information," said Newman. "What made you even give a thought to putting them together?"

I shrugged. "Well … I looked over the photos I took on the morning of the murder, several times in fact. I couldn't see anything that looked even remotely helpful. Then Tammy told me about one of the paper's photographers who'd had some important images deleted and was able to recover them with some very sophisticated software. My buddy Charles here and I had had a conversation about that software a few days later. With my new laptop, I also bought an image recovery package. I had deleted some of the images from the morning of the murder, but I recovered them, and when I did, I found the thing that had been swimming around in the murky water of my memory." I looked from the chief to the detective, for effect, I admit. Shameful. "And the image of a jacket bearing the Folly Police emblem."

Both the chief and detective made little sudden intakes of breath. I knew then that I'd gained a foothold.

"So there you have it, Chief," Charles said, head raised and shoulders back with pride. "Obviously, I was critical to finding this solution."

We all looked at him, but I was the only one who smiled.

"You want to hear what's so ironic," I said, interrupting Charles' moment of fame. When no one said anything, I assumed they did. "If McConnell hadn't burned my house; if he hadn't broken into my *new* house; if he hadn't taken my notes from the city council meeting and destroyed my laptop—all efforts to prevent me from discovering the truth about him. If he hadn't done all that, it would never have entered my mind that I knew anything about the killer. I was quite content to believe the killer was far, far away."

There were silences in the conversation now, and so far, no one had asked how Charles just happened on the scene. We didn't bring it up. I don't think they wanted us to ruin a good story with the truth.

Charles leaned over to me and whispered behind his hand, "'If you don't say anything, you won't be called on to repeat it.'—old dead President Calvin Coolidge."

I offered to download the video and burn CDs for them. They quickly agreed to that. Something about chain of custody, said the chief. And it gave the Boy Scout in me something to do. They asked why I had burned two extra copies. I said, "Habit."

With that, the detective looked at me with a wry smile that I thought cast a shadow on my veracity.

"Finally," asked Chief Newman, "why didn't you just call the police? You did a mighty foolish thing."

"Chief, I agree about foolish," I said. "But look at it from my side. Who could I trust? I suspected that *some*one in your department was involved. I didn't know but what it was you." I hesitated, and then ventured, "I've heard that you and Detective Lawson are … shall I say *close?*" Instant stony silence, quickly exchanged glances, and two barely perceptible smiles. "So how could I go to the sheriff's department? I was a target. I was in danger. I had to act on my own."

That was what brought our meeting to an end. Detective Lawson said they would stay longer but had to make a visit to another local resident, a developer— "former developer" she said—named Frank Long. The officers reluctantly thanked Charles and me and left the house shaking their heads.

When we heard the cruisers' engines purr away and Charles and I knew that we were safely alone, we looked at each other, wiped our brows and grinned.

"Mr. Photo Man, you sure know how to liven-up our peaceful, happy island of Folly. Are you sure you have to leave Friday?"

I nodded. "Afraid so, but I might be back sooner than I thought. In fact, I *have* to be. You've got to teach me how to use that video feature on the camera." I looked at my watch. "I'd talk longer, but I have to make a phone call before it gets too late. How about breakfast tomorrow at The Dog?"

We agreed to meet at seven, and I almost hugged him, but thought he might be embarrassed.

I dialed Tammy's number. I may be a slow learner, but I knew I'd better call before she heard about tonight from someone else.

After we talked, I slept better than any night since I arrived—except for one.

CHAPTER 33

My next to last day of vacation finally arrived. The sun shone with greater enthusiasm. The birds were singing in tune and at the top of their little lungs. I even heard the soothing roar of the ocean. Life was grand!

Charles was waiting for me at The Dog. When I walked in, I saw he'd taken a seat at my favorite table and had a steaming mug of coffee in his hands and one at my place. This morning, he wore a long-sleeve black sweatshirt with NYPD in large white block letters on the front. Funny! He was deep in conversation with my favorite wait staff person sitting across from him and didn't see me. No telling what his version of last night's activities had become after a few more tellings. I didn't care.

"Good morning, Amber, Charles. Mind if I interrupt and have some breakfast?"

Charles sat back in his chair. "Good morning, Mr. Photo Man. It's about time you got here; you're only ten minutes early!"

Amber was smiling at me in an especially benign and beautiful way. She got up and came and gave me a sisterly hug.

"I'm glad for you, Chris," she said quietly.

"Glad for what, Amber?" I asked.

"Oh, that Charles saved your life. That you've found you a house here on the island. That we're going to be friends for a long, long time." She paused and looked at Charles. "In fact, this morning, Chris, you're buying Charles's breakfast—it's the *least* you can do."

The steady stream of visitors began. The regulars—the two city council members, and "Cool Dude" Sloan, the owner of the surf shop—came to the table and expressed shock about Officer McConnell and Frank Long. They apologized on the part of Folly Beach for what I'd been through. That was very kind of them and, of course, unnecessary.

Chief Newman came in and walked directly over. Bent forward and with both of his big hands planted on our table, with a kindly smile, he made his announcement in a semi-confidential fashion.

"I knew you'd be here," he said. "I wanted you to be among the first to know that we took Mr. Long into custody last night. Detective Lawson has him in jail in Charleston. I don't think you'll have to worry about running into him anytime soon—like in this lifetime." We chatted a little longer, and about the time Amber returned to our table, he left.

Amber said she'd known all along there was something strange about McConnell. I didn't ask if she had noticed that back when they were dating or if it had come as a recent realization. And then I told her that she had provided an important clue in figuring all this out. She was pleased. Then she gave what I thought was an extra-long look and smile at Charles, and went about her work.

"You know, Mr. Photo Man," Charles said with a light in his eyes, "she might be smarter than I thought."

From the angle of his gaze, I could see that he was noticing her other attributes as well.

Breakfast even tasted better than it had all the other mornings I'd sat at this table.

✳　　　✳　　　✳　　　✳

After a couple of hours at The Dog, I walked home, and as I began packing, I had mixed feelings. My usual tinges of depression at the end of a vacation were competing with the euphoric feelings that surrounded what happened last night.

Both my conflicted feelings and my packing were interrupted by the ringing of my phone.

"Good day, Mr. Landrum," blurted the familiar voice of Bob Howard. "I've got something to show you. Are you available in, let's say, ten seconds?"

I didn't even answer. I just clicked *end call* and walked out the front door—knowing full well that the Plum Cruiser and its proud owner were at my curb. I wasn't disappointed.

He greeted me before I was halfway to his car. "When in the hell are you going to stop trying to scare the shit out of me? I can't leave you for more than a few days before you manage to get someone to try to fry, shoot, or drown you."

"Good morning, Mr. Best Realtor in the Second Largest of Three Small Realty Firms on Folly Beach. Thanks for coming over to check on me."

He piled out car with a folder in his left hand, came round the back of the car, and gave me a huge bear hug. He laughed and said, "Enough of that warm and fuzzy shit. Mr. Landrum, turn around and take a gander at your new home!"

The bank had accepted my offer. Frankly, I was a little disappointed when Bob told me I wouldn't have to return to Folly, that I could do all the paperwork from Kentucky. I thought I heard him say he was glad I'd survived last night. But it could have just been my imagination.

*   *   *   *

I couldn't leave without saying bye to my first neighbor. I walked to Bill Hansel's house hoping to catch him at home. He was there. In fact, he seemed to always be there; I wondered when he honored his students with his presence.

Bill was one of the few people around here who actually said the appropriate words at the right time. I always welcomed his directness as an antidote to the constant barrage of *Follyspeak* from my other friends.

"Thank God, you're okay," he said in that signature calm voice of his. "I didn't hear what happened until this morning." He clapped me on the shoulder and let his hand rest there a moment. "Want some tea?" he said. Then he motioned me to sit down at the picnic table where we had enjoyed our wine and "little hot doggy things you eat with a toothpick" a few afternoons ago.

Our conversation under the shade of his live oak was a crowning moment of peace after a long stretch of trouble. We talked a little about the events of the last twenty-four hours. Most of our conversation was about the last twenty-seven days. He was pleased that I'd got the house, but was sorry it wasn't closer. Only on Folly were three blocks a long way away.

*   *   *   *

That afternoon, Tammy came down with a sudden case of bronchitis and called in to the paper sick. I was pleased how quickly she recovered. By the time she crossed the Folly River, the ocean mist had cured her. Amazing.

Amazing would also describe our night in my new house. Like Bill, she was direct, but showed it in much different ways. We didn't have any tea. Nor, thank God, did we have any grits.

CHAPTER 34

My last day on Folly Beach—for now anyway—began early. Tammy had to be well and at work by eight, so we were up and walking on the beach before sunrise.

Speaking of mixed feelings! Tears of laughter and sadness shared the same faces as we said good-bye. I promised to call when I got home—regardless of the time.

I wanted to leave by ten and still had a few other folks to see. I didn't really have time for breakfast but went to The Dog to say bye to Amber. I wanted her to know how much she meant to me and to wish her the best. I also wanted to tell her to spend more time with Charles, that she wouldn't regret it. I think she had already figured that out.

When I got to the house to finish loading the car, Charles was sitting on the steps. I knew he would be. He had my camera cleaned and neatly packed in its case, and tried to give it back to me. I told him I thought the camera was very happy here and didn't want to leave. He said he'd noticed that himself. I told him that, in addition to the camera, he needed to keep a close watch on a certain waitress at The Dog and on her son. He'd pondered that too, he said.

"Where's your cane?" I asked.

He shrugged. "At home. Why would I want to carry that heavy damned thing around?"

We laughed, and believe it or not, I hugged him, and he hugged back.

At last, not being very good at leaving, I just said, "time to go," and he walked me to the car.

I pulled away from *my* house and looked in the rear view mirror. There he was with the camera to his eye, photographing my departure. Or, maybe a candy wrapper lying on the street.

I turned on Center Street and slowly headed toward the bridge and off Folly Beach. But before I got to the bridge, I heard the short, quick burst of a siren and saw an unmarked police car behind me. I pulled over and got ready to argue about what law I violated, when Chief Newman approached my window.

"Chief, what did I do wrong?"

"Nothing, Mr. Landrum. I wanted to catch you before you got away. Thank you for helping catch McConnell. I hate it that one of my men was involved in a murder, and that he created so much misery for you. If you hadn't been here and so persistent, he would have gotten away with it." He put out his hand, I took it, and we shook warmly.

"So thanks," he said. And then he said, "Oh, by the way, my daughter wanted me to thank you."

"Daughter?" I said.

"Yeah, Detective Lawson." And he grinned. "See you the next time you're back. We'll try to make your next stay more uneventful."

I watched in my rear view mirror as he made a quick turn and waved, heading back the other way. The chief had left me flabbergasted. "Daughter!"

Laughing at my faux pas two nights ago when the four of us were gathered around my table, I pulled back onto the road and again headed out. As I approached *The Boat*, once more I pulled to the side of the road. I took out a sheet of paper and wrote a shopping list—a Tilley hat for Charles; send him a computer; and buy two long sleeve sweatshirts to send to this, my new best friend, one from the University of Kentucky, and one from the University of Louisville.

Then I sat there and allowed my mind to retreat to that time when I first saw *The Boat* five years ago, and then more recently, a month ago. At that time, little had I known what Folly Island would bring me in those thirty days. But I'd do it again in a heartbeat. Well ... maybe I'd not try to photograph the lighthouse at sunrise!

Twelve months, twelve days to retirement. I'll have to do something to speed that up.